The Cult of Relics

Devôcyon dhe Greryow

Alan M. Kent

evertype
2021

Dyllys gans/*Published by:* Evertype, 19A Corso Street, Dundee, DD2 1DR, Scotland. *www.evertype.com.*

Trailyans Kernowek © 2010–2021 Nicholas Williams.

Kensa dyllans/*First edition* 2010: *The Cult of Relics: Devôcyon dhe Greryow.* ISBN 978-1-904808-41-1 (aden gales/*hardcover*); ISBN 978-1-904808-79-4 (aden vedhel/*paperback*)

An secùnd dyllans-ma/*This second edition* 2021.

Y kefyr covath rolyans rag an lyver-ma dhyworth an Lyverva Vretennek.
A catalogue record for this book is available from the British Library.

ISBN-10 1-78201-304-0 (*The Cult of Relics*)
ISBN-13 978-1-78201-304-4

ISBN-10 1-78201-305-9 (*Devôcyon dhe Greryow*)
ISBN-13 978-1-78201-305-1

Nyns yw radn vëth a'n novel-ma marnas fug-lien. Yma henwyn, persons ha wharvosow portreys ino ow tos in mes a dhesmygyans an auctor. Mar pëdh an persons, an wharvosow ha'n tylleryow ino haval in fordh vëth dhe bersons, bêdhens y bew bò marow, dhe wharvosow bò dhe dylleryow i'n bës gwir, keschauns yw hedna yn tien.
This novel is entirely a work of fiction. The names, characters, and incidents portrayed in it are the work of the author's imagination. Any resemblance to actual persons, living or dead, events, or localities is entirely coincidental.

Olsettys in Minion ha New Pelican gans Michael Everson.
Set in Minion and New Pelican by Michael Everson.

Cudhlen/*Cover*: Michael Everson.
Delinyansow hendhyscansek in mes a:/*Archaeological drawings taken from*:
"The Exploration of Grimspound: First Report of the Dartmoor Exploration Committee" in *Reports and Transactions of the Devonshire Association for the Advancement of Science, Literature and Art*, Vol. XXVI, Plymouth: William Brendon and Son, 1891, pp.101–121.

Contents

Preface to the 2021 edition

When *The Cult of Relics* emerged in 2010, those readers who followed my work were surprised to see both its form and content. In terms of its first edition, my publisher and I decided to present the novel in a bilingual format, both in English and in Cornish, making it the first novel to be presented in this way. Ambitiously, we hoped that this might represent a new way forward for literature in Cornwall, as well as asserting the fact that Cornwall was a bilingual (maybe even trilingual, if we include Cornu-English) country. Placing Nicholas Williams' stunning translation of my novel into *Devôcyon dhe Greryow* and having the two languages face each other was a new challenge. Time moves on however, and perhaps with this new edition there is an opportunity now to present the two versions of the novel each on its own. We have grown used to new novels being published in both Cornish and English in separate editions.

Whatever our intentions and what we were doing with *The Cult of Relics*, it seemed to please some critics. The novel gained positive reviews in as illustrious a publication as *The Times Literary Supplement*, as well as the more Cornu-centric magazines and newspapers. This was gratifying to see. One important issue here was to show that Cornish-language narrative did not necessarily need to resort to Medievalism, Arthuriana, mining, or lamentation. Our aim was to make Cornish a contemporary language which could deal with any topic. That is why *The Cult of Relics* was such a suitable novel for this process.

The story here was connected to the first Gulf War, and is told via three narrators coming from very different backgrounds. If Cornish readers were expecting me to repeat what I did in *Clay* or *Proper Job, Charlie Curnow!* they were going to be disappointed. Only one of the characters here is truly Cornish, the archaeologist Robert Bolitho. I wanted the novel to have a post-modern collision of characters and ideas, all linked by the layers of time, and connected somehow to the story of *The Mayflower*. It is therefore more than appropriate that this new edition is published just over four hundred years since the *Mayflower*'s sailing.

While the novel is perhaps not how I would write now, a decade on, it was an important developmental text in my own literary journey, and I hope that it showed a new way forward for indigenous literature emerging from Cornwall in the opening decades of the twenty-first century. I am still very proud of what was achieved in 2010, as I am also with this splendid new edition.

Alan M. Kent
August 2021

The Cult of Relics

Ne was ther swich another pardoner.
For in his male he hadde a pilwe-beer,
Which that he seyde was Oure Lady veyl:
He seyde he hadde a gobet of the seyl
That Seint Peter hadde, whan that he wente
Upon the see, til Jhesu Crist hym hente.
He hadde a croys of latoun ful of stones,
And in a glas he hadde pigges bones.
But with thise relikes whan that he fond
A povre person dwellynge upon lond,
Upon a day he gat hym moore moneye
Than that the person gat in monthes tweye;
And thus, with feyned flatterye and japes,
He made the person and the peple his apes.

Geoffrey Chaucer
"General Prologue", *The Canterbury Tales* (1387)

Amid the storm they sang,
And the stars heard, and the sea;
And the sounding aisles of the dim woods rang
To the anthem of the free.

There were men with hoary hair
Amidst the Pilgrim band:
Why had they come to wither there,
Away from their childhood's land?

What sought they thus afar?
Bright jewels of the mine?
The wealth of seas, the spoils of war?
They sought faith's pure shrine.

Felicia Hemans
Landing of the Pilgrim Fathers (1826)

I

The First Offerings

Robert

Come close.

No.

Closer.

That's it. That's better.

Now I can begin. There was, once upon a time…

No.

Stop.

Let me explain.

See, each of us has a tale to tell. What governs our tales to be different is too lengthy to explain here. It is just that they are, and this—for what it is worth—is mine. Others may tell the tale differently. Yes, there are others who may tell a not dissimilar tale, but that is not my concern for now. This tale is not a pleasant one. Indeed, there are sections of it which may appal you, or scare you even, but you may still like to listen. It concerns myself—albeit as a kind of onlooker, a metaphysical voyeur of a sort—and two others.

No.

Hold on.

I am wrong. Make that, *three* others. Another exists, or existed once, or exists in me. But before I can begin (My God, here, I feel the way I used to, when I read lulling and lolloping bed-time stories to my son; when he was still scared of the dark and afraid the bogey-man might get him) I need to frame the picture for you. As well as this, I need to give it depth and a sharper clarity, and—dare I say

3

it—some perspective, in order to tell you this fad, this tale of mine. Bear with me then. Listen carefully...

The world is still waking. Much is lively, and has been for millions of years. As much—possibly even more—is still asleep, still slumbering soundly, undiscovered and unexplained.

Time, yes, that old devil, controls what will waken. It is also controls what will sleep, and then that which will reawaken again. Man is also waking, a yawning, slouching creature rubbing the sleep from his soft, Chinese eyes. He once banged greasy animal bones together. He now orbits the airless void around the earth listening to the works of Igor Stravinsky and Lennon and McCartney. His worldview has opened its eyes, and he has sat up straight; his back rigid. The bed of darkness is passing. Dreams on the way have been strange, from the crucifixion of Jesus Christ to the discovery that the Earth is not flat, but round; from bloody, barefoot treks up Holy Mountains, to the discovery of new lands and worlds that once he never knew existed. The dream has been disturbing and dislocating. The dream has been both good and evil. The dream is also the Hope.

We are all travellers—more precisely, hopeful travellers. Our soles have been toughened and the leather of our sandals has become cracked and flayed. See the flakes of worn skin and our bright eyes. It is the oldest story we know; each of us on his own odyssey. Yes, our odysseys do link, but, for the most part, we wake at our own rate; discover our own dreams. We take what we are given, and try to find more. Our objective in this is to heave the human condition that one tiny distance more out of the gritty, black bed. Even while I speak, and while you listen, the human race has changed and evolved from what it was a mere second ago. We are all altering the pattern, life-tapestry-treading, weaving our way, dodging the pitfalls of natural selection. Oh yes, it is not only the sea iguanas and finches of the Galapagos Islands it works upon.

But for the most part, the darkness rarely lifts. We continue in a stumbling blindness, pathetically holding on to what we can, as if clutching some fragile banister, absurdly constructed from only sugar paper. The dream then swiftly swoops to yellow-tinged memories, and we grasp tightly any relics: the things that warm the cockles of the heart—gifts we were given, some keepsake, that dress, that photograph, and that battered teddy bear which you cannot let go. We mysteriously alter and become those people who keep their worn-out shoes, gain a sudden passion for antiques, and recall that record you first danced to. You remember when you first felt *it*. Yes, *it*. Call it sentimentality. Call it whatever you like. We are yelping dogs, chasing our tails and licking our wounds. The past shapes and forms us, so much so, that sometimes we cannot distinguish it from the unrelenting, stinging present.

Frightening.

The relics then, are what we seek: the objects of veneration. They are those items we hold in esteem.

Remember the way we searched for the rotting bones of St Peter, digging down through the dusty, high altar through webbed catacombs of decay to the Apostle's grave, or any other of those Saints; or the way prime-time television blasts us with yet another scientific dating of the Turin Shroud? We are in synchronicity still with Polycarp's relics, Paul's handkerchiefs, Pieces of the True Cross, King St Stephen's right forearm, the remains of Saint Cessianus… The list is endless.

Q: What for?

A: To make the Darkness go away.

To be with Him—whoever "He" is. God, maybe. As if that notion could offer some sanctity in the final round up. Those objects are our sanctity now, in our present, ever-increasing world of anomalies. Some call this insanity. For those seeking sanity, escape may be better. This is the one reason for travel. In the same way pilgrims left their warm and buttered homes in order to deny the Parish Priest his monopoly over their spiritual welfare, we too, are still pilgrims. The object of the pilgrimage has not changed. The Medieval package tour remains, mutated into the thousands of sun-seekers who fly south to the Med every year. Escape is what they are after. The opportunity to forget. To find themselves.

And yet somewhere, in lifting one's dull body out of bed, someone might still wish for the true journey, the real way forward, the journey to genuine enlightenment, the seeking of the Promised Land. Perhaps somewhere, at some time, someone has sought this. You may have met one of these people. You may even be one yourself. They are, however, few and far between. These types, these one-offs cannot be defined as wanderers, who merely seek some sacred place. No. They are the ones more awake than the rest of us, and any remnants of them must surely be worth preserving.

Wait…

I cannot continue the tale now. There is more to say before I begin, but that is the frame of it. It is not always the case, but with this picture, you must know a little more of the artist, warts and all. I'll be as honest as I can.

My life has been an absurdity. I say "absurd", if only to generate your interest, though more probably your sympathy. After all, for most of us, life consists more or less of birth, school, work and death. Fortunately, there are some pleasantries on the way. I name love as one; sex as another, but even these charming, lacy things fade when you reach my age. You should know that I am sixty-four years old. But no, I say absurd for a reason. You see, my main interest in life has been in death. A strange preoccupation I know. Go on, laugh. Initially, I suppose death can be a morbid topic, and not the best way to begin any tale (let alone this one), though you'd be surprised just how many things do begin after a death.

I mean, you are, by now thinking of skulls, coffins and of a great unknown. Another void. But remember, when death finally comes knocking, they say—and I believe it to be true—that it is a great release. And then consider the gloomy, though somewhat ironic thought, that once you are born, you are, in fact, dying. Once that is accepted, death takes on a different note. Fear of death is a farce. What was it John Donne said?

"One short sleepe past, wee wake eternally,
And death shall be no more, Death thou shalt die."

Do I sound metaphysical? Then so it must be. It is, as we used to say in the Navy, "uncharted waters", though they should not be dreaded.

Uncharted or not, I always had a soft spot for the dead. I've had it ever since my childhood. See, my father worked as the coxswain of the St Ives lifeboat, back in the '20s and the '30s. I knew the gusts of the Atlantic, knew the feel of every dirty swell that came in, and snatched the lives of many. I often stood on the quay in the dawn, watching them carry the drowned across the gangplank. Death's been with me a long time then, stalking me and holding my hand. He is part of my tale.

Maybe now, and in my professional life, I would be more correct if I said the *pasts* of the dead. The dead's lives. The dead's loves. The dead's writing. The dead's anecdotes. And how do I know of the dead? Easy. I am a magpie. I collect things that glisten, things that shimmer. They are things that have passed. I love things like the frail skeletons of beech leaves, which as a boy, I used to collect back in the woods over Nancledra, and then the barnacled wood found over Gwithian. Once, in my early fifties, I had a penchant for old news-papers. I used to look for them in car-boot sales and markets. There is something very satisfying in reading events you know of already, like those fairy stories or folk-tales your mother or father read to you when you were a child. You know every word, every turn of phrase. You long to interrupt but know you mustn't. And yet still, they enchant you, even as the adult.

Above all, I suppose I am a collector of the words of the dead. Words are manageable you see. Words in sentences. Sentences in chapters. Chapters in books. Books in shelves. Shelves in libraries. See how I like everything to be pinned down, organized. Of course then, I read their books, the books of the dead. I had a swirling ado-lescent gurgle of Shakespeare, Dickens, Hardy, Donne and all those other frail literary leaves who wrote of the dead. But even books are not permanent. Paper decays. Just think of all the books along the way which have gone. Disappeared into dust. Thousands. Millions. And remember the Inquisition...

Stone is better. It lasts. See then, it is with the stones of the dead that I have spent too much of my adult life. My specialism you might say. Perfect iambic pentameters carved exquisitely on the grave-stones and tombs of the dead. Prayers and poems in memory of somebody. Epitaphs. I still spend countless hours jotting down humorous and interesting verses from the shady churchyards and echoing cathedral tombs of these islands.

"You and your stupid tombs..." father would say, "better if you was out on the water boy..."

His words didn't have much effect. I am his eternal disappoint-ment. See, professionally, I am a Professor of Archaeology. Well, ex-Professor of Archaeology. I am recently retired you see. Took the deal they offered. Almost thirty years at Bristol. Thirty bleddy years spent with mould and dust. My specialism: graves, tombs, shrines—Medieval, Early Modern, Modern—I'll take whatever they throw at me...

And this, oddly enough, is the reason I am here, in the city of Ply-mouth, in the county of Devon. I have come to find the dead. My discoveries, as you will learn, have taken me far and wide, yet it is here that I know my friend Death will change me. He might even come to me, for I am near the sweep of his scythe now, so to speak. I'm not twenty-one any more. In fact, it was at that age, that I was first in this city, taking the bo'sun's pilgrimage down the tight, salty streets of Stonehouse and Devonport, and along to Union Street. We walked on the wrong side then. Some tales to tell there, once upon a time… in the early 1950s…

But wait.

I drift again. I do that these days… drift like a boat upon the Atlantic's swell…

See, in such and such a place, not far and not near, not high and not low, there was once…

No.

Robert. You must stop. Be truthful. Tell the truth.

So… what I really wanted to tell you was how the dead are still among us, and how we are all bound hard and fast to the past. See, you know that some pasts are more important than others, and here, in this city, I sense an incredible past; one that is stacked up in rows, a domino history. But other thoughts too: of a present equally as huge, and of a future, infinite. And think of me as what you like—call me an old fool—but I feel like a molecule encased in some school chemistry room gas chamber, jumping around like children these days on those inflatable bouncy castles, with all these other bouncing molecules and ghost molecules (are they anti-matter?) from another time. And there are the present and the future leaping around as well.

You will see then, that I have a very different notion of time to everyone else. That will become even clearer very soon. Time, I believe is not governable, not graspable, and neither is History. History is not just events past. History is past, present, future. I have travelled here on a pilgrimage to that.

This then, is a homage to time and its swirling tales.

It is between these unmanageable and unaccountable forces that I am sitting. I am in that part of the city they now call the Barbican. It is the year of our Lord, 1994. It is September. It is where Tudor, timber-built houses almost touch on their upper storeys. It is the contrast to the rest of Plymouth's post-war, ready-mix nightmare. I am between worlds and times. I am at the end of the domino topple. It is an ethereal place. I feel good though. I am sitting quite still, gazing—no, more staring—across the grey, still waters of Sutton Pool. There are chip-fed seagulls above me, white, shrieking, shitting things. I am next to the Mayflower Steps. It is here, that *they*, and *he* departed. You will learn who *they* are, and who *he* is, soon enough.

I am between old and new worlds. I am not quite a split personality, but close. I am living, not in the past, but among the past. I feel closer to the dead, closer to them than I have felt in a long time. I am holding their hands. I am reading their broadsides. I am with the whistling ballad-sellers on the quay. I am like them, trying to tell stories.

Let's see if I can remember it all, as it was told to me...

Once, long ago, in a time that will never be again, and will never come back...

When I get back, I will tell her how lovely it has been. I will say to her—because she had not my contemplation of the past—I will say, "You really must come down to the Barbican with me some time..."

"Yes," she will say. "I must... some time."

I have already confessed to you that I am a pilgrim of a sort. What I have not told you is my real name; the name everyone calls me now: Bob. Not Robert Bolitho. But Bob. Cut down. Trimmed. Already a relic. You must have demanded that by now; a label with which to hold me, like some tiny biological specimen. It's not that easy though, because throughout my life I've had a selection of names, so much so, I've never really known which one is correct: Robert, Bobby, Bob, Robby, Dad, Son. Yet, I do not have a crisis of identity. I do know myself. You will learn that as we continue.

And something you should know, my marriage is not a happy one. Perhaps you have guessed that already from my tone. Forgive me please if I call my wife "*her*" or "*she*" (I know for a fact, that she speaks of me in a similar way).

Her name is of little consequence to me now. I sometimes wish things had turned out differently. Such is life. It is a gamble and you only have one chance. The numbers on our respective dice thrown were not what we wanted.

This however, is not to say we are divorced, or separated. Far from it. We tolerate one another, in a kind of vague symbiosis. She tolerates my ecclesiastical and archaeological quests around the country, and no doubt, my lack of lively conversation. I tolerate her garden centres, shopping adventures and her male friends. I have never really known why things have worked out this way. We did try. Thinking back, our son noticed it very early on (a story for later, when it is dark). But we stayed together. It may be a kind of respect for the happiness we once had. After the War it was—the late '50s and the early '60s. I think it was something to do with her always being happy with what she had: the semi, the child, the Labrador dog, that first Morris 1100 we bought. But for me—and I shan't kid you about this—it wasn't enough. You may wonder then why I do not have religion. After all, in religion, I may have found something spiritual. Something more. Proper stories. Stories to run lives by. Indeed, there was a time when I thought that was important to me, after something that happened here... in Union Street, but no, what I seek is beyond the material and the spiritual. That has always left me out on a limb, on the periphery. I am a cold planet.

I remember that holiday we once had at Barry Island. When was it now—'69 or '70? Our son and she would always be on the pleasure beach rides—rickety, whirling things, but I would never venture on. I never needed the autonomic kick. I was always the incongruous onlooker on the side-lines. Never the participant. She used to say I was old before my time. Perhaps, but at least I never suffered the agony of middle age. I sailed through that with a full wind behind me. It's just another breezy ocean to cross.

While I am talking, I ought to mention that one of the reasons I am here is because it was in Plymouth that I did my National Service. I put in for the Navy. Or rather my father put in for the Navy for me. Six weeks of square-bashing and then Able Seaman Bolitho on leave. A childhood spent in rural Cornwall had left me with only a few limited ideas about drink and women. During leave, I encountered both here. In one sense, I have come back to re-live those days. Odd, because so much of my life has been a pursuit of regaining innocence. Odd, because it was here that I lost so much of it. After that, I could no longer be a participant, but only an onlooker.

These intermingling and yet also related reasons are why we are here, but there is another. It is late summer, and we are to stay for a while.

Then we are to return to Oxford—a town-house in Summerhill (that's where we moved to after I retired). It has been a long time since *she* has been to Cornwall or Dartmoor, so we are bound to visit there. St Ives maybe—for old time's sake. Here however, we have quite an ornate room in a Victorian-fronted hotel on the western edge of the Hoe. It is called, of course, *The Armada Hotel*. I think the room itself is a bit too big for what we wanted, but she likes it. It is on the left side of the hotel, with one window giving a view of the Sound; the other towards the Brittany ferry port at Millbay Docks. Below the other window, on the ground floor are the kitchens. Each morning, I wake to the smell of fried bacon, than gaze at the cracks in the plaster ceiling.

Earlier, and she is talking to me from the misty shower cabinet. I can see her thin, white body. I imagine her sinews and muscles; her skin reddened by the steaming hot water. I hear little gasps from time to time. I see her hand lunge for the de-odorizing soap on the shelf above the sink. In and out, I hear her annoying humming. I am only half-listening. I am reading *The Guardian*—an article about post Gulf-War Kuwait, but there is a fly annoying me. She is telling me about her plans for the morning. I grunt affirmatives to her. She is planning more shopping, more money on her store cards. As you know, I have come in the other direction, away from her. I say eagerly, "You really must come down the Barbican with me some time."

But she knows me. She knows my over-keen voice.

Her words are lost, as I finally line up my aim. The fly is squashed into a yellow and black pulp on the net curtain. I am annoyed with myself for the mess I have made. But then, as I have already told you, I always had a soft spot for the dead. And do I really need to know what she is saying in the shower? She is probably calling me names.

Bob is what they called me in His Majesty's Navy. I am in a Bob kind of mood today. A bob-a-job happy-go-lucky, all right-my-son sort of frame of mind. I have been Bob Bolitho quite a lot lately, rather than Robert Bolitho, or Robby, or Bobby. It might be the holiday, or it might be the fact that I am back here. I say holiday, I mean, we are permanently on holiday now. I am at that time of life when you know there is very little to come, and you spend most of your waking hours dreaming of what has gone before, and most often, how you would have changed it (I am, after all, in the middle of my seventh decade!). I do not then believe in reincarnation. If there were such a phenomenon, then we would have not learnt anything about relationships or the control and taming of our stupid, infantile emotions.

Hold on. I am rushing. Pause and reflect on what I have said in my offering for a moment. You will need to know more of me. What makes me tick? Where I am from. And where, as the Americans say, I am at. Anyway, it seems there was this…

Jude

Journeyman, or rather Journeywoman, is what I like to be called. The world calls me all sorts of things. Most of them are abusive and derogatory. "Slut" and "Slag" are two I got labelled with just last week. "Weirdo", "Fucking Gypo" and "Hippy" are others. I care little though. I know what I am. There is no pretence in me, nor is there any malice aimed at others. Live and let live is my motto and I wish others would live by it too. I suppose they find us eccentric or dated, like '60s' relics or drop-outs. You know the headlines in the tabloids. They call us, and always sneeringly so, "self-styled travellers" or "new-agers". But that is not the reason. No. It is because they see us as "other". We are dirty and unhygienic. Filth. Scum. That's more it. We do not fit. They feel threatened by us, as if our presence might encroach on their sanitized existence somehow, and worse than that, change them; make them think differently. Or that my partner Pete might run off with one of their children. Abduct them in a moment, like he's some kind of Pied Piper figure. That's it now isn't it? Be different, and you're some kind of paedo.

But I ask you straight, are we not the same as them? Don't we have eyes, bones and blood? Are not our children as innocent and as beautiful as theirs? I am afraid I cannot answer these questions. It is they who must answer. Then again, I suppose we do look odd, out on the road, on the "trail". When I stopped off for some water, I could see the whole of our convoy silhouetted against the skyline; Pete standing close to some wild ponies, my friend Sarah's children playing follow my leader, the dog beside them. I hear his friendly barking, and the deep chug of our rainbow-painted bus up the windy hill. Sarah is in there, cranking the worn gear stick. I picture the wooden bender tent-poles rolling around in the back. I hear a tiny sound—Pete playing his penny whistle. The children are clapping and singing. You know that kind of clapping, just for pure joy, for pure life. I have been disillusioned at times, but when you see that, that's when it is all worth it. They wait in a line at the top of a height, the sun's orb slipping down behind them. The ponies swish the midge flies away. I dump the water canisters in our homespun bus, and walk on with the kids chattering. About this, about that. And so, it is just us—the way I prefer it to be.

There are three of them, all Sarah's, all from different partners. So yeah, you're probably judging her already. A slag, eh, who is scrounging off the state. How many? How young? Shouldn't they be at school or something? That's the problem with society these days. People, like us, who do whatever they like. No responsibility for their actions. Think what you like: there's Adam, who is twelve, Cari, who is seven, and little Ally, who is four. I challenge you to find three more wonderful children.

See, this is not just some vague desire to return to a rustic, Pagan way of life. It is more than that. It is what we all truly believe in. It is another way of living. You'd call it an alternative lifestyle I suppose. So, yes, talk to me about being "Green" and talk about harmony with nature, but then, we admit, we are sometimes as guilty as you are. We cut down trees. We burn wood. Our bus uses diesel. Not exactly good for the ozone is it? What our lifestyle involves is something older; even older than the bent trees formed by the westerlies. Maybe as old as the stone tors here on Dartmoor. The old way, and our way, is to give back something to repay nature for what you have taken away. There is a traveller I know, who when he takes something from nature, he gives back to it a drop of his own blood.

We do not pursue such ways, but we do try to give back. We scatter seeds. We use older, fallen trees when we can. We try to live alongside nature, not against it. Like the Indians of North America. Like the Celts, yeah? It is giving back what you take away, and it is not just take, take, take—the selfish way of humanity—but give, give, give. And when those who scorn us, those who slam shop doors in our faces, learn that, then maybe a real new age can begin.

And what did we hear today: "They d'piss on the food, so as it's thrown out the back, then they d'take ut."

Our reputation is tarnished though. I can't deny that. There are those among us who have leapt on the bender bandwagon. I have met them at peace fayres and camps around the country. They are on some other mission. They seek some of our entities: the anarchy, the drop out, the rejection philosophy, but do not last. They are takers, with us to pose, to show the world they can live without the extras. They play the game by another set of rules than me. Yes—and you may be surprised by that—we have do have our rules. Ours is a society, an alternative one maybe, but we must also have order. Our rules may be different, but they must not be broken. We kicked a guy out once, because he drank too much. Spent too many days asleep in the bender. He would never work either. Takers then, who break our principles and give us our reputation.

I will tell you of one such taker later on.

"Jude, we'd better make camp now. The kids are getting a bit tired…"

It is Sarah who shouts this to me from the driver's window of the bus. She is younger, yet hardier than I was at her age. I mean, she drives the bus. She does some of the engine repairs as well. She is never afraid when there is any trouble, yet somehow, the convoy see me as their leader. I don't know why this strange notion has come about. It was perhaps because of that winter, a couple of years back, in Wales, when nothing went right. Yes. My suggestion was that we should claim benefits—against our rules—but then, it really was do, or die.

There may be another reason though, because I have no children of my own. I am infertile you see. The seed, shall we say, finds no root in me. No hold. My man knows this, yet has stuck by me. Do you see the irony yet? It isn't lost on me: an Earth Mother who can't be a mother.

Little wonder then that in order to compensate for my sterility, I have always tried to make myself attractive to children. I wear bright colours. I plait my hair like Rapunzel. Maybe I do live in a fairy tale. It is because I need to feel some of that instinct, to find a woman's reason for living. To bind myself to them. And so later, when the fire is animated (night is always the best time), and when we are all sat around it, the children will come to me. They will plonk themselves on my legs and use me as their armchair. The little one Ally, will play with my hair, and they will feel loved and warm. Then they will ask us. Pete is the better storyteller than me, but tonight it is my turn, and so they face me.

"Tell us," they will say. The same words always. "Tell us. Tell us a sto-o-ory..."

Tonight it is no different, except that the adults are listening, and you are here too. And so, a story. Forgive me, if I appear long-winded and embellish it, but then, that is my prerogative as teller I believe. It is as part of this art, as a keen eye is to painting. So... Once upon a time, when I was young and beautiful, and that hasn't been so long ago, as you can see....

Are there enough logs on the fire to last the night?

There are? Good.

Then listen...

Our route this time has not been a straight one. We have meandered down the skinny, staggering, elephant's trunk peninsula of the South-West, beginning at Salisbury Plain, then following it west in haphazard fashion. You will by now, have guessed that our object of highest reverence is Stonehenge. People of my kind believe it, and other such places to be the relics of a more sacred time. Sacred crumbs, all these stones then, from the moors of Penwith in Cornwall to the heights of Dartmoor. They are the salvage of our original knowledge. And yes, there has been the usual sordid battle between ourselves and *English Heritage*, the police and Wiltshire County Council, as to whether we will be allowed to see the Solstice. I viewed it with my father as a little girl, a long time ago, and so there is not the voracious desire in me to worship. Others are different though. Pete, I know, was anxious to see it. So yeah, us Neo-Pagans—we follow the ritual year.

We stayed about two miles away. A site had been designated. That means other travellers have just chosen some convenient land. Not the best way of carrying on, I'll admit. The landowner was up in arms about it, but as usual, the authorities have done nothing to aid the influx of people. We arrived artfully, before the vast majority had travelled east from the Glastonbury Festival.

On the actual day before the Solstice, we keep the children inside. The police are there, with growling dogs and sweaty horses. We have no argument with them. They are only doing their duty. They uphold the law, but then the law—and it has always been the case for travellers—is an ass. I mean, talk to gypsies about it. They know. Of course now, we are trespassers and can be prosecuted. Here, it all gets confusing, because there are others involved: local councillors, farmers, the government, two gangs of Hell's Angels down from London, and they are kicking the shit out of each other (some fool trashed another's Harley chopper), as well as the police.

This is when I get disillusioned, see. I suppose it is like all religion, for in a way, this is our religion. You have to fight hard for it, the same ways Muslims fight for it now, or Christians once used to. Only it doesn't feel like that, when you have come merely to see the Solstice, and the crowd is pushing and shouting. There is bad feeling in the air. This is because of the Bandwagon Hoppers, the takers. We are fighting amongst ourselves as well as authority. So it all seems so awful, that we come together for peace, to celebrate the Earth's power, and all we do is fight, and hurt one another. That is really when I feel like getting out, cleaning myself up, and doing the Nine-to-Five. But then, when, on that morning all the aggression has gone, and you do see the sun come up, the rays emanating through the spaces between the stones, that's when it entrenches you. It drives you further our way, elating your hopes and resigning your fears. It makes you feel alive, and not just living for the sake of it.

So 'Henge (notice how I call it 'Henge. It is our way. More familiar. Our place of worship) is like those other places, the places set out by ancient men and women which have survived. Newgrange and Avebury are two. Boscawen Ûn and the Merry Maidens in Cornwall. The stone rows, pounds and crosses of Dartmoor. There are thousands more. As time goes on, they are more and more beautiful, standing there, objecting to what is happening. They are symbols of a past reverence, hating the helter-skelter of concrete pushing ever-outwards from our cities, computers guzzling information, and money and corporate bonuses ruling the heart. That is why we journey to such places. It is because they stand alone, because the wrath of modern humanity has not touched them, because they are symbols of everything we love, just as, say, yuppie harbour-side developments are symbols of all that we abhor.

This is behind the reason why we have taken the way to Okehampton at Exeter, then onto the Princetown Road. This is why we have come to Dartmoor. It is truly an ancient place. It is why we are happy, why we search, why we strive, why we dance to a different beat; a more primitive drum.

Dartmoor scares us in some ways. Yes, even us, who have spent nights and nights amongst hooting owls and the murkiest dark you can imagine. It has a blacker presence.

You see it first as an all-pervading darkness; the shadows of high summer thunderclouds on the moor-land. In the distance you can spy one or two of the tors. But we are not there yet. We come to a halt in Mortonhampstead. There's a name to juggle with. The place is a traditional, small moorland town, and the folk there glare at us with eyes as hostile and chilling as the Moor itself. We are not welcome. This is nothing new. In fact, the pensioners call us Gypsies. They have no other terms to describe us. They know our type, or think they do. We are no different. They wait for us to go round the village knocking on doors, selling lucky heather or clothes-pegs.

We stop in the central garage for diesel. The place is small, yet almost as ancient as the Moor itself. It has old-style pumps still— aliens with fingers in their ears. The owner glares at us. His face is ingrained with the dirt and oil of two decades. A cigarette is stuck in the corner of his sneering mouth. The same boiler suit for the twenty years as well. Before he has a chance to say anything, Sarah is out of the bus. Her boots stomp down the steel stairs, her self-made earrings catching the light. I am dressed the same. I don't realize it, but to him, I suppose, I must appear as an odd combination of male and female. Hermaphrodites then. As mutants, we hand him our money.

"Thirty quid," Sarah states.

He takes it. Our money is not mutant. We always do this: pay first. Saves any problem. Sarah checks the tyres. I watch the old man. He must wonder who we are. I know this, because I used to think that way once. My mother took me to London. There was a beggar-girl. I still remember her face. I was seven. You wonder why. He was thinking the same about us. He was thinking of what things have come to. Then, his expression changed, more friendly, but when he spoke there was somehow still that bitter tone beneath it.

"Stayin' long be 'ee?"

I answer in the same tone, "No. Just passing."

It is phrase I have used countless times.

He places the oily hose back onto the petrol pump. I screw the cap back on the diesel tank.

"Thank you," I say.

He manages a grunt back.

We are not refused from walking into shops here. We have seen it though; experienced it. You get some places where they put up a barrier: "No travellers allowed". You've got to laugh really. It's always stuck next to the "No dogs allowed" sign. To get around this kind of behaviour, you dress slightly differently, or go on ahead before a main convoy gets into town. So, we know what Apartheid is. Someone always calls for the police as well. Up country, we know some of them personally. Almost a formality. No doubt it will be the same down here soon. The West's generally a bit friendlier though.

When I return from the shops, the bus shadows a police car. Inside it, a radio crackles. There are two young constables, not long out of training college. It is their first encounter with our type, I believe. I suppose the bus does look incongruous. There is a vague kind of search going on: a token look for drugs—cannabis and "E" mainly. A few townsfolk are watching, though our children and their children instinctively play together. It's a new one for them here. We're clean apparently. The police can do little. We're harming no-one, though they guardedly advise us to move on. There is no staying overnight. Pete gathers the children and the dog, and we push on. We take it slowly, keeping the bus at a creeping pace, letting the traffic pass by. It's always better this way. How can I put it? You get the feel of the place better. We watch the villagers' expressions turn to ones of relief. We are unwelcome guests: Banquos at the banquet. Layabouts. Scroungers. Then, you are already used to abuse. You are hardened by it. Sometimes, it is strange not to receive any. Once in a blue moon, there's a farmer who'll say yes, or a place that doesn't treat you like dirt. But then, it's the old argument isn't it? Get a decent haircut, tidy yourself up, and get a proper job, and you'll find we're all right.

We'll take the abuse thanks.

So, you must have questions by now. You must desire more about us. Where, for instance, do people like me come from? Tricky. I have lots of theories there. In some ways, we are the last remnants of the old country traders who used to peddle their wares around the country. We're not true Gypsies. We know that. We have much in common with them, but they are, in a sense, more special than us. See, there is none of the true Romany in us, and neither is there a tradition. We, in a sense, are the founders. We are making tradition.

There is, however, a wander-lust. So, maybe ours is just as special. It is a misty morning, a darkest-before-dawn lust. An old wandering...

You might have seen some of my type. We sometimes call ourselves traders, because we are. We do not sell to one another. We trade. We barter. We swap. Money is not irrelevant, but of less value to us. Our convoy makes earrings and jewellery. The "business"—if you can call it that—does relatively well. But then, our time as traders is comparatively short. There is one trader we know, who goes by the name of Trader Wally; he is from the Brecon Beacons. He has been trading for the last fifty years. He has the face of a disciple and the philosophy to match. I hope to emulate that. Peter does his performance, his shows, his storytelling, wherever we go.

The only place you can say we are from is the "other" society. We are all from there. Joining us can be slow and strained, or it may be quick and simple.

Plenty see the romance in us: the open road and all that jazz. But that is no good. What is needed is a desire, a very real desire for an alternative existence. You must want a freer land. That is what we want, and this is how we shall evolve. And as to our rise—for there is a rise of us—I don't know. Perhaps more people have the strength to let go, to free-fall, to get out of the rat-race.

My story is different. You will see why. I am also older. Even though Pete is my man, I know very little of him. He was the storytelling, rich boy escaping. A weekend hippy. He was the lad who felt too much the pressure of following his father: an intellectual type, so he said. I know nothing more. It is all I need to know. He is, what he is. Now, I feel his dreadlocks, and kick his peaty boots. You might call us husband and wife, but with us, there is no need of marriage. He is my man, and I am his woman. That is all. We have faith in each other. How many of you have that?

Our main companion is Sarah, who you know by now. The three separate fathers have long since gone, over the hills and far away. That is Sarah's only regret. She always seemed to pick the Bandwagon Hoppers. She is as hard as nails though. At Stonehenge, I saw her kick a copper right in the balls, then go running across the field to breastfeed her baby. She is still young. She may yet change, and go her own way, but somehow, I do not think so. All I can tell you of her is that she had a scrappy upbringing in Shropshire; a divorce, and then a harsh grandparent. She rebelled like crazy, but became the mother she longed for. When I think of Sarah, I always think of a night in a pub in Cornwall, not long after I met Pete. A man was asking her what she did for a living.

"I journey," she had said.

"What for?" the man asked.

"It's what I do best."

She was right. It was what she did best. We all journey. It is what we all do best. And so, Sarah put the bus into first gear, and we rolled on; Pete aiming an extended middle finger at Mortonhampstead.

Eddie

Holy shit. Dude, or dudette, you don't know me, thank God. My name is Hopkins, Edward Hopkins. Back home, people call me Eddie. I know others though who call me a dickhead, or give me the finger from the sidewalk opposite if they see me. I'm a photographer. I am a capturer of images. I am a magician. I can hold time and make it solid. I can falsify. I can juggle with reality. I can manipulate. I can pretend. The camera never lies, they say. They, whoever they are, are wrong. I'll do whatever the fuck I like.

It hasn't been long since I got back from my second trip to Iraq. Six months though, in fact. It has taken me that long to recover. Things are unbelievably fucked up there. It is really like something out of a horror story. Nearly got myself killed more than once. First time I was there, was in the Gulf War itself—heading up through Kuwait with the Marine Corps. Somewhere there, are two of my cameras. I had to leave them behind on that final push with the Corps to the north. I like to think of some old native boy finding them: the twentieth-century finally entering his patch of desert. I told the Agency I wasn't going back. So I am on the move again.

My life has permanently been in flux. Thirty-fucking-four years and it seems like the whole lot of it has been full of Kuwaits, Iraqs and other war-zones. You name them: I've done them all: Nicaragua, Mozambique, Palestine, and then that little trick of Saddam's. I have no real roots. You'll learn that. I am a spore drifting around the oceans of the world on its eddies and currents. Sometimes I stick, the way dry thistles do to wool. It's then that I make images. I'm not an artist. I'm no Andy Warhol or Paul Klee. I just make images. I am an image-maker. I am a voyeur. I like to watch. Then, I click.

You know a little of me now. Let me tell you more. I am an American. You may have guessed from the accent. But I'm no fully-integrated, constitutionalized, turkey-on-Thanksgiving, get-on-your-horse-an'-go-get-'em American. I mean, I'm a blemish on its record of otherwise perfect humanity. I smoked dope in the last year of my New Plymouth High School behind the chemistry classroom. I'm no new Republican if you get my meaning. Bush, he's a fucking asshole. The only reason we bothered to bail out Kuwait was for the oil—but then you knew that, didn't you?

But for my sins, I am American. I was born in the state of Massachusetts, not far from Cape Cod.

My parents owned a twenty-four hour diner on the coastal trucking route heading to Boston, next to a liquor store where the hobos sat, and where my father worked on Johnson's farm at the weekends and the evenings, to earn a bit extra. I grew up looking across the grey Atlantic, over to Europe. As a kid, I used to believe I could see it. Then though, I didn't know the world was round. Didn't know about distance and what it can do. I used to look out from the stony beaches for the *Queen Elizabeth II* coming across. The nearest I got were the hulking, rusty oil tankers heading up from the Gulf to the St Lawrence River; all sexy names like the *Texas Lady* and the *Sargasso Princess*. I was a romantic kid see. Still am, I suppose. First went to New York City when I was ten. I ran away from home after my grandpa died. The police caught me tagging my name on the aluminum billboards in the subway, with a couple of kids from the Puerto Rican ghetto. That was the coolest I think I have ever felt. With them. They could tell I was from out of the city: me in sandals and a hand-me-down checkered shirt from *Wal-mart*. I looked like a complete hick.

Let me give you some more to build your picture of me. Put a little light into the viewfinder as it were… I lost my virginity at fifteen. I guess I was always a little over-developed for my age. She was seventeen. She told me I looked like Jim Morrison. Amazing what things like that can make you do isn't it? I mean, I'd been blasting out "Strange Days" and reading the Lizard King's lyrics for a few years. It was only natural. She worked in the local 69 gas station. We used to watch baseball together, when my mother and father worked the late shift. We watched a game and then walked together. We made love on that same stony beach I used to go to when I was a kid. I couldn't resist looking over her shoulder, out over the grey water. I guess we weren't meant for each other long term.

I grew out of all that though. I got into cameras and photography. See photographs are like poems: Haiku-like, and compact. They last forever. You capture the moment, then that's it. It's there forever. After I left school, I went to New Plymouth College for a couple of years to learn to do it properly. My folks had wanted me to do better. Pa had an eye on me doing something at university but I never had the discipline. I didn't want no jerk-off Professor telling me how to do things. I just managed to scrape my way through. I had a shit-hole of a first job, doing wedding and graduation pictures for smart-ass families from the other side of town, all kids with their eyes on Yale or Harvard. "Hopkins for High-quality prints" the ad ran. I jacked that in soon enough though. There was no future in it, and then, well, then, I still wanted the paparazzi. I wanted to photograph tight-butt babes getting in and out of taxi cabs, showing me their legs.

Yeah, tits and ass shots for the glossies, that's what I wanted. Now though, when I go back home; I always look in the window of the old store. It's been unused since I hauled ass out of town. There's still one of my cards on the window sill, so I suppose there's still a part of me there—a piece of me, yeah?

And now, you're wanting a piece of me. But I am not there now though. Oh no. That has passed. I am thirty thousand feet up. I am drifting. I am being the spore again. I am sitting next to an old crotchety couple from DC, who are going to see their family in Manchester, England. They are sleeping. Most people around me are sleeping, breathing dull air into their blankets, trying not to feel the turbulence. I am awake. I am eying up the stewardess. She has smooth, tan-stocking legs; legs that speak to me and cry out a woman's difference. She is my type. I'd like to take her thirty thousand feet up: mile high club, yeah? She looks at me. I smile. She knows nothing of my perversions. I want to stick to her, make my thistle ladder her tan stockings. This is a fantasy, but in any case, there is not the time now. We will be landing fairly soon, and this is only a mid-air collision on a flight of fancy. We are above the ozone shattered cloud still. It is incredibly white, like the earth is still encased in a wrapper of innocence. I want to photograph that cloud, but I would have to lean over the couple from Washington, and that is just too much like hard work for me right now.

You know a lot about me then. You know I am a thirty-something, lecherous, good-for-nothing, lazy photographer, and you know I am in an airplane, more precisely the 07:19 Virgin Atlantic 747 from Washington to Heathrow. The flight takes about seven hours. There is about an hour to go, by my reckoning. I order another drink: a Southern Comfort, coke and ice. I tell the other passengers who look at me, that it calms my nerves. They look at each other and think of terrorism and Gaddafi. Such areas of existence are not my concern (not now at least…). I live for the moment, but then, you should know that by now.

When I doze, I can feel the stewardess-stimulated pheromones dying in me. I do not dream. I cannot recall the last time I dreamed. It must have been before my experience of Iraq. You don't dream there. I'm on edge, like you have to be. Every five minutes I wake and hear moments of life: snoring, coughing, farting, talking, someone hastily walking towards the closet. This has gone on for the length of this flight. It is a habit I picked up in old Babylon. In the desert heat, you are wary, wary of anyone who can slit your throat, so you always sleep with one eye open. Eventually however, out of the window, I see not clouds and sea, but land. The crew inform us that it is Ireland.

A while later, we are lower. We are above England some place. I am thinking of sparkling Princess Diana and green Wimbledon. I am thinking of men in derbies with black briefcases and of The Beatles, Monty Python and Shakespeare, and all those other clichés of time and place. I am here. We circle above London's urban limits, and then the plane drops height to land. We land smoothly. When the loosen seatbelt sign lights up, I am the first to stand up. Keen, see. I have arrived. I have a mission. I smile at the sexy stewardess at the door. I say goodbye, and imagine rubbing ripe strawberries and fresh cream into her milk-white generous cleavage.

England awaits.

There is a new term now, which perhaps describes me. It is normally applied to an accent: "Mid-Atlantic". Perhaps I am a Mid-Atlantian. Sounds good doesn't it? As though I was conceived of the ocean, born of seaweed, and raised on the tide. Then again, it sounds as though I belong to nowhere, caught between two poles. I think the latter more correct. I mention this, because the sweaty baggage handler takes the piss out of me. I have asked him if he knows where the flight-cases containing my equipment are. As always, I got them billed and insured separately from my other luggage.

"Oover there siirrrrr…" he says pointing to a desk on the other side of the baggage collection zone. He mimics my Massachusetts accent in the question with his answer. I don't blame him. I would have done the same had I been him. I collect my two battered flight-cases and then, once other airport formalities are completed, pushing a yellow-handled trolley, I head outside for a cab. Without thinking, I take a last look back for that stewardess hoping she must just want to share a cab with me. She is not there. Outside, I see obese, middle-aged bankers with my longed-for derbies and briefcases. I laugh. They are my mission. The brief for this assignment is a doddle. Take a break, they said. I have to capture Britishness for the organization I am contracted to. Their magazine is called *Day to Day* and it's a kind of trendy, office coffee table rag that sits in companies' foyers, for the rich to read while they're waiting.

I mean, what the hell is Britishness now anyway? It's strange. I do it myself even. Americans seem to speak only of England, yet they actually mean Great Britain. I'm goin' t'try to stick with this, although forgive me if I slip. See, America, or rather the people who buy *Day to Day* have a passion for Britishness, for antiquity, for a culture they think has deeper roots, longer memories and remains. I am here to snap that. My editors think that Britain might be changing with its further integration into the European Union, and they figure our readers might want some feature on it. They want a definitive study yeah, running across four or five issues.

I did the same thing on Iraq the second time around. An in-depth photographic study. You try to get the essence of the place at that time.

As well as that, I gotta tell you. I am on a personal mission that they know nothing about. It is nowhere near as grand as what they ask of me, but I have waited a long time to come here. I told you how I used to look at the Atlantic Ocean whilst that gasoline girl and I greasily screwed.

When I used to come inside of her, there was something else that drove me—something else that used to make me tick.

It was something my grandpa told me.

But I can't tell you yet; not just yet at least. I have to prove it myself. Now, I don't know… but I will find out.

My thoughts about these two interrelated missions are interrupted by a shout from a cab driver. He asks if I need one. I do not answer. I am still tied up in all these thoughts; but instead, instinctively hold out one of my flight-cases. He sees the affirmative signal and takes the trolley from me, loading the weight luggage into the trunk. I guess I am disappointed. I wanted a Cockney "Cor-blimey" geezer. I wanted to talk about London and the War, jellied eels and the state of the bloody roads. Instead he is Asian, from Pakistan. He tells me his equally as interesting a story instead, in word-perfect English. This was how he joined his brother in a place called Slough, a journey across two continents, just to be part of a taxi firm in London. While he talks, I sit back and watch concrete. I give him the address where I am to stay. He knows it. The journey will take forty minutes. I relax. I watch blackbirds on the side of the highway. I am enchanted as we pass a Morris Minor on the M4. These are the myths of Britain you see. I watch for my first red bus. I have already slung a camera around my neck. The lens cap is off, and there's higher resolution film in. This is me. An American in London. Stranger in a strange land… or… and I'm weighing it up, a more familiar one?

Earlier, I said that you do not know me. At least now, you do know something of me, or at least you think you do. I mean, I could be telling Cockney "pork pies". You wouldn't know now would you? It's like I was working with a guy once, who specialized in manipulating photographs. It's becoming easier now, with new computer technology. I mean it could be as simple as making a polluted, grey San Francisco sea look beautiful for tourist postcards, or it could be as crucial as changing military photographs for the right result at the Pentagon. No civilian casualties is always a good result. Nothing then, is that certain, and everything is a myth. That's something I've learnt. And yes, those pictures you thought would be great, never come out, or those you thought were plain awful turn out on the front cover of *Day to Day*.

I can play with myths as well. I mean, you must have an idea of America. You must know its myths, its survivors, its legends, the things that have stayed in the collective conscience: diners, *McDon-*

alds, Reese's Peanut Butter Cups, Beef jerky, *Twinkies* and *Budweiser,* the great outdoors, Route 66, "Sweet Home Alabama", James Dean and Jack Kerouac. Then there's garbage cans, dumpsters and Vietnam vets. Yes. That's us. The same way Britain has its myths: "Evenin' all" policemen who don't carry guns, red telephone boxes, fish 'n' chips and black-faced chimney sweeps, who still exist. And, of course, the Royal Family. They love all that, you see, back in the States, and if I want to, I can alter it any way I like. I am a recorder of myths. I am a modern scribe; only my goose quill is the SLR camera, and I write with pictures.

Follow me.

Follow me. Come on. I want you to take a trip. Yes, a road trip if you like. I spoke of another mission as well, as the recording of myths. To explain this mission, I need to tell you of other journeys. America is a country based upon journey; journeys to get to it, and journeys to cross it. Ask the Native Americans. Ask the Mexicans. Ask the Puerto Ricans. Ask the African-Americans. Ask the Europeans even, if they care to remember. If their ancestors were still alive, you could ask the Wagon trailers, and then those who headed to the Klondike. They would tell you about journeys, and searches for paradise. It's all about the quest for the Promised Land; their push westwards, ever onwards, across the Prairies, across desert, across the Rockies, across canyons. And did they find it? At first, it was a never-ending story. Then, they came to the Pacific—another ocean to cross. There, they found California. You tell me if they found paradise. I'll let you decide, man.

Zip Hopkins journeyed. Zip's my grandpa. Zipped everywhere as a kid. He wasn't the first to journey—not by a long chalk—and he could never have been the last. I used to go up his place as a kid, a few miles up the coast. Used to stop by to help him saw up his mountain wood, or feed the few horses he used to keep in a paddock there. He'd cook me up some waffles then, when we'd done enough work, and the night was coming down. So we'd sit there, with me pouring on the molasses and him muttering on. Some people are called legends, but my grandpa really was a legend. Had he been discovered, he would have become a myth. Some folk would say he used to go on, and on, but most would still listen. He always had something to say. Give him a decent whisky, and it was like a dime in a jukebox. The favorites would come on then, replayed like scratched records. Zip was respected see. He had another name: Doc. My father even used to call him Doc sometimes, but most of all, you'd hear it down the bars in town (you still do on occasions when people reminisce about him to me).

"Doc, you coming in for a beer?"

And I hear his deep voice, "Nope. I ain't got the time. Takin' m'gran'son Edward up t'see the horses…"

And this was me. Edward. He always called me Edward. Never Eddie.

I must explain my grandpa's other name. He was called Doc by the old timers, who remembered his ramshackle medicine show. Yeah, he had this mountebank stall he'd set up. Of course, by the time my grandpa had started up, everyone has seen through them: bottled water in most cases. Doc was no better—a relic from another Age. My father was embarrassed by him, carrying on an idea that lead nowhere a century ago, and had gone half-way across a continent for nothing. It probably went back further still, to holy water and saints' relics; all psychosomatic medicine crap. Picture him. A noisy audience. He would calm them first of all with his voice, and then their bodies would be topped up with his so-called patented Vitamin and Life-Enhancing tonic. The old snake. Sometimes, I used to come back down to his farm after I had been up the diner with my mom. He would be in the old barn, repeating to himself his old selling patter, seeking something of his youth.

"Get yerself some of Doc Hopkins' finest Vitamin and Life-Enhancing tonic," he'd whisper, as if it could still cure all evils. "Genuine stuff y'know… from the age-old secret recipe."

It was his greatest time. He told me that one time out in Tucson Arizona (Yeah, the fool would travel that far…), he had sold his entire stock to one little ranching town. Bought the lot. Apparently, such was the power of the tonic, the birth-rate tripled nine months later. Later, after he died, I could remember us clearing out his barn. There were hundreds of moldering bottles filled with God-only-knows-what. He sounds romantic. Old school yeah. But now, here in London, when I think of Zip or Doc, I think of a small-framed pathetic old man, who was riding on the final wave of those people, who still had superstition, and the old ways. He might have been the last for all I knew. The Indians knew him too, but that's another story for later.

No, I am romanticizing him too much. My grandpa was a waster too. Spent his money on liquor and drove my grand-mammy into an early grave (I never knew her). She died aged forty-three. He went on nearly twice as long as her. Something else I remember about him as well: he never went grey, like time preserved him. Always kept his jet black hair, with cropped dustbowl sides and a centre part. Had a shoe brush moustache as well. When he talked, his mouth disappeared under a cover of coarse hair. He used to tell me all his secrets. As a child, I felt he was wonderful. He would set me up with those sugary waffles, and then turn the oil-lamp down low. He spoke slowly, the tones resonating around the woody kitchen. He had a voice that was Walt Disney jolly, yet always in control, maximizing the effect of every word.

Now, I can see why. Those words were his life. He had very little else to show for his eighty-odd years. Times he's spent in New Orleans or Chicago; weeks of his life on railroads to some crap-hole of a mining town in Montana or Utah. Such tales: the day he bumped into Richard Nixon, Muhammad Ali, Gregory Peck. Yeah, right. They loved this down the bars down town—and so did the impressionable me.

I was ten when he told me about our past, and about the Hopkins family. About where we came from. He showed me old things he and others before him had kept. Relics, yeah? Real old shit, and how he came to develop the tonic. He took me down to a hill beside the coast. I know I had my eyes opened that day. He altered my view on life. He made me feel important. He knew himself to be important, and the story that he had been passed down through the line, to be important as well. He knew he would be talked about when he went on. High School was irrelevant compared to the things he told me. He would spin me some nonsense about how he came to be himself, how he came to be named, how they came to live on this peninsula, and you never knew if it was the truth or not. He said I had a special bloodline, and a history. Perhaps then, I am not the spore I make myself out to be. Maybe my spore is just without direction.

Shortly after he told me all of this, my grandpa died. They found him slumped on the earthy barn floor, trying to lift a hay bale. A heart-attack. In his pocket was a half-empty bottle of his patented Vitamin and Life-Enhancing tonic. He believed in his own voodoo, see. I didn't stay for the funeral. In fact, I have not been to any funeral, not even my pa's. See, I like to keep my distance from death. I did take one of his tonic bottles though—just for keeps. I packed a kit-bag, and got on the early morning bus journeying to central New York City, for bright lights and city nights...

II
The Indulgences

Robert

Somewhere, I have mentioned that I have a son. I have also hinted at my estrangement from him. This I now accept, and have done so for some time. He has always sided with his mother, and so it is she who keeps in contact with him via the odd letter, the occasional two-minute long phone calls, but there are never any locations. He could be in any cardboard city for all I know. Since his teenage years at least, I have always been a mere annoyance to him, a kind of vestigial appendage, no longer needed. No, I am just a wily, eccentric academic who should take things easier. I did my utmost with him, but she always took the lead, though the actual estrangement began long before I stood watching them on the strawberry-and-cream coloured dodgems and the rickety roller-coasters of Barry Island Pleasure Beach, where we holidayed that year. See, I had no opportunity to prove myself as the male of the species. Our son noticed this from the outset. In family games of cricket, on Sunday afternoons, she would always bowl me out for a duck, with not a single run made. And she, well, I would spend all afternoon trying to bowl her out. And then, I could only bowl underarm, pathetically daisy-cutting the ball along the innings.

Be warned—or perhaps you may know already—children are clever onlookers. They look more closely. They watch you to test the rules of life for them. They watch you play the game, and then hopefully, they will play it better. I then, could not have played it very well.

Now that I am old, it feels strange to have featured in his child-hood spiral, to have done things with him. But then, that is the bane of every parent. It is the stirring and horrible voice of truth. There is no real thank you. Everything is accepted. You are the parent, and you are the provider. So while he grew up, I had another name: Daddy or Dad, but do not read love into this relationship, for it was never like that. No, for Dad read "money", and then see where I stood—there, on the extremities.

This afternoon I will read. I've been asked to review a new book out on *Death in Fourteenth-Century Western Europe*. Some bright young spark from Cambridge has written it. So, I will play with the words of the dead once more. It may have some bearing on a paper I am writing. There is a conference coming up this autumn on "The Archaeology of the Canterbury Tales". Do you know Chaucer? You must do. He of "Whan that Aprill, with his shoures soote, The droghte of March hath perced to the roote". I know him well, but archaeology will make him real; bring him back from the dead and make his words live. Somewhere earlier, I told you I do not believe in reincarnation because if there were, we should be more skilled in the way we lead our lives. Well, if I am a reincarnation of someone else, then I believe I might have been from Chaucer's age—a medieval man. Here I am see, also on a pilgrimage. I don't have any wish to walk barefoot, as it were, to my shrine. No, my pilgrimage is an escape. I am denying just as Chaucer's crew did, others' spiri-tual guide over me. My son and wife's monopoly over me hurts. I am denying them just as other pilgrims in the past. What were their motives? Just the same as mine: to see new places and experience new things, the servants' impatience with the master, of children with their parents, and husbands with their wives. This is the correct notion of humanity.

You know that I am an academic. Well, you know how that goes. I won't bore you with the institutions I have progressed through, never kowtowing to stupid business managers and clueless heads of department. But what did I end up as? Well, Reader, then Professor in Archaeology at the University of Bristol. So, I spent much of my time writing stupid papers on stupid digs. In fact, I have played with words for most of my life, games with sentences and card-tricks with paragraphs. I was being oh-so-bloody clever. I messed around with them for days on end, just to set up some paradigm or thesis. Endless books too: tracts which now sit in dusty rows in my library that I never read now. Let me advise you now: this is not a sensible thing to do with your life. You end up confused and bewildered, as I am sure most of my students were. I often wondered what they really thought of me. It has been a few month's now, since I retired—or rather took "early retirement" i.e. was asked to jump ship.

I'll spare you the grimy details. I might embarrass a few people with my mutterings, opening to many dingy cupboards with skeletons in them. It was then, with the opening years of my career, that I first became interested in the dead. All those early digs, ripping up skeletons of the past, who had been carefully placed in the earth.

This naturally led on to elegies and epitaphs—the structures and similes of the dead. And so then on to mossy graveyards and ivy-clad tombs. I have walked this country's vast Victorian graveyards, through marble monoliths and Celtic crosses, past angelic sculptures and pseudo-gothic sepulchres. Not only here, but most of Western Europe. Oh yes, you might say I know the architecture of the dead more than anyone else alive. People now say I am the world expert. This is how I discovered the words of the dead. It is in such places that I found how the darkness of then can affect the light of now. I have spoken to a thousand mourners and guessed the thoughts of a thousand more.

But wait. My penchant for tombs and stones has much more than just an academic interest. I believe it began in the mind of the sensitive, voyeur child. I'm not even sure I should tell you this, but here goes. Once upon a time, in my St Ives childhood, I came across this courting couple, making love amongst the gravestones of the cemetery above Porthmeor Beach. Imagine—she has propped her chalky back against a subsiding gravestone, and he was about to enter her. When she leaned forward—and I shall always remember it—the green moss on the stone, had stuck to her back. I shouldn't have stayed, but I watched them do it. And something then, told me that I was watching something intolerable, something so disgusting that my innocence abhorred it, but I still wanted my innocence ruined, the way we all do. But then later, I knew it to be rather beautiful, making love, making life among the watching dead. For many years, I had a fantasy of doing it myself with her there, right there above Porthmeor, while the waves of the Atlantic could watch us, but she would never have had that. It was always a lights out and a fumble under the bedclothes. She is still self-conscious after all these years of marriage. And now that all our bits sag badly, we can't even do that.

And then that other time, that time with the Navy when we put into Lisbon. We'd all gone out. There was this girl. She had wanted us to chase her through the graveyard. She was rich beauty that one. It was ethereal, diabolical almost, and I regretted that I didn't actually do anything. Oh yes, she had wanted all of us. Me included. She had straddled a stone monument, and the boys queued up to fuck her. I loved the way she hitched up her skirt and, and clambered onto the stone, and they lined up. It was like some kind of gothic *South Pacific*.

"Have me…" she had said, but no, being me, I resisted and walked back to the ship. I still see her eyes in my dreams.

And so maybe, that is why my life has been devoted to death. Sex sits well with it. I knew that my life could never be quite the same after those discoveries. You are hearing the thoughts of a disturbed mind.

She knows nothing of this, of course. She thinks me repellent enough already. But I know, and that is all that matters now.

When you are my age, the small things do count. The larger ones—so they tell me on the cheap stickers on sale in the tourist shops of the Barbican—can wait until tomorrow.

Tombs and gravestones are dying you know. They are going the way of their occupants. Now, cremation is the way to go. It's less messy. Less of a reminder see. There is nothing to be tended, or kept; except to polish the urn. But graves are where my heart is. It's odd, but the graves I like the best are the ones where the grass strangles the stone, and the lettering is but a dull shadow. Those are always the interesting ones; the ones no-one cares for any longer. I have another memory from childhood here. I always think of it when I see an overgrown grave. It is a picture of me as a boy (all short trousers and scarred knees) and my great uncle. Jack, he was called. Jack Bolitho. He had some notion about tidying two distant relatives' grave. I remember loading all the tools he had into this rusty wheelbarrow, and driving the five miles from our place to the dark churchyard at Nancledra. The grave was there, a simple marble thing for two people. The blackened concrete had cracked where the grass had pushed under it. I was still a boy remember. I was too scared to look down the lichen-infested cracks in case death stared back at me. Uncle Jack's pick cracked it open, and I saw him replace the heavy slab. We hacked all the seedy grass down, and cut the fruit bramble back. But once it had gone, the grave looked terrible, pathetic even. Overgrown, it had looked majestic, like a tumulus. I felt my distant relatives turn in their grave. Jack thought it looked proper, but I never forgave him for what he'd done.

Though my interest is in graves, you will see that by nature, I am not really a morbid man. I rarely talk about my interest now. Even at dinner parties at Bristol, when people asked me about my research, you do not say gravestones and the dead. You turn the conversation and get onto gardening and travel, and how good the food has been. It is a fallacy I do not mind keeping up. I like to keep the peace.

I am aware, of course, that some day, not too far off now, that death will come and knock on my door. Then he will flick his scythe and I'll become my life's work. But I do not want to go the way of most men. My wife signals from time-to-time that I should make "arrangements". She knows I am not interested. I seek a different kind of death. Let me try to explain. Have you ever noticed that we find so few bodies of dead animals? They chose somewhere undisturbed and sacred. Here, I am thinking dormice, sparrows and spiders. What becomes of them when they pass away? And those elephants' graveyards, where those creatures track when they know their ends are coming. That is how I want to go. I shall find a thick bramble bush where I may simply rot in peace. Think of it as the perfect archaeologist's graveyard. I cannot think of a better way to go.

So you have learnt quite a lot about me now. You know about my son. You know about my complexities and associations with regard to the topic of death. You know my most intimate perversions and experiences. We all have them, so don't judge me. Now though, I am ready to continue with why I am here. See, after death, comes always life. It is the way it is…

I have heard that Plymouth has given its name to more towns and cities than any other in the world. There are seventeen Aberdeens outside Scotland. There are twenty-nine Londons outside England, but can you believe this? There are forty Plymouths. It's hard to contemplate I know. Forty journeys heading out from the choppy

Sound into the Channel, and then away. It sounds too fantastical, as fantastical as Corineus and Gogmagog wrestling up there on the Hoe all those thousands of years ago. Over the years, hoards of rum-filled sailors have made the break, to go onto the tiss-toss ocean, only to arrive at some distant place and recall what they had left. It must be the grasp for something, the reminder; that amongst the primitive can be found the civilized.

Consider, for example, New Plymouth, Massachusetts, where William Bradford and the Pilgrim Fathers set out for. He remembered the place that they last left. Aided by a Native American, the so-called Squanto, they negotiated a treaty with Chief Massasoit, which helped to ensure the colony's success. Yes, colonial power at its height. Bugger the Native American names. Name it Plymouth. Aye, she has seen them all, this city: Sir Francis Drake, the Armada, the *Mayflower*'s blow across the ocean to a new continent, a new history. Consider the warships she had seen, the crews piped aboard, Chichester, and then the coming home. The soundtrack here is the one of voices of gulls, the clank of the gang-plank, and the dip of algae-draped ropes into the water. But Plymouth is richer than that, for she is a variegated city. She has many colours and she changes like a chameleon. There are parts of her I thought I knew, but which have changed immeasurably. There are parts I thought I would never go… and yet have.

How best to approach Plymouth? There are many ways: across from Cornwall, or down over Dartmoor's brown edge, or even follow the River Plym to its mouth, past the twin towers of the Prince Rock power station. No. The right route is from the sea, so you can ease in on the frothy tide, eying the barber's pole that is Smeaton's Lighthouse, and grand Eliot Terrace. You observe the dip of the tide in Sutton Pool's harbour, that place where so many have set out; the harbour encased by the black and white, topsy-turvy Barbican, a remnant of another time, and something to treasure. I always wonder how the hell it survived the bombing. Yes. By the sea is the best way to approach. Coming home on the tide. A timeless thing. Biblical. You want to be in there I think, wound up with them all, swirling around with the past's glory: Hawkins, Grenville, and Raleigh.

This is where they came to. This was the place where the first Elizabeth ruled. I like to picture them unloading wonders from far-off lands. Raleigh standing there, smoking a cigar, standing like W. C. Fields, amazing the townsfolk.

"Look what we've brought back this time," I can hear him saying. "Come and see. Come and hear our story…"

I always do that when I am down there.

But this is insignificant. I want to tell you more of my time here. My time seems better, but then it is often like that. Everyone's time is better than everyone else's. Because you were there, it was better. In such things I like to be selfish. I was serving in Plymouth in the early '50s. This was before archaeology. Before any of that. I was different then. Almost another person. But wait. I don't want to tell you this. You have heard all of that before from others. I want to tell you of us, all of us, in our blue, just-pressed uniforms heading up from East Stonehouse. Yes. Then, Plymouth was a real city, a grand place built upon years of wear and neglect. Despite the bombing, chunks of it were still there, shouting out its old-fashioned glory. You never realize it at the time. Now see, there are only fragments left. Think of Charles Cross church in the centre of its roundabout, encased by multi-story car parks and a dual carriageway. The war did gut the city centre though. Some relics though: Derry's clock, the Bank, the Palace Theatre and the Guildhall. They are still there along with the Barbican. They are pieces of time that should have ticked away years ago. But stand they do, and Plymouth rose behind them, and now she flies again, her concrete proud. The Luftwaffe's *Heinkel He 111*s helped build modern Plymouth.

But back then, a lot was still there, the way I always had Plymouth imprinted on my mind. Yes. Union Street. You will know that, I am sure. Its reputation travels before it. It is an odd place, like a quarter of a mile of South-West Soho. I think it used to be our place then. Real places you know. Sawdust for a reason: to soak up the vomit and sodden, spilt beer. It had romance then. Brown tiles with crafted brewery pints on them. Stained-glass windows. The smoke of ten-thousand cigarettes tucked in the corners. Illegal boxing matches. That bloke from Cattedown, who when he went to the urinal, had trained his dog—a Jack Russell terrier—to piss when he did. That boy wandering around all evening asking for tuppences until he had enough for a drink. Bars where men stood who had seen every sea twice, and three times if they were sweet-talking some girl sat on a bar stool. Is that right? Or do I wear rose-tinted spectacles? Perhaps there were fights. Perhaps the place stank of sick, and beery piss of the Matelot. I loved it though.

The last time I looked, there was one left. Caw d'hell (I hear my father say this)—the women the boys used to meet in there! Rough as rats. "The Albert" I think the place was called. Now, it is wedged in between some tattoo shop and a kebab house. It's all gone now though. Fun pubs they call them. We were heading back that way in a taxi the other night. We could only but watch Gaudy Cinderellas and acid Prince Charmings down there on the pull. No different than us I suppose. But there are bouncers on the doors. The pubs' gaudiness saddens me. There are kids (they do seem much younger now) dodging us. The police vans wear black riot shields over their windscreens. I see the toppling structure of the Old Palace Theatre, her mosaic frontage as regal as ever. The shows I saw there! Her past is ignored by the clubbers underneath. She is renamed "The Academy"—a new nightspot. I gaze wide-eyed at it all. I'd be lying. Yes, I would be telling a big one, if I didn't say I was looking for the ghost of that bloke and his dog. Now wouldn't that be a find for this archaeologist? Other ghosts too—but I'll leave them still buried for now.

Jude

Those outside us are not close. As the universe pulls apart, so follows its people. We develop. We grow. There will be a day when we are autonomous, when we will need no contact, when we will need no voice, and when we will need no touch. Nothing more will be needed. Each will have his or her own private space, and that is how life will go. We need to rebel against that. We smash it. We vandalize it. We pull it apart at every opportunity. We crunch it into pieces on the ground. I do worry though, that we may be going against the laws of the universe: the big-bang and all that. Nonetheless, we hug. We are close. As the universe pulls apart, and leads to bigger explosions, we stretch out hands, straining and trying to catch it. We are trying to pull the pieces back in. Our indulgence is this then. This is what we cherish.

I need to tell you this, because of our ultimate fear—the one we confess most freely to ourselves—is that we will lose everything, and it will never be regained. This is like learnt stories. If the teller dies, then they die too. They are lost. I suppose then, I do believe in the record. I believe in the passing on of knowledge. The trick though, is the sifting, the slow swirl of the bowl. We want the hidden truth to come to the surface, to poke out at us, as bright nuggets of gold. Note, that the sifting is the true skill. It requires adjustment, and it takes time to learn.

I learn it through many ways. Rebellion at first; the reactions against the norm. But then you have to replace the norm. There has to be something to hold, to share. So we adapt. We have become a different creed—a new species. We rise early, when the rest of the world is still asleep. We sleep when the world plays. There must be problems when we collide. Here's just one…

May Day, and we tried celebrating the Beltane with fire. The old Pagan way, the time our forefathers and mothers welcomed the return of summer by constructing huge bonfires to strengthen the power of the sun. But they wouldn't have it. The authorities moved in. I sat there in the ashes, freezing cold water from a fire hose streaming onto me.

So we pursue, yet we are pursued. I mean the educational authorities hunt us like tracking dogs. See, Sarah's children do not go to school. Oh no. We believe that artificial. We throw de-schooling at them, but they are not interested in our apparently anarchist tendencies. We are troublemakers. Be we educate here. We home school. We spend hours with them. We show them things others cannot teach them. I would lay money on the fact that our children are much brighter than other children of the same age.

See, we want human beings, not machines, not fuses to fit into a nine-to-five rack. Our children will not blow. They will learn wisdom and vision, hand-in-hand with algebra and past participles. I am a good teacher, because I am still a learner. I reflect on my practice. When learning stops, then teaching soon follows. That is when we shall send the children to school. That is when we shall leave them at the gates, and the jaws of society shall swallow them.

That is why is it best to sift, to look more closely. To filter. To find the real, and not the fool's gold.

Eddie

I've been to places on this crumbling relic of a planet that would make you violently and physically sick. Places where man's inhumanity to man is at its peak. You know where I mean: the axis of evil—Central America, South Africa, Burma, Iraq... to name only a few. Yes, only a few... At times, I have felt like the messenger boy on some sadistic errand, and I have said to my photo-journalist self, "Do I really want to show the world this?", and so sometimes, I bin film that I do not want the world to see. So the pictures you do see are only the scrapings of the surface. Yes, we are all guilty of that, of not seeing, or not wanting to see. Talk to me of evidence. Oh sure. Evidence. But do not rely on the proverb: the camera can lie.

It was in New York City that I bought my first camera, from a sleazy pawn shop somewhere across in the Bronx, full old 78s and Les Paul guitar copies, with their strings missing. It was a Kodak Brownie. I had stolen some money from the till in mom's diner; the same money I had used for the Greyhound bus fare. You see, I didn't want to know how Zip had died. I bought a film. If I couldn't have Zip then I was going to "do" this city. I spent most of my time in the older parts of the city; in the ghettos, as they were then labelled. I think even then, I could see the beauty of those tumbling, grey-brown apartments with fire escapes clinging to them like some kind of steel ivy. One place I managed to get into, after an elevator ride, had not been touched for months. There were still ornaments and clothes left: statues of the Virgin Mary, boxes of candles, a Bible still open. The family had been evicted. Immigrants who couldn't keep up the payments. There were little pieces of their lives left; this Puerto Rican family who had come to find work, come to find their Promised Land. There were hundreds of them in this part of the city. They were aliens, slapped down in the middle of late twentieth-century nastiness. Maybe that was better than where they came from, but their faces told me another story. The bubble had been broken. Their dream lay in the filthy gutters. America had enough immigrants now. They were "eroding the culture". I heard that coming over on the plane. Spanish would not be an official language of the country, despite the high numbers of people who spoke it in pref-

THE CULT OF RELICS

erence to English. The States don't need any new pilgrims. That's Bush for you. All they want are cultural ambassadors of the right kind: English-speaking and white. Don't dare ask for a quarter-pounder in another tongue.

Further down the same streets, at the dead ends, are the real tragedies—men and women who have nothing more to give. I was with the worms of the Big Apple, ragged, torn, coughing creatures huddled together. These were the creatures that told me all they really wanted was to be loved, or held, instead of being shunned and ignored. Had I known, I would never have walked down there at that age (I would certainly never do it now).

I don't know what they thought of me, except my camera thrilled them. It was like a wand. They lined up and posed—all black teeth smiles, bad-breath tales; relics amongst the relics of urban architecture. Mere shells of humanity. Hobos. Scum. I used up a whole film on them. When I was sixteen, I looked at the photos again, and threw them out. I couldn't believe I had taken them. They scared me. It was the terror that lay beneath their smiles that got to me. But then, perhaps going down there, to that community, is why I am never sick when I visit these places. I know I lost my innocence early. Perhaps I lost it earlier than I thought. Hardened me, when I was still a child.

Explains a lot really.

Useful, when you're in my line of work.

How I got accepted into the gang is a different matter. But I was part of it. I was sworn in as a brother. Duke was the leader; a black kid with a retro Afro. He must have been impressed by this puny white kid in their territory. They were the products too, of a society that no-one wanted. They were pure wastage. I thought they were cool. I too, came to be accepted, as another waste part. I was another deviant. We did the subway trains with spray paint. Tagged the fucking lot. But it was not that which made them cool. Tagging, was merely fun. No, what made them cool, was their identity, their unity, their togetherness. They had nothing, and yet they belonged to something. They were part of something which had its own set of values, its own way of living. Its own sexuality. Its own religion. They didn't give a fuck for anyone else, because no-one had ever given a fuck about them. This was their culture, their devotion, and it was as fundamental, and as real as the long sheath knives they carried at all times. And yet sometimes, smiles as bright as the blades. So if you ever come across them or their progeny in the street, then toss them a buck. I might not have survived if the police hadn't caught me spraying a train by flashlight in an Amtrak marshalling yard. I'd still be with them (perhaps I am still in a small way).

I often wonder what happened to Duke. I imagine him sometimes. Had he turned it around? Maybe working for some youth projects, discouraging gang culture, or maybe have gone the other way—dying from some infected needle. Can I possibly get over to you the sense of freedom they gave to me; the sense that not everything is cut-and-dried. We all have cultures. There are as many cultures as there are people, and they may be there for all sorts of reasons. I do not believe I belong to any culture now though. I have seen too much. I am no longer objective. I have to say then that I have never really discovered my true culture, the one that I should fit into. I was just a vulture feeding on others.

They took me home. I had been away for three weeks. My father nearly killed me. Mother said Zip had been buried. I went to visit his grave. I felt I had aged ten years. In my coat pocket, I had a knife and a camera. Not much has changed.

The knife I gave to a Chaldean nun in Iraq, and that first camera sits on my mantelpiece at home.

Somewhere along the line, the long line of my family from the year dot, my own father, Henry Hopkins, had lost what I can now term the "Hopkins' zest for life". He was a more simple man than his father before him, and I somehow always felt his life to have been overshadowed by grandpa's. He was a good man though, and rarely complained of his lot in life. I say "was" since he too, died a couple of years back. Natural causes. Nothing spectacular. His life was one of inconsequence, a continual tedium of seasonal work on the farm that seemed age-old—as old as that first Plymouth colony—then helping out at the diner when mom went shopping, and on the late shift. So primitive. I could imagine prehistoric societies living on similar lines. He spoke little, and his one and only passion in his life was old farm machinery; the startling innovation of his youth. Green and yellow *John Deere* tractors, plows and seed drills made him drool.

There was a time once, though, not long after Zip died, when my father opened up, blossomed into the man he never was, like those desert plants which only flower ever hundred years. It was one day, while we were out gathering in the corn. I was down in the field, throwing up cobs to him on the trailer. I heard him chuckling.

"What's up pa?" I asked him.

"Oh—something Doc told me once," he laughed, and I could see the narrative well up inside of him, like some old magic.

"What? Tell me…" I pleaded.

My father looked at me. He sighed. I felt him think. Suddenly now I was a bit older, he could tell me. This is when stories make sense.

"Well once, Pa got this thing see, this object see, that makes his Holy Water; his tonic right? And he makes a deal with one of these gentlemen to sell this stuff… There was a Reverend around these parts then. A Reverend Whitworth. Well, your grandpa sold this tonic to the good people around here. And he told them… you know the way he did it… that if they bought and drank enough water, they'd be cleansed of all their sins, an' that it would make 'em—you know—fruity for love…. Well, old Billy Farrell (a man nearly ninety years of age) was first up there. Paid the money and drank the water. Said he felt like a million dollars. And do you know, the whole town bought this stuff. The Reverend, a Protestant sort of feller, he called grandpa all sorts, words you wouldn't expect a man of the church to say.

"Yes—language children shouldn' hear and that grown men should never use. The water went so goddamn well that Whitworth had no-one turn up to church. And your grandpa, well, he brought another couple of cases full of the stuff inta town…"

His voice petered out. I could tell the sadness rising. Then we both laughed a crying kind of laugh. A desperate laugh. No more was said that day. I carried on throwing up the corn to him.

That story reminds me of another I must quickly tell. In Great Britain, you are lucky. Religion is not rammed down your throats like it is the States, and where gleaming, sticky, lovely game-show evangelists ask you to send in your money for God. Flick through the television channels and see how many Christian channels there are, preaching and eventually asking for a credit card donation. In America now, there is no magic. Religion, like everything else, had only a temporary hold. America has seen every tacky mania. Every fad. Every "in" television show. Every social trend. One fad, however, is dropped quickly for another. Fads seem to run in circles.

Things are "in", then "out", then back "in" and then back "out" again. American society is based on this enormous dance of hokey-cokey.

As well as fads, we have cults. You may know something of cults. More hokey cokey. More mumbo-jumbo. They are frightening though; more real than fads. Cults may be religious or materialistic. They begin when one person suddenly realizes that there is somebody else who shares their interest. Think of the ones so far: The Children of God, Hare Krishnas, The Moonies, Scientology, Jehovah's Witnesses, Satanism, The Rajneeshis, and The Mormons. These cults are not flashes in the pan. They are as devotional as those that existed in the Medieval world. They are long-lasting lifetime obsessions. Followers of cults are determined people. They travel great distances to meet, gather at conventions and dress in cult fashion. I speak then of all kind of cults; all those others who lurk out there in the deserts of New Mexico and Arizona. And then, there are the new cults, the icons of our age, who become the cults of tomorrow. Jedi religions. *Star Trek*. Do you know that if you are a Trekkie you can visit the future birthplace of Captain Kirk in Iowa? So we are at the "beam-me-up" stage of cults. You cling on for a hold, things are slipping and sliding. See, religion and pop culture are merging. Think of Madonna. Think of Elvis and the Temple of Graceland. And you know what, those religions of the world—all the big ones—Christianity, Islam, Buddhism, Hinduism, Judaism—what are they really? Really, they are nothing more than cults that just got big.

Cults are mad though. There is, I feel, no future in being part of a cult. Though each one has its beliefs and heroes, the cult is inevitably self-destructive, because if we all joined, then you would no longer be a cult. And there, lies the paradox.

I don't plan on stumbling across one in the near future.

III

The Steps of the Master

Robert

I have made it. The journey of my meagre pilgrimage is over. I must now reject the world, take penitence and seek my cause. The strange thing is, I am unsure of this pilgrimage: the actual reason for me being there. I wonder if it is some holy reason or not? I have come to a town, where the Pilgrim Fathers, the very beginning of a new land and age, started from. But this is no Lourdes, no Mecca, no Croagh Patrick, nor Bethlehem. This is Plymouth, plain, concrete and steel Plymouth. And yet there is a presence, and I see that presence. My reason then is complex. I will attempt to fill you in on my confusion and hallucinations. Now hear this…

Imagine tiny Plymouth in the seventeenth century. Think of the town then. Think of a winding, mouldy estuary, and busy Sutton harbour. Think of ships creaking and heaving in. Think of men just glad to step off the sway. Don't think of romance, for that is not here. Leave that to novelists. Think harsh. Think brutal. Think of four, brim-full cutters side-by-side in the harbour, their softwood masts blocking the view over to Cattedown. Think of decks below, so tight, that you have to bend double to cross them. From the castle, you can just see the fishermen, and across Catwater to where Fort Stanforte rises. In the town, on the greasy quayside, characters speak, talk, get drunk, piss, make love, catch pox, eat, and remember. But this is not any rough rag of a story. See amongst this seafaring bowl of humanity was "He". See how I am constructing. Writing another paper. Weaving. Digging. Imagining. Will that do for you or not? I ask you in this very place, at this very moment: can you tell the truth from the fiction anyway?

You do not know him yet. Indeed, I don't know whether I know him yet either. What I am convinced of though, was that he was there. Of that, I am certain. I feel it in my bones. He is important and I have much more to tell of Him. I only know a little of what he looks like, and I am still unsure whether he was bearded or not.

Twice, I thought him an old man. Twice again, I have dismissed this. I have discovered more along the way. I think of him with brown eyes. No. Dark brown, or even black eyes. Anyway, eyes which give no reflection of the sea. They are eyes which just take in "things". Eyes that do not give away any secrets. I see him, sat outside the sailors' taverns on that year's sunny days. I see him larking with seagulls, pretending to kick them. I hear them cawing back to him, abusing his presence. From what I know of him, I see him tall, yet slightly hunched, with a slow stride; a casual movement of muscled arm. I see him as a skilled man, one however, who then cared little for his "profession". You will learn why, soon enough.

He wears not the grand clothes of those who arrived that day. His breeches are torn, and his stockings are black, and old. He wears no wide-brimmed hat with brass buckle. His, a simple skull cap, if anything at all; strands of long, straight hair escaping from beneath. His collar is small, and roughly cut. Their beards are neat and triangular. His is not. Their women are tightly-bodiced, with woollen skirts, linen blouses and aprons. They are not the bawds of the Sutton alehouses that he knows all too well.

His language is coarse: the dialect of sea-life, the tavern and travel. Theirs is refined, rhythmical and soft, though perhaps occasionally, snatches of it are heard in him. As their ship comes in, or rather returns, he drinks his last drop of warm ale, and steps outside. He says his cheery-bye to the maid. Out there, he hears creaking. The shipwrights and water-tighteners are being called for. Those refined speakers and smart dressers are complaining. The name on the ship is not clear. Is that *Pee'd well*? No, *Speedwell*. Ah yes. Separatists. Those from Holland and elsewhere… travelling people. Those who he had craftily sold shot and tobacco to, only a day or so before. There was a great commotion around the quayside, as though the very Apostles themselves had docked. A stranger to them all, he sat down, then bent his legs over Sutton quay, staring first at the flotsam and letting it wash over his mind, then peering out to where a second ship silently cut her way in. He knew this one, and would know her better still, by the end of this tale.

Here then, begins "The Stranger's Tale". It is full, as are all good stories of strangeness and charm. It is a tale that has survived, or at least the crumbs of it have. I am the one who has collected the crumbs, and re-made the cake. As yet, I have not told you the year. Here, have it. It is 1620. Now you know? I see Stranger, bouncing his knees like a child, watching history come in.

What is the second ship's name?

The *Mayflower*.

The *Speedwell*, to Stranger's point of view, appeared over-masted for her size, though even he admitted that her sailing should be strong. Activity on the quayside was frantic. It seemed that her Captain had brought her in because they had already had several problems coming down the Channel. They had stopped at Dartmouth already, he had heard.

He knew they were Separatists, and even though they had been persecuted, most knew of their foray to Leiden in Holland, and people there gave them hospitality. In Sutton, in Plymouth, many knew of these whims of people to cross the Atlantic, so this was nothing extraordinary. Maybe an anticipation of something more… but only maybe…

Though the leak was on the starboard side, he had heard that there was indeed, a hole, large enough to put his fist through. She was leaky as a sieve, and the crew knew it. They were presently shouting at each other. She wouldn't stand a gale out on the Atlantic. Tempers were flared. Faces were red. He could not help but laugh at the comedy of these usually calm, religious men arguing with the hardened, stubble-faced sailors. There had been worry as well over the Captain submitting them his accounts. Apparently also, he had refused his passengers to go ashore, in case they ran away. He was a worried man. He acknowledged Stranger, as he walked across the plank. Stranger was known. The Captain spoke to the leading passengers in an enraged tone.

Passengers on board the *Mayflower* began to disembark. They were friendly if spoken to, but kept themselves to themselves, preferring hours in dedicated prayer. The crew, meanwhile, were looking for men to undertake the repairs. It was a golden opportunity.

He stepped forward, and his name was taken. Behind him came a voice.

"Be 'ee registering fur the work then Stranger?"

He recognized it instantly. It was the voice of Moses Brimicombe, his companion. Stranger had been waiting for him.

"I can't make a killun' on me ballads, so I'll do the same as ye."

Moses was a small-built, weasel of a man, who sold a hotch-potch of broadsides, varying from the serene to the downright obscene, on a creaky, battered barrow he heaved from day-to-day around the waterfront.

"I've a new collection of Marvels and Portents, but they," he said, pointing to the travellers, "are not interested. What am I to do?"

"Same as me. Help with the repairs…"

Moses wrapped up his ballads in sacking to protect them from the damp, and took his barrow back to an opeway where he stored it. He and Stranger were of a common type of man in Sutton. "Odd-jobbers" they were known as; more commonly just "Jobbers". Found right the way down the coast, from Dartmouth to the Scillies, they were men who could repair ships. If a swift job was needed, then they would work through both day and night. In return, the jobbers expected a high return with regard to payment. Stranger—and there were many more like him—idled their wicked days away in the inns, in Stranger's case selling tobacco, then waiting for the next ship to come in. This was the way: make your month's earnings on one rush job, and drink it down. Only a certain type of man became a jobber, and Moses and Stranger were prime examples of the type. Many of them were drifters; men who had no real hold anywhere. The work itself would begin tomorrow. For now though, the crew and travellers were engaged in scooping out the salty water from the ship's hold. The jobbers would not do that. It was not their job.

At night, although the two ships swayed in the harbour, the town felt no different. A few more windows had the light of candles shining from them, but the town's streets were no busier.

"They'll be up a-praying," Moses commented.

"'Es. Their choice," Stranger said. "Reading of the Word…"

"I consider myself a religious man. Are you Stranger?"

"I have religion," replied Stranger. "But then, does religion have me?"

This thought, too complex for Moses, left him unable to respond any further. Instead, he just grunted and closed the door, the Channel wind catching it and causing it to slam. All those inside the inn turned their heads. Recognition showed in their faces. Stranger. They needed him. The coughing began. That was the signal. Moses ordered up the ale, but another jobber at the bar paid for them. They had come to the inn for a reason.

"Who's for it?" Stranger asked.

The cry went up.

"Line up then friends, and show me your money."

A queue of heavy-breathing men lined up.

"The Stranger here has a substance of such glory, you will ne'er see the like again," announced Moses.

"Come, come, good fellows, watch me…" said Stranger.

They peered intensely, as Stranger sold them the goods. He took a small clay pipe and pushed it into his mouth. A table was given to Stranger. He dug deep into his pockets. He felt the softness. Smelt that smell. Then, in one clump he brought it out. It was a large pinch, the result of a lucky deal with a Rigger.

"To-bac-co," Stranger announced, chewing the word.

Moses grabbed a handful, and pushed it into his own clay pipe. He took a light from a wax-oozing candle, and sucked. A smell entered the inn. It was a smell that was to follow man in his history. Moses coughed and looked satisfied; his stem sticking out from a smiling face. They watched him take the pipe out, take a sup, then replace it. It looked good. They would have some. They would have the lot. Guineas were exchanged. The Harbour Master would not approve, but then, he would know nothing if no-one told him. People here did not tell tales. Within ten minutes, not a strand of tobacco was left, and the door slammed shut once more. That's what he was then, this Stranger: a dealer in drugs.

Next morning, they arose early, heading down past the London Company house, and onto the quayside. In his breeches, Stranger felt a few crumbs of the tobacco left. In the other pocket, he felt the money. He put his hand in the money pocket. The rough-necked helmsman gave then a small gundalow to take around to the starboard.

Other jobbers climbed over the sailors' chests lashed down on the main deck, and began work on the bulwarks. The worn waistcloths were removed and the repair work began. Moses ripped out the belaying pins on the side, working upwards towards the main deck. The others worked downwards. It was coming in a bit. Summer's hold was lapsing.

When they had removed their section of pins, Moses and Stranger were told to move around to the stern. They took it easy. There was no hurry. One of the jobbers swung ropes down, and others worked from the inside out. The hole has been larger than they had first anticipated since the wood has turned rotten. Behind them was the endless line of lodging and warehouses, stretching towards Eastgate. On the quayside at mid-morning, the Separatists met. The townsfolk called them "Saints", because they prayed so often. A religious murmur could be heard above the activity on the *Speedwell*. Moses and Stranger were wedged between the two wooden hulks of their ships.

"She's not well," Moses remarked, stripping layers of rotten wood off the *Speedwell*'s hold. "Not well at all…"

"Her tiller's rotten as well," noted Stranger.

He stood up in the gundalow. Moses steadied her.

"Rotten to the core, she is," he added. He sat down, and felt with his arm underneath the waterline.

"Beneath as well?" questioned Moses, his eyebrows arched.

Stranger nodded.

They could make this survey last most of the day if they were careful. Easy going. It had been wise to come down early. The earliest down, had the best jobs given to them.

"She'll make the crossing for them," Stranger said, pointing to the *Mayflower*. Then, he looked at the *Speedwell*.

"They must think God will guide them in this wreck. She won't make it past the Scillies even."

They edged the boat around the port side, between the planking, and the quay wall. Above, a conversation was ensuing on the foredeck. It was between one of the Separatist leaders and the Captain of the *Speedwell*. There was already talk of swapping ships. The Separatist felt the *Mayflower* should go it alone. The Captain disagreed. The repairs would be done. He was confident of the jobbers he had employed. Moses sniggered, then re-adjusted the tam o'shanter on his head, as the Captain looked overboard. Oilcloths were now being used for sealing the wood. Cutters had been brought in. Rope was being tarred in between the planks.

"I have a feeling about these people," Moses said.

"What?"

"They mean something."

Moses' eyes burned with adventure and intrigue. Religion even.

"No. You deceive yourself. These are mere fools who like so many others seek the glory of the New World, and will fail."

"But surely sometimes, you must take a chance…"

"Take the chance yes, but make sure you win. That's what I do Moses. I make sure I win. Winning here—means not going with them."

Sat on a mooring post above, they became aware of the presence of a man who had been watching them. His face was difficult to see, because his wide-brimmed hat shaded his features. When he realized he had been seen, he became self-conscious and walked away, like a scuttling crab, his feet clicking on the cobbles.

"A Saint wasn't he?" asked Moses.

"Aye," said Stranger.

"He was listening to us."

"Let him listen. He may learn some sense."

The Helmsman leaned over the side of the damp vessel, his thick beard trailing and whiskery.

"Trimming tomorrow then lads?"

"We'll be there."

They gently winged the leaky gundalow in, moored her, and clambered up the steps to where a few men were already dancing to the evening's jigs.

Listeners, I do not dance here. I do not pipe you the wrong tune. This is imaginative reconstruction, yes. But it is something of what I believe happened here. I have the facts, you see. I have merely embellished them for you, made our journey, our trek together, more comfortable. I "told" instead of just "said". There is a difference, you know. You have now learnt of Moses, and the man I name Stranger. He is Stranger, because he is a stranger to me still, as well as to you. I have not yet discovered his true name. So, do you wish to hear more? If so, be still and silent, and let me spin you the yarn…

The men were dancing to a hurdy-gurdy player on the front, next to the Island House. The minstrel was jolly and sung with considerable gusto; one of Moses's boughten ballads. Children sat listening to him on the steps, playing chequers. The younger ones toyed with hoops and sticks. Having had enough of the activity, Moses and Stranger walked back up the narrow, fish-stinking streets. They turned into North Street, where the timbered buildings became more common, and where gentlemen's clothes were finer: silk and collars instead of sacking and cheap sailing boots. Through an ope they entered High Street, passing a dray of freshly-landed fish. On the front, a bell rang telling the town another auctioneer had a consignment of pilchards for sale. From the top, they could just make out the webby rigging of the *Mayflower* in the harbour, and across the way, the frenetic boat-building at Cattedown.

It was whilst watching this view that Stranger first saw her. The "her" was a girl, not that old to be fully a woman, nor so young to be a child. She was between ages. Her cheeks were red, her collar wide and her figure encased in black. So, a Saint-girl entering this end of town. Rare. And a girl to change lives no less...

This was not what Stranger thought as he meandered his way over the hay-strewn cobbles, occasionally flinging hoops back to children, who knew him to always be up for such tricks. But then, when they turned into the final ope that lead to their lodging house, he became aware the she was following them. He told Moses. They walked on, and then hid behind a leather-oil barrel, left outside a stable. She was frightened, they could tell. Her frame was tentative and nervous. She stopped at the ope entrance. Stranger watched her closely. She entered gingerly at first, then more steadily, with growing confidence. Moses stood up. She jumped like a frightened grasshopper, caught in the blade of a scythe. He removed his oily hat.

"Yes?" he said.

She was startled. Her eyes bubbled into tears. Her skin went goose-bumpy, like the feel of the pebbles on the quayside.

"Yes?" he repeated, and then, "Can I help you?

"I seek a man, a bearded man. You were with him."

"You seek Stranger then."

"Stranger?"

"Aye—he is known hereabouts as that."

"Where is he then?"

"He is close. Why do you wish to speak with him?"

"I come on a message from my father. I don't know why. It is he who wishes to speak with Stranger."

"Then Miss," came a voice, "if your good father wishes to speak with me, then bring him here. This is our lodging house."

Stranger stood up, and pointed to the white-daubed upper storeys of the Stable building, where on the very top sat several nesting seagulls.

"Do you know anything of his business?" Stranger asked.

"None, save that I know he has a task for a man to do before we leave for the New World."

"What kind of task?"

"I know not. Honest sir."

They were interrupted by another jobber, who shouted Moses' name out of the top floor window, and sent showering down a bowlful of warm piss.

"Oy, missie!" the voice went. "Don't ye be associating with them two misfits. The very devil's cousins they are."

The urine fell onto Moses, and he shook his hairy fist at the culprit.

"I'll have 'ee, ye bastard!"

The girl became pained again. All at once, she said, "I'll bring my father here at five and twenty to eight. The prayer meeting finishes at half past the hour. Please be here."

She walked away quickly, not looking behind at them. She was obviously scared she might be caught there.

On their way up to their room, Moses ran on ahead, up the rickety stairs to the upper lodging room. He was shouting outside the piss-thrower's room.

"I'll have 'ee ducked in Sutton Pool before the day is out y'bugger!"

From deep inside the room, there came a gleeful, throaty laugh, rich as blood. Revenge for that misdemeanour would come later. Now, puzzlement at what the girl had said to them was their chief concern. What had a Bible-abiding "Saint" to do with them? They were jobbers, with the occasional killing made from tobacco. That was them. Dealers. That was what they knew. Nothing more. Although he would not confess it to his companion, Stranger felt a tide turning though; a spring-tide, warm and drowning, and a high one at that. Moses took a ballad off a shelf and began practising it, while lying on his creaking hammock. The words were sweet and soothing, but inside Stranger's blood twisted. What did a holy man want with him?

In the corner of the room, they kept some bread and provisions. Stranger hewed off a chunk, and ate it, swinging on his hammock to the rhythm of Moses' ballad. This lodging house was as good as any. They had seen worse. They might see better, but probably not. The worst of it were the floorboards. They were uneven, and the gaps between them were wide. It was easy to see down into the room below. A woman lived there with her three children. She had come to Sutton from Exmoor and was presently engaged in bathing the children. Soft crying could be heard alongside delicate dribbles of water. She had told Stranger and Moses that she was going to get onboard one of the two ships that had come in. Well, what more for her could be found Devon? She might as well take her chances in the New World.

"They're good people," she had said about the "Saints". "The youngsters'll have a better start in a new land, than here... what with their father over the hills and long gone."

Moses went down there in the evenings. For comfort. For her. For him. He crept down there stealthily, like ship's rat. She was lonely, he used to say. But so was he. There were jokes about it at breakfast. It was odd, but all the women liked Moses. They liked his voice see. That was it. Loved the fact that you bought ballads off him; ballads which allowed their minds to escape whatever drudgery of their present life. Not that any of them could read. That was not the point. Just owning the ballad was the point; that and being able to treasure it. That was the important thing. The escape. Then later, perhaps sing it. Pick it up from some more educated person. You could pay ballad-singers down at the front.

Stranger had never had a woman. He had a cold soul. It was as if instead of skin he was covered in a layer of hard scales. Emotion seemed to pass him by. Love avoided him. That was because he was a wanderer. A traveller. A Journeyman. He had no master. Wherever he went, the women did yearn for him, but he always had to go, as if he were afraid to plant himself, and tell them who he really was. And he was no young man, was Stranger. He had been there when they brought the first blacks over. He was well-read in the debates of the day. He was, as they say, in all senses a gentleman, but yet a scoundrel. Drink was his escape, and if there was a hardness to his face, then it was the drink that had sculpted it. He had been to sea for much of his life, but he knew the land of the Britain equally as well. He had been to the very tip of Cornwall, and boasted how he had seen the highlands of Scotland. No-one disbelieved him. Devonshire, he knew not like the back of his hand, but like the swirls on the pads of his fingertips. Moses never understood how he could remember so many maps and places in his head.

"My brain is full," he would say. "I know not how your pour in more, my friend."

Their conversations had nearly reached this usual point, when they heard a straining shout from below, which told them that the "Saint" was outside. At the door, Stranger was greeted by the girl, and an old man with a stick, dressed richly, and with a white beard. He had blue eyes and pink skin.

"You are Stranger, are you not?" he asked.

"Aye. You are?"

"No matter for now. Let me in. Only then, will I tell you my business…"

He was anxious and forceful. Stranger lead them up the steep stairs to their room, the old man's feet still scuttling. Down below, one of the single mother's children was crying; teething most likely. Stranger offered them a seat, but they would not accept. The old man stood leaning on his walking stick, half-supported by his daughter. For a while, there was a tense silence. Then, the old man gathered his wheezy breath and spoke.

"I sent my daughter to find you because… because I have heard you are a man… a man, shall we say, of many skills. You have no master, and are free, and yet you rule you life well. I learn of you around the quayside. I have heard many things… It was me who saw you working on the *Speedwell*."

"I remember you," said Stranger, nodding. He recalled Moses and him looking up from out of the gundalow.

The old man continued speaking.

"You will know then, that we seek a new start in the New World, where we may live according to our beliefs. We then may worship as we choose. The King will not allow reform, and so we fled to Leiden.

"You will know perhaps that a valued friend of mine, Mister Brewster, set up a printing press there, so to publish and then smuggle books and pamphlets about our belief back to England. This is where I worked. We now have permission to emigrate. I pray that

54

we may make it safely, and with some haste, before the Atlantic winter sets in."

"You tell me all this sir, but I already know of it. Come, what do you want with me?"

The old man looked at his daughter. From under the bulk of her wide coat, carefully hidden, she produced a metal box, richly engraved, the size of a fish dray. To Stranger's eyes, it looked instantly like a reliquary. So now, Puritans with reliquaries. What was the world coming to? This was proof enough that it really did move in mysterious ways. The evening light caught on the reliquary's lid, and produced a shimmer on the creamy walls of the room, illuminating the dead flies caught in the webs of the room's spiders. The first thing they noticed about the box were the engravings on the outside of it: strange letters and images of copulation that neither could understand. The letters had extra loops or swirls, or else were completely different to the alphabet Stranger and Moses were familiar with. Stranger had seen strange markings before, but none like this. The markings carefully edged the box, a phrase on each of its four sides. He did, however, decide that the symbols were holy.

"Sir," the old man began again. "Well will you be paid, if you take this box, and hide it for me. Do not ask why, or what is enclosed inside. I have one hundred guineas. These you will receive, if you veil the box for me."

"The contents?"

"As I say, I cannot release that. I have a vow to keep—one sworn in my youth, during a different age... when... well... things were different. The two keys to it, I shall keep myself. As your honesty goes before you sir, I plead you to do this for me."

The old man's face was doleful and enquiring.

Stranger looked at Moses. Moses nodded.

"Aye, sir. I will do it. Do you have any thoughts as to where it shall be hidden?"

The old man was more certain now.

"In the ground. Buried."

"I see."

"You see, we cannot take the box with us. It was hard enough to bear it from Holland, without others seeing. But also, it contains a thing of value, beyond the journey. If we sink, then what? No, it must stay. I do not send any of our fellows to do this, because I do not wish them to know of this item. You know, of course, that our kind, does not tolerate such items…?"

"I know it well sir… My grandfather talked often of the times when all such items were destroyed here in Devon and Cornwall…

"Aye," chipped in Moses. "Many marvels were destroyed in that age of discontent…"

"You will do it then?"

"Yes."

"When you have done it, find me, and give me notice of where you buried the item. Then you will receive the money. Where do you think of burying it?"

"Toward the Eggbuckland?"

"No sir. That is too close. It must be further a-field. In the wilds…"

"The Moor," Moses said in murmur.

"Yes," said the old man. "That is better. Far from people. Some-where it may sit for a very long time. If I, or someone else, in the future, may return here, then it would be useful to know its where-abouts. Draw me a map."

"A treasure map then," noted Stranger.

"You might say that."

The old man paused for breath. After he had gulped in some of the dry, evening air, he continued.

"Art thou solid not to tell of this deed?"

Stranger nodded.

The old man turned to Moses, "And you?"

"Aye. Solid enough."

The old man nodded.

"Then we shall go."

The daughter passed the reliquary to Stranger. It was heavy, solid and smelt old. Not of the recent past, but of a generation before; a mustier, darker smell, as of precious stones when they are first dug from the ground. Like tin, which the streamers on the Moor released from the ground. Stranger tested the lid. It was held firmly in place.

"Wait. Your name sir, so I may find you?"

"Carver. Pretend you have come to see me on some shipping mat-ter… Ask for that name, and you will find me. Sirs, I wish you good night."

He turned, taking one last look at the reliquary, and then Moses and Stranger watched as he and girl exited their lodging room. The girl smiled at Stranger as she closed the door. In silence, they listened to their footsteps as they spiralled down the rickety steps to the street below.

The reliquary seemed to say much, but spoke little.

"What have we here?" Moses asked Stranger, beckoning to feel the box.

Stranger carefully passed it to him. Nothing rattled. It was as solid as a capstan, and felt almost as heavy.

"I don't know my friend. What I do know is that we must leave the morrow for the Moor. Go down to the quay and tell the helmsman we shall not be there in the morning. He will curse us both, but here we are offered one hundred guineas. Enough to set us up for life— and a fine swap for an easy task. Hurry…"

Moses' spindly legs went into action, and he left Stranger and the box alone. He placed it on the floor. Then, in his mind, he pictured his map of the Moor. He saw lines and tracks. He looked at his fingertips. Yes, he knew a place he had visited before; a place that had a history already, a place where he was now going to dig. There, he would add a smidgeon of history, and a pinch of the future.

After that, are you with me then?

Can you see the shape in your mind's eye now? Of this, there is more to come. Ah, but be patient. My art is not easy. No-one has told me this story. This is no Cinderella, Rumpelstiltskin or Little Red Riding Hood. I have had to construct it out of nothing. But then, facts do often come stranger than fiction, so listen, and I will tell you how I came to believe in Stranger and his tale. It doesn't bother me one iota that you may consider me to be some kind of conjurer, con-man, or trickster even. You will allow me then, to carry on, to dip into my top hat and produce a white rabbit, or uncover the green pea from under one of three cups. Take a gamble. Come on now. Though, perhaps in this one, you have no choice. By listening, you are becoming a part of this tale, becoming conjoined to it. You have become grafted on. You have joined, dare I say it, this cult. You have a "like interest". You are treasuring my word, watching them being spat from my lips. I'm your preacher; your cult leader, your guru. You are looking for meaning aren't you? Just like me. We both step into our possible pasts, right?

So, I tell you have these events, these possible events. But before I began, I realized that for a tale of this magnitude, and this disbelief, it is not enough just to give mere fact. Fact is for the court room or one of my stupid papers for the *British Journal of Archaeology*. I play with bigger toys here: fragments, myths and superstition. I love it see, toying with history, and teething with antiquity. Saliva dribbles, the way it does from a baby.

I need to make the cult more real. I want you to see Stranger and Moses standing next to you the way I do. These pair, remember, are not a fiction. They are not characters which merely exist from a once-upon-a-time to a happy-ever-after. They were blood and bile. Now they are dust. This is the way they sing down to me, and this must be the way I tell it to you. Remember, he may change during my tale. We may learn more. We may then have to erase, and redraw the sketch, until it is correct, finally adding the fine detail.

Now that I have confessed this much, I feel I can tell you something more. I have walked the Barbican's streets today, like some demented old warlock. I mutter to myself, I know. I hop-along. I bounce. See, Stranger is a kind of master, and I like to follow in his footsteps.

Jude

I think people believe we are outdated, out of touch, or unreal. Or at least, that is the way they see is. It's not that I mind it exactly. It's just that they don't quite understand what we are about, and that annoys me. We're after something. I can't quite even put my finger on it, but we are after a different existence. It might be an older one, even something left over, something that hasn't quite gone, something that isn't quite dust. We have just stopped things going too far. We prevent the dust from settling. We salvage.

We have camped at a place named Grimspound. I have more to tell of this grim-sounding place later.

The boisterous children are all over me. They cuddle and hold me tightly. For the most part, I am their favourite plaything. They like me I sense. They like the bits of me left over from elsewhere. They like to feel me. Smell me. Cari and Ally dangle from me like money-spiders and see the world from upside-down.

The Moor is warm still, and not yet wholly in autumn's grip. We are between seasons, in that last hot phase of the summer. It is harvest: the time of the gathering. This is an important part of the ritual year for us. Remember that ours is a different culture from yours now. It never used to be, but it is now. The fire is the centre of it. Fire is everything to us. We gain our light in the dark from it, our warmth, our togetherness, by sitting around it. Wait…

Let me stoke it more. Burn your flames a little higher.

Just as it is a curious culture, we also cross continents. Pete has the tepee set up, and in untwisting the thick oil-cloth that covers its supports. It is straight from the Plains Indians, this design. Sarah sits Buddha-like next to the fire where she is cooking rice. There are touches of Indian, Celtic, African and Chinese in us. Our culture cuts time as well. We slice through it like a taut cheese wire. I am certain of this. We cook in great vats and black saucepans. Sarah spoons our food into bowls, but there are cans of beer beside her. There is an irony here, and a dislocation. You can see it, of course. We still have difficulty completely letting go. She's using a plastic spoon to dish out the rice into a tin dish. Sometimes, it feels that we are not just travellers, but time travellers as well. When I think of this I see us, floating amongst objects, or maybe objects floating amongst us. Whatever. One day though, when the time is right, we will let go completely.

We have pulled off the main road. The public cannot see us. There's a forest plantation of pine. We will collect fallen timbers, and dry needles for kindling.

I think that's when we all like it best. The kids asleep. Us outside. Us, and the night. No-one else. Not anything. The coughing smoke rises, and stings your eyes; incense of the night, but you stay, because you know it is right. The black soot is whispering. The fire is crackling.

Once, once upon a time, there was a television. We ran it off our small generator. It went. We decided we no longer needed it. We had a ceremonial trashing of it, at a recycling centre. When it went, an outer skin peeled off, and it felt like I had shed the twentieth century. I came out a changed creature. See, what we seek is something more special. Better than the rest. But then, you will know that by now. You know something of our way.

But us. What of us? You have observed the scene; this quasi-medieval convoy of no-hopers, fakers, hobos and ragamuffins. Later, you may see us perform our theatre and storytelling. You have seen the cauldrons hissing on an open fire, and you have watched us polluting the air with our diesel-fuelled bus. You will have tsk-tsked at the children with the shaved sides of their heads, and their starry earrings dangling. You will have not helped but notice Pete's tattoos on his forearms and neck. You will have watched our lurcher sniffing and barking. You can almost feel his wet nose. You will have seen all that, but... But what of us? Well, we are more complicated. We do not jump time, like the scene before you. We can jump barriers. Sometimes though, we do not bother to jump. We barge through. Other times we go around. More often, we go back.

We ask no more than anyone else. In fact, we ask for less. Because of this, others become annoyed. They are dissatisfied with their own lot. We are inexplicable to them. We are people on the edge, and they want to hold us back. Protect us. In the same way the rock clitter drifts down the slope of the tors, we are on the fringe. We are chunks apart. We function as a transitory territory. We have no roots, or shall we say the roots we had, have long since been dug up, and thrown away. Perhaps eaten. Imagine that: eating your own history—cultural cannibalism. Let me think carefully. Yes, we do that. We are cannibals. We strip a life to the bones; the bare bones of living. Call it scraping an existence. That is us.

You will learn more of us. Some of us have massive roots which have been gobbled up, or left open like storm-fallen trees. I sometimes wonder why we have not died, but onward we live, and onward we go. I hated them when they printed "so-called travellers" first of all, but now it rings right. We are not sort-able, not box-able. We cannot be pinned down. We are confusion; the merry-go-rounding wind that swirls around the black tors. That's us: the wind.

Eddie

The address I am travelling to is insignificant. For your information, and because I know you need it, it is *The Grange Hotel*, Holborn. The taxi eventually drops me at the rear of the building, where I enter double doors into the lobby. The place is decked out in Egyptian crap, like Pharaoh had the design job. You know the kind of thing: mock Sphinxes and images of pyramids; meaningless hieroglyphics in the lifts. It is just an impermeable surface for me to settle on for a day or two, until I am blown on again. Tomorrow, I am to meet with my "Media advisor" in London to suggest some of the better places to go and "image-make". But I rarely take notice of these advisor types. Usually, I follow my own instincts, whatever and however awkward they may be.

On the way across London, outside of the taxi, I eye glorious women in tight-fitting suits and plaited hair. So this is the epitome of British femininity right now? At some traffic lights, when we have to stop, I stare at one girl. She is slim, her legs well-shaped, hair neat, with spectacles. I picture her going home to some terraced house for a cup of tea and some BBC Radio One. Chat with her housemates on what a terrible day she has had.

Perhaps you have noticed that my name has a curiously British ring to it. I have never really grown used to it. Hopkins seems so prim and precise; a positively excellent surname. A poet wasn't he? Gerald Manley Hopkins. Or the Witch-finder? Hopkins too. Or it sounds like some official in the Ministry of Defence at Whitehall. And Edward. So royal isn't it? Like the prince. It is a name that doesn't fit the owner. I should have another name. However, when I think back to Zip, he was always the one who called me Edward. Never Eddie. "Edwaaard". Yes—that's the way he would say it: long "a" vowel sounds in the middle.

We get stuck in traffic jams. I am here. I close my eyes and ease tension out of my body with a stretch. Is that the jet-lag kicking in? Maybe. I am tired, and feel irritable.

"What's the hold up?" I ask.

"They've closed the street down here today, sir. Road works…"

There is patience here. British people do not honk or get out and shout at the buddy in front of them. They remain quietly calm. It impresses me no end. I will watch the people walking on the sidewalk—in particular, of course—the women. See, I haven't been with a woman for a while now. I split with my last girlfriend, Stacey, for the second stint in Iraq. She wanted marriage and kids. I wanted adventure still. The two could never have mingled. But I miss her.

She was a model. No big time stuff. Just clothes catalogues and that kind of thing. I longed for her at night down there in the marshes, bedded down with the Shi'ites there. When the swamp mosquitoes bit in, I dreamed it was her teeth. Now I look, but I've given up trying. I think maybe that I've had my fill. I screwed around quite a bit when I was younger. Those were stupid-ass moves. I could be dead, or HIV positive and counting the days.

I begin to sweat. I have already noticed that there is no air-conditioning in London. I push down the window and undo my tie. My pants are already damp. I see my reflection in a shop window opposite. The image is broken by passers-by, but the face looks okay. I do have large bags under my eyes. I can see these in the driver's mirror. They seem to have always been there. My hair grays at the side, though at least I've not lost any. I give what that first girl used to call a "mirror-look" and push back my hair. Yes, I do look like Jim Morrison—still.

The air is now a buzz of voices, though the jam is clearing. We pass by hoardings and typical main street shops. There is not far to go to the hotel the driver informs me. We are in Russell Square. He speaks to a voice on his radio in a language I don't understand. We move again. He drops me beside the hotel. I pay him. There is just enough for a tip. I have been a good fare for him. I enter the airy foyer of the hotel. I pass Pharaohs and hieroglyphics. Despite this, everything is very British. I hear a voice I have heard a thousand times at the movies.

"Can I help you sir?"

It is the receptionist. I fumble. I drop my baggage accidentally.

"Yes. I have a reservation. Hopkins. Here's the confirmation…"

"Mr Hopkins, I'll just check that for you… Yes… I see… Please can you fill in this card…"

I complete the information she needs.

"Room 306—on the third floor…"

A porter helps with my equipment. I have no change to tip him.

I lie down on the bed, and dream of British women bobbing up and down on top of me. It is all like the waves of the Atlantic and I am drowning, ever so beautifully.

I told you America's tale is short. I lied. It isn't really, not if you count the Native Americans. They are as old as any group: the Celts, the Aborigines, or the Egyptians. It isn't always sweet though. It is a brat of nation at times; a spoilt child. It is young and inexperienced, yet underneath, under all that bravado or stars and stripes and wholesome and heartfelt presidential messages, it has begun to develop a soul. It is maturing, but our problem is how we sweep away our past too quickly. We are built from a people who wanted to escape their pasts. We are afraid of skeletons in our closet.

You'll see one day, one of these days, someone will really have a pop at us, and that's when hell will really be let loose. Somewhere like New York or Washington DC. I can see it now. Then we'll really have to look at the relics again, re-examine and grow anew. Ten years, twenty years, who knows? Some time in the new century for sure. But that day will day come. Then we'll all be scrambling around in the rubble, looking for relics.

See, America's drive is always onward and outward, not inward and beneath. There is always that longing for the way things used to be, but too much the American seeks the frontier. Always pushing. It's not stopped out West either. You know our quest for adventure. You know the Space Shuttle. You know Captain Kirk. Our next frontier is space, and we will be there, putting our feet down on Mars, terra-forming the bastard and wrecking another paradise. Whether our soul will be there, is a different matter altogether.

You see, I do believe most Americans have no sense of rootage, no sense of footing. Maybe that is why we are cheap and nasty and why I dream of strawberries and what it would be like to fuck Princess Diana. When I cross the Atlantic, I cross a frontier. I go back in time. I am the polarity of my forefathers. I am crossing one world to another. And do you know what I like best about it here? Do you? It is the old things. The traditions. The way of doing things. The fiber. The exactitude. The morality. I mean, here, I can let go because of it. Become someone else. Learn a little of myself in the process.

Like the way it was in Iraq. I lied. There was a girl. She was the first I had met since the break-up with Stacey. Brown skin. Aztec eyes. Tits like temples. Led me through the backstreets, with the guerrillas. Not really on the side of the Allies or Saddam's. Just on their side. One day, she took me to see an ancient city, just outside of Basra. I can't remember sweating so much there. Out of the desert floor, stood these statues. She told me they were the ancient ones. They were as tall as the sky, and they had been there longer. And then, I was someone else. It was the way those crumbling figures stared at me. I was someone else. I should not have been there. I was some odd piece of bone and gristle thrown down here. She wanted me to love her, to take her away from all the hurt, all the broken, exploding oil wells, all the strafing and cluster-bombs, and all the fighting, but I couldn't. I had no place, no time, and it was too beautiful to do anything. I was standing between times and I could not, for the life of me, make any move. Yeah, a complete cluster-fuck of paralysis.

I was telling Martin all this earlier...

Martin is my "Media Advisor" over here. We met today for the first time. He works for the Mag in London. He's a similar age to me. Mid-thirties. Gay. He's got two kids though. He's left his mark. They will be his legacy, and they will be able to look at his relics. Mine, well, my tale, my legacy, my relics are not finished yet.

He tells me he's just left his wife though. Come out. She came home and caught him and a client fucking. It wasn't a good scene, apparently. I've only known him for two minutes, and already I know this.

We meet in an inauspicious office just off Portland Place. He's got the regulation prints on the wall of splashing dolphins chased by an environment-damaging oil tanker, and a high-tech desk lamp. I look rough. I sampled the hotel bar's beer last night.

"The South-West's good," he tells me. "You ought to go down there. Devon and Cornwall. Really lovely. You really ought to..."

He bites his nails while he speaks. The tips of his nails are twisted and compacted from so many years of closeted nibbling down on them. He does not know me. I am a filthy encumbrance on his pristine day and environmentally-conscious dolphins.

"So, what's best?"

It's one of the questions you say when you don't have a fucking clue.

"Oh, anywhere!"

This is my "Media Advisor" advising me where to go. A grand a week for this kind of thing. Asshole.

"The time there will be plenty of people on holiday. Capture them, and you'll have some great shots. The Brits are always at their best then. Do anything for a laugh, you'll see..."

"I see..."

. "I mean that's after you've done London… But I mean there are other places. Newcastle's a good bet… and Liverpool too…"

We talk a while longer. He speaks crap, this guy, whole lumps of it. I do not work best like this, but then, you know that by now. You know I am a spore: a disgusting, filthy, mushrooming spore.

"Family then, Eddie?" he finally asks, once the official part of our meeting is over.

"No. 'Fraid not…"

Spore. Yes. Something romantic about that, and something very horrible too. Fungus. Perhaps that is me then; living on dead things. Resistance as well; to heat and cold, and jerk-offs like Martin.

"I hope you get some good pictures," he offers.

"Me too. It's a long way to come otherwise."

I lean forward to shake his hand. It is sweaty and slimy.

On his desk is an object. It is small and insignificant, yet it draws me closer. Martin notices my interest.

"It's a paperweight," he says.

I pick it up. He watches me carefully.

"From the *Mary Rose*," he says, "a Tudor warship that sunk in the Solent… The first to be able to fire a full broadside of cannons…"

"The *Mary Rose*: wood from the upper gun deck," I read.

I leave his office, thinking of the person who might have stood on that knot of wood. How depressed he might have been to know that the wood would end up in some swank media office in London. I think of sailing ships and gundalows. I close the door, leaving him biting his nails, and posing with a chunk of old wood.

Outside in the street, I head into *Waterstones* bookshop. Inside, I root through maps of the South-West. I'm taking Martin's advice, but also some of my own intuition. I see lines on a page. Random places. Grid references. Co-ordinates. Navigations. Ways to journey. Names, almost as old as those in Kuwait and Iraq.

"Can I help you sir?"

That voice again. An assistant looks at me with a benign smile.

"Yes—these please."

I buy a cheap holiday guide to the South West, and on Ordnance Survey map of Dartmoor. I give him a twenty pound note. He gives me the change and mumbles a thank you. So I have co-ordinates now. All I have to do now is get there.

Once outside, I buy a newspaper. I will use this as a prop. I will wander around aimlessly pretending to read. I will sit on park benches. Occasionally, I will say hello to people, who will, in all likelihood, ignore me. Sometimes, I will snap. There is another reason for buying a newspaper. It is my birthday today—August 25th—and I want to keep a British newspaper. So I am celebrating with headlines about child-molesters and Lotto and page three tits. I want to take it back with me, and keep it the way I wish Zip had kept things for me, for when the spore finally settles.

IV

The Rejection of the World

Robert

You need to step back with me, and take a leap into the past. It was a while ago now, but clear as a gleaming bell in my normally dim memory. We're on another holiday. This time: the Lake District. The early '70s. Climbs and lakes and standing stones and slate quarries. Us, in a small cottage, near Lake Windermere. It was all like stepping back in time. Wood-smoke and walking. Like a real family ought to be. The sort of thing advertisers present. Our son was with us then, before he went away. Before the final break. Although, he was into his teens, we still connected. I'd just been appointed Senior Lecturer. Digs on Anglesey, and yes, another at Barrow in Furness—a Viking burial ground. That's how we'd been in Cumbria. It was, you might say, a more happy time. I view it close to my Naval days, in the sense of wonder it brought to me, and in the loss of that wishful perennial: innocence. It was a time of some kind of easing reconciliation between us all, between what had gone before, and what was to come. It was one special moment. Honey-wrapped. I felt I had never been so in love with my wife, despite her companions, and finally, my rebellious offspring and I had mellowed. There was a mutual acceptance. Those were… the days… But I ramble. This is of no relevance now, for in the next few years, it was all to pass, and so once again, I push forward to the present.

I had a phone call. The desk put it through to our room. The voice at the end was desperate, yet familiar. Something of interest, he had said. In fact, the voice was a former colleague of mine from Bristol.

Bill Evans was a crusty old dinosaur, yet still a survivor. He was in charge of Methods and Techniques in the Laboratory. He was like me, a battler against time and wasteful educational spending, and had something of a reputation for interesting finds, the same way I had for inscriptions concerning the dead. Indeed, we spent the best part of the last decade putting a book together on significant burial sites of Britain and Ireland.

Of late, some television programme on Channel Four had wanted him to be a contributor. He'd told them where to go. He was a real archaeologist he told them; not some media toy.

"Harbour redevelopment," he had said. "Seems some construction workers down there have found something. I hope to be down myself soon, but can you check it out?"

He gave me the OS co-ordinates and who to speak to. So, some rescue archaeology then. The very worst kind. No time, no money; reaching around in the dirt, and vaguely hoping to pull out some survivals. My memory fares me badly here. I think I asked him what it could possibly be that would warrant him contacting me over the summer vacation. Normally, we'd agree to give it a break, and let our batteries recharge, so to speak. Something about a tomb; interesting inscriptions. Someone had advised the Site Manager to phone someone at Bristol, where they specialized in such matters. Such is the haphazard pattern of discovery.

My wife, refreshed by the holiday, and now ready to return home to Oxford, was somewhat annoyed at my request for us to stay longer, and to have to unpack all her things again. The call came in the evening, around seven I believe. I had to be pulled out from dinner. We spent a good hour on the phone, but now that conversation is sketchy. You don't realize until afterwards do you? You don't think you'll ever need things like that again, so you throw them away, the wasteful fools we are. It was a Barbican redevelopment scheme, knocking down some of the disused warehouses on the Eastgate side: eighty-five luxury flats; oh, and a business hotel. In fact, the hotel was nearing completion. Views of Sutton harbour and the Sound. Very swish.

The flats are there now, comfortable, fully-fitted, double-glazed, designer homes for upwardly-mobile young Plymouthian couples to share their lives in. They have blue-framed windows, each with balconies, and have a wave-line painted beneath the roof. *Drake's*

Lodge is what they've named it and the hotel complex. A pristine waterfront development. The right image you see, for the Plymouth of the twenty-first century. I was there for the opening, but that's later.

It seemed that *Drake's Lodge* was being built on the site not only of some nineteenth-century warehouses, but also an older piece of holy ground, where a small cemetery had once been. It had only been discovered now, because the foundations for the Lodge needed to be deeper. It was no normal graveyard. There were no graves, but the impression gained on the phone was that the men had stopped digging when they found some kind of tomb structure. I hold the notes now in my hands. Scribbles whilst I was listening; twists of indecipherable black ink.

I could have walked to the site that evening, but that would have been pointless. The place would have been boarded up and fenced off, and would have a thick padlock around the gates.

Bill would be down with a team as soon as possible. Probably post-graduates, with nothing more to do over the holiday then get out their trowels and trenching tools. I had to be patient that's all.

I didn't know it, but here was the pivot. Yes, a very definite pivot, that was about to change my life. You do not see them at the time. Most of us are blind to them and utterly foolish to ignore them. There are these points which change us, and alter our lives immeasurably. You think getting married will alter your way of life. You think that having children will alter your way of live. But these factors do not alter it. No. They don't change it, like other things do. Marriage, children, they merely impinge upon it. They snatch time from you. Here then, was my chance to snatch—and in Plymouth too—where my wild oats (pathetic though they may seem) were sown. Now, finally, a stalk of life from the past.

That night, after I had put the phone down, and plodded down the thickly-carpeted stairs to finish dinner, I babbled to my wife all night. She is, of course, used to my verbal meanderings into the realms of the dead. But later on, I could not sleep. She managed to drift off, but I got out of the hot sheets and sat in the cool bay window. There was a clear, white moon above the Mount Edgcumbe estate, and a few boats in the Sound. The torches of night-fishermen could be observed on Drake's Island. I could hear the waves. I heard the flotsam on the beach. Crab's claws, broken glass, seaweed, plastic trays, binder twine, cork, driftwood… all relics. And that night, although I did not really know it, I prayed—prayed hard—for other things to be left; things from another age.

I was at the site before the workmen arrived. They viewed me with suspicion. I knew they thought of me as some kind of bumbling old fool, about to put a stop to the job. After gaining a hard helmet, and some Wellington boots meant for visiting surveyors or councillors, I stepped over lengths of rusty scaffolding, and ready-mix trails. The find was where a further level had been dug to accommodate a car park beneath the proposed apartments. A rough, muddy track led down there. There, the earth changed to a dark colour, and it became damper, as though Sutton Pool were slowly soaking in. I followed the Site Manager, a tall man named Steve Morris, with a small birth-mark on his neck. He was friendly and curious. It was he who had the sense to stop any further digging. I thanked him for his fore-thought.

"It's over there," he said.

I remember seeing a JCB excavator propped on its greasy, extended legs, with a rear shovel poised to scoop downwards. As I approached, the men lined up around the find. The size was initially disappointing, but then, they generally are. I advised them not to clear any more soil until the archaeologists from Bristol arrived. They would excavate it properly. About a metre down, in a small trench where the JCB has been digging, was something made out of a crafted, dark slate stone. There were some details around it; all dec-orative, yet with no writing. The top slab was covered in earth, and the white footprints of misguided site workers, who had stepped onto the slab from above, were clearly visible.

I felt an air of expectation. They wanted me to explain. I didn't really have a clue at this point. I was merely the scout.

"The lads uncovered a slab at one point… a sort of plaque, but we have to leave it because that corner was coming in," said Morris. He pointed to where the JCB stood.

"I only know about inscriptions really…" I said. "That's all…"
Anticipation still.

"It's definitely some kind of tomb though. I can't tell its date yet… but it's been here a while."

This was more of what they wanted. I'd have to bullshit. It could have been Victorian for all I knew—Edwardian even. The Site Manager made a gesture for me to look closer. I lifted my glasses in an effort to look more studious. What they wanted was the tale behind this; the reason, as did I. When the men realized I could do no more at this stage, they gradually drifted back to work. Mixers were cranked and cement started to be scooped again.

I stayed there, my eyes scanning the surface and fingers feeling the stone. Below, it was hollow, or felt hollow. The decorations were well-carved. Some money here. Behind me I could hear the blare of Radio One, as the masons started laying block again. By now, my clothes were dirty. She would curse me when I got back. I could do no more. Walking back across the site, I nodded to the Site Manager, stripped myself of helmet and boots, and re-entered Plymouth's concrete.

A generator could be heard on the harbour front, and a posse of hardened men and women stood around the trench. They stood beneath bright arc-lamps, and talked of other successful digs. That one in North Wales. Another in Bristol itself. This was another on their time-line; flotsam on the surface. Bill was down there, back aching, but not complaining, and carrying on like the old trooper he was. He still liked to be in the thick of it. I believe this was two days later. The bugger had even managed to squeeze a bit of funding out of the developers. They were usually keen to put some money in, wanting to avoid headlines which might state how their development had destroyed some priceless find. I felt somewhat an outsider. No longer part of the department, and just there to decipher the inscription and ideology of death if there was any.

The trench was being excavated meticulously now; the post-graduate team working in shifts. Now, though, they were in a position to lift the slab off. Inside there was one main coffin, and two ancillary ones, next to one another—a possible couple, and their child. They were all puzzled though, as to what had caused them to have been covered so thickly and buried so deep, almost below the tide-line.

The city council archivist had come up with some information. Previous digs confirmed that the place had been a burial area, but most of the graves had been removed in the latter half of the last century, when the warehouses were built. It appeared from notes then, in the *Proceedings of the Devonshire Archaeological Society*, that the graves were really of little interest, so the dig then had not gone any further.

Some samples were taken away to be analysed. Bill got them turned around within forty-eight hours. Carbon-dating gave the first crumb of evidence on this particular tomb. The dating given was early seventeenth century. 1615. Possibly later. There is discussion of the electromagnetic surveying, and the ground-penetrating radar being used. Soundings are being taken. Calibrations are adjusted.

When the actual moment of opening the coffins came, Bill asked that the arc-lights be switched off. He preferred it like that. You'll see… It was early in the morning. The wharf was silent. It was better this way, with only torches and touch. Holy? Ethereal? No, grave-robbing actually.

The main coffin was opened first. Four of the team pushed the lid across. A further group grabbed and cushioned it. Inside, like a Russian doll, a smaller coffin. This time, it was wooden. Wooden hinges. On top, there was a finely-caved cross; a real craftsman's work. The stone has preserved the wood very well. A few sections had rotted around the edges, but on the whole, the condition of the sealing was excellent. A body could be expected. I remember watching Bill, lick his lips at the feast. I watched the intense concentration on his face, probably reflected in my own. He knew that in an official capacity, at least, this might be his last find.

It was the shock that got us. There was an expectation of a decaying, dusty, mummified figure. A skeleton at the very least. Dust even.

Instead, nothing.

Bill laughed like I have never known him laugh before. He couldn't believe it.

"Someone's playing a trick on us," he managed to say.

Some members of the group, and the younger Masters post-grads were totally dislocated. Their eyeballs darted from side to side, tongues out like cartoon wolves, rapt in amazement. Within the space of twenty seconds, this had now suddenly became a puzzle beyond what any of them had experienced before.

The coffin itself, though finely crafted, was utterly empty. Death had not paid it a visit.

"Try the others," requested Bill.

Although the outer stone coffins were simpler, and the wooden coffins inside more roughly made, they did contain skeletons. I think we all expected another joke to be played on us. But no, they contained death un-named. A few fragments of burial gowns survived on the skeletons.

With this done, the erection of a temporary shelter began. This took us up to mid-morning, and was the most tiresome stage of the operation. Next a Portakabin was brought in to store any further finds, and the area was fenced off.

I walked back through the site with Bill. We discussed the mystery.

"I haven't an idea," he said. "Honestly, it's like death for death's sake, no more, no less."

I confessed my own ineptitude to him. By now, though, although I did not know it, I had become wound up in this tale, and I wanted to discover, or at least theorize the reason. I had found my drug, and it pumped around my worn-out arteries and veins. At this stage, I did not realize how easy it was to become addicted.

"Time for breakfast. You want some?" Bill asked.

I nodded, stepping over a smashed concrete breeze block.

After Bill and I feasted on bacon rolls and coffee at *Cap'n Jasper's* on the Barbican, I slept for most of the day. I heard the door go during my morning's doze, which meant she had gone out.

I have not told you yet. Sadly, I believe she was having some kind of affair at this time. I say "some kind of" because that is all it is. She has not the presence of mind for anything but this. Hers is a tea-shop, walk along the promenade, garden centre sort of danger. He is a retired army officer. Decorated. Fought in the Falklands. Pure opposite to me. I imagine Brylcreemed hair and a hard jaw-line.

I am woken with a call from reception. Bill is downstairs. I tell him to come up. He had news. They have recovered a plaque on the side of the tomb, which was previously inaccessible. There's a date: 6th September 1620. Instantly, the connection is made: the Pilgrim Fathers. The body supposed to be in that tomb died the very day the Pilgrim Fathers left. What a day to have died on; a day when past meets future. Old world meets New—the very eve of the modern world.

How do you react to this then? One stitch has been pulled through, but it is hard to find the thread still. I am juggling with time, and the mystery of the *Drake's Lodge* "non-body" is still in the salty air.

The summer high tide was causing us problems. Already brown seaweed was being deposited at the harbour end of the site, over the barrier which had been constructed to keep the sea at bay. Morris explained to me how a lot of work still had to be completed down there, and that the discovery had delayed work on a barrage that was due for construction. The Harbour Master was consulted. A further couple of feet could be anticipated. That really meant problems. That height would cause the water of Sutton Pool to trickle in over the find. Workmen were already clearing tools and equipment away.

Between all this activity, the team stood puzzled and perplexed. If the tide did come in over the tomb, then the damage caused would be irreversible. Then if the recovery was now rushed, it would probably be damaged anyway. The choice was impossible, but a decision had to be made.

By now, the dig had gone down quite far. A few extra pieces of wood were found. Everything was bagged, sealed and labelled, and taken up the slope to the Portakabin, to eventually go back to the lab in Bristol for analysis. The site was now slippery and waterlogged. A decision—more financial than anything else—is made to leave the tomb there. The JCB backs up. The tent is taken down and our team move onto higher land.

When the tide actually comes in, we watch it sluice into our trench. Everyone's face is solemn. At least the coffins and artefacts are out. The earthy sides of the dig crumbled as the water lapped at them. There was no other way really. There was not the time to dig it out properly. That was a six month job, possibly even longer.

I was asked to a take a phone call. It was the press office at Bristol. They wanted a run-down on events, for the newspapers and television. I gave them the details. But none of the media would understand, nor would know of its real significance. Then, at this point, as Sutton Pool washed over the site, neither did I. I am now the flotsam being carried back and forth on the tide. I am the helpless. I am, as my wife would so bitterly say, "beyond help".

Jude

Fission and fusion. Pete and I were talking about these forces one day. We always have good conversation. Real talk requires effort. It demands listening and response, not two people talking at each other, but with each other. Don't you think it's true—no-one listens anymore?

I'll try to tell you what we were saying.

You may want to group us, separate us and put us into a neat box, like a different species. That is the greatest mistake of the human race. We are all too busy dividing humanity, slicing it up, carving deep, evil chasms which may never be closed again. But then, it is easily done. No matter how much I fight against it, I still find myself doing it. There is an urge to compartmentalize. We work by clichés. I find myself doing it now. The whole of our order is based upon this. Think about it. Walk down any High Street. Search out the "types" and destroy the whole. The list is endless and a mistake. All of us are too keen to write labels—me included.

Fission is too easily achieved. It's like riding a bike. Once you have learnt, then you never forget…

But then, no matter how you fight against it, or how you turn you back to it, or reject it, it still happens. This is because human nature is tribal. It is that primitive. Beyond all the sophistication, behind all the plastic, the good health, there is something darker and immeasurably malignant; something infinitely dark and continually pushed under, and placed deeper. It is something that caused people to cling next to those who feel the same way. There is a desire to clan, to walk together, to unite. And the most important part of that is the exclusion of others, whether you are at the top looking down, or as is the case for most of us, the bottom looking up. We love exclusion; making cults. It gives us our whole well-being. So yes, we sneer, and we laugh. No other animal does that. Humanity is out on a limb. Somewhere we have developed our consciousness above and outwards of our planet. We are too busy coming together to see where we are going. We are so afraid of being left alone that we will do anything not to be. We will find the like-minded. We will laugh and joke. We will be happy and our lives will be fulfilled. To reject that, takes everything and more.

Fusion then, is a different skill altogether.

See that, can you?

Eddie

Zip, that racer of his youth and fertility god of his adult life, told me about the Indians. He secretly desired their way of life I think. He certainly understood them, and could feel their sense of betrayal. They had always felt an ease with my family, as if we were kindred spirits. I remember him bringing back Chiefs with plaited black hair, home for supper from reservations miles away. You see, the Indians are both a proud and bitter people. Proud, because they still defy the white man, still cannot be boxed in or controlled. Bitter, because it is their sacred land and nomadic history which had been over-run and invaded. They are the remnants of an age of peace, an age when humanity was in harmony with nature, when no-one ransacked the globe. They belonged to the land. The land did not belong to them. They knew the gateway to the spiritual world. They were there with the Aborigines as a truly ancient people. Older than you or I. They will be there when you and I are gone, and we are but dust.

He took me out West once, to Arizona, where the sun seems to spend its time higher in the sky than anywhere else I have known, to meet a Chief whom he knew. He had some morals my grandpa. I mean, he would never sell them his tonic water. He knew they had their own religion, and he would not make one step to interfere with that. I feel he liked them because they were old, because they had a history, though he would never have called it that. It was because they had their own culture; their own rules. They had their own past, and stories, from times we cannot contemplate. He took me to Monument Valley. The Indians used to go there, to carve symbols in those left-over stumps of rock. Like Totems. I liked those mesas and buttes, relics of a former land surface, caused by differential weathering. The right landscape for an ancient people. The same sort of symbol as Uluru for the Australian Aborigines, right along there with these places I'm heading for on Dartmoor...

See, before these reservations (we say reservations, but we mean rural ghettoes), they were a portable people; people who moved on to where pastures were greener, and so matched nature. You know the picture here. Brown and white horses ridden bareback. Tall, dragon-stitched tepees and patched leather wigwams. Everything mobile and portable, so they could travel and wind their steady way, wherever they saw fit to roam. But then, time has passed. Now, they are just second-class citizens, children of campers and *Winnebagos*; that or the guardians of casinos and gambling emporia. Yes—check the social security statistics in the states: the worst health-care, the worst unemployment, greatest alcoholism, ten-fold increases in obesity and diabetes.

They try to keep it; you know, the traditions, rain-dances and totem-poles, but it is being continually gnawed away. The erosion caused by contemporary American culture is a powerful force, a fast-flowing river, larger than even the Mississippi itself. I always felt what a come down it was to see the Chiefs gathered around their caravans and buses. There should be a fire, and instead of cone reefers, they should be passing pipes of peace.

What I find saddest of all, was that before the white man arrived, before he placed his cold foot down on this warm land, the Indians were satisfied enough. It was the ocean that brought the white men, carrying them from the sad ports of Europe. And then more came, then more, then so many that the Indians lost it all. So it was pre-historic bows and arrows against guns. Really, it was children against men. It was the old world taking over the new world, and it was the whole world that suffered. I've seen that again and again… See any similarities in Iraq? One day, you know, the children will fight back, and when they do… well… look out.

There is one story, told by the Great Bear Clan, called the Fable of the Water Clan. I will re-tell it to you the way Zip told it to me. A long time ago, some people travelled across the Great Water in canoes that had giant sails upon them. They had come because the rules in their old land had become evil and selfish, and because they had a different way of worshipping the Great Spirit. The Bear Clan treated them as brothers and sisters. They treated the strangers well.

"Come and live with us, and share our land and ways," said the Great Bear Clan, "and you shall be called people of the Water Clan."

The Water Clan told tales of corruption. They said, "This shall not happen here."

As the Water Clan moved across the land, they met new people until finally the people knew each other from sea to sea. In each place they always remembered their balance with the Great Spirit.

When a man called Ford discovered an invention that could move people about and cultivate the land, they said, "This is good if we use it well. We can feed hungry people in other lands. We can visit one another and so our hearts may be as one."

When the Water Clan members heard that the people in their old lands had gone crazy and made weapons that killed people, they came to this land, were taught a balance. Everyone learned a balance with the Great Spirit, and the world became green and beautiful in his joy. The Great Spirit looked to the Earth, where all the creatures knew their place and purpose, and was glad to see happiness.

"It is good," he said.

This is how it should have been. You can tell the truth to someone else.

That's the story, see.

And that's what happened…

Now it would be fine indeed, if there were more, but there isn't.

That's about the top and bottom of it.

V

The Growth of a Cult

Robert

The heady days of summer whisk in and out again far too quickly. Hardly have we exposed our milky skin to the heat then we have to cover it again. Ours is a land where weather rhymes have a good deal of meaning. The climate is fickle and childish, and on the day that Stranger and Moses began their task, she was playing them up with the fury of a baby's tantrum. When they began, the weather was calm and sunny, but by mid-morning, a gale lashed against their flanks, and wind scooped between their horses' legs like a ghoul. They are journeying, much to the annoyance of the crusty helmsman, who is short of two skilled jobbers. The repair would now take that much longer. He would tar their names vehemently, for letting him down like that. Moses did not argue. He just told him and left.

Good horses were expensive, but the stableman below their lodging knew Stranger well, so dropped his price. He paid the man with some of the tobacco takings. A few people had been surprised to see them on horseback; not least Moses. Stranger they knew, would occasionally do such things. He would set off, then return a few weeks later, with new goods to sell, or to barter hard with. That was his way. But Moses Brimicombe too? Now somethun' must be on.

The horses were well-shod, and their hooves echoed over the black cobbles. They swung past the butchers and a small piece of consecrated ground for the rich, and then upwards, across the plain to the north. They crossed Terrior drawbridge and were soon outside Sutton. So, northwards they made their way, following the course of

Francis Drake's Water, the town's new, fresh water supply. The slim road ran higher, until the houses became mere crabbing boxes and the people sparkling shrimps during the mating season. However, they could still just make out the Separatists' meeting down on the quay. Amongst them, they knew stood Carver and his daughter. Their destination was two, maybe three days hard journeying across the toughest part of the Moor, across mire and mountain both.

Haste was essential for the *Speedwell* would be departing soon. Stranger knew he had a week at least, probably a bit longer until the "Saints" left. He wanted that money. That was all.

The previous night, he had not slept well. Temptation to open the reliquary was enormous. The box was a silk-wrapped fly held on a spider's web. He was that arachnid. He confessed earlier to Moses that he had tried it. He had tried picking the locks, but even when one seemed to click, the box would not open. Another system was present. Only Carver would know how to operate that. Besides, he knew all that was asked of him. Luck would not be pushed. It was against Stranger's rules. He took few chances. Presently, the box rocked gently with each step of the horse. It weighed down the animal on the left side, and to balance the horse, Stranger rode slightly cocked to the other side, his right leg dangling, the sole of his boot occasionally catching any long grass.

The Moor then, was not the picturesque place of beauty we now think of. It was a place that few dared to cross. There were a few tracks, ancient travelling lines; one coming down from Tavistock, another from Okehampton. Besides that, it was just moor-land; mile upon mile of rock, heather, bracken, grass and peaty soil. There were more trees but many of these were being used for ship-building in Sutton, and would shortly disappear. Those that had been logged already has left swathes—mile upon mile across—of stumps, and destroyed forest. In summer, the Moor was less ominous, though the weather does change quickly. No sooner than some height and distance had been obtained, then the weather could come in harsh and the sky turn a magpie-black. A thunderstorm was cawing.

They crossed to the north-east, following what seemed some kind of trading path. They could tell this by the occasional wagon tracks in the soil, just past Leather Tor. Some old boy had come up here with 'oss and wagon to see the Moor folk a few days before, because the wheel-lines were relatively newly etched in the earth. Some of them might not have seen a soul since the winter, though they were bright enough, and self-sufficient. Most of the folk up here felt the town to be too full of greed and lechery. How perceptive they were.

A few miles into the Moor, near Crane Hill, they met a man taking some cattle to trade. He was clearly fearful of them, and crossed out of his way to avoid them. Soon, the tors became great beasts of stone instead of tiny hillocks. The ground became wetter, a more waterlogged subsoil evident. When it finally rained, the sun never quite went away, but kept a dazzling brilliance before them, so the two of them followed the edge of the rain as it fell, and tracked across the ridge they rode upon.

There were no major towns upon the Moor, only scattered villages of six, maybe seven homes. All the cottages were constructed of granite rock—hardy, yet primitive. When the two of them passed by such homes, the women called their children inside, scared of the two figures in black.

They knew them to be townsmen, full of evil most likely. Outside of Sutton, jobbers had a reputation somewhere below child-stealers or slavers. Woodcutters watched them solemnly from beneath the tree canopies. They swung accurate, heavy axes, and were best avoided.

A stone clapper-bridge took them over a small river, and then they galloped the horses up a larger hill. At the top of the hill, Stranger stopped and checked his sense. He seemed to make some calculations as well. Stranger carried no compass. Being originally a mariner, his guidance was by the stars, the sun and a triangular-shaped device, made of metal, which he always carried on such journeys. Moses saw him use it the night before, one eye closed, one hand moving an arrow, and the other noting down the measurement. Before them was a brown ocean. To the west, on the horizon, a small cross could be made out. Yes. The Abbot's Way. His directions were correct.

"Why not bury it here?" asked Moses. "Surely it would save us much time?"

Stranger looked at him. Moses already knew the response he would get.

"No. There is a place where I know other things have been buried and also found, where I have been before. That is the place where this must go."

Passing a few more cold-faced cottages at Swincombe, they decided it would be time to rest. They had done well that day. Much of the journey had been covered. They made camp near a small settlement. Older girls, innocent as the sun itself, came out to see who they were. Moses gave them a wave, but they were all too quickly shooed in. The wrath of their parents' glare fell upon them. Men feeding heather into their thatch came down ladders and put away their peat ridges ready to be sewed onto the apex. The hazel spears used for thatching were left scattered on the roof, regardless of the rain.

"A warm welcome here then?" joked Moses.

Stranger and Moses were not ill-equipped. They had an oilcloth, which they trapped down by stones, making a triangular tent in which to spend the night. Their asses were sore after the heavy riding. Moses had a long piss over by the horses, while Stranger made a turnip broth. They had some rough tea leaves—another line of Moses' emporium—which made an inviting brew. Their view faced westwards, and they watched the sun pale and sag in distant Cornwall, as they ate and drank. A good ale would have been better, but that would have to wait for now. When the eerie nightfall finally came, Moses collected the box from the horse and brought it into the shelter. Rest came easily. Actual sleep came slower. The Moor is an odd place. It has deceiving ways (I know from my own experience). It has been so for many centuries. It will do, for many more. At night, it was cold, in spite of the fire they'd made. Moses could feel the horses shivering. He hated to think of the place in the full depths of winter. He resolved to think only of their lodging house and his weighty share of the guineas that Stranger had promised him.

And so, they had joined the greater plan; this divine yarn. Got involved you might say, by mischance, in this strange pattern of events. But that is often the way. Sidestep a little, and you are doing something else. Go on a little more and your life is irrevocably changed. You start something. Begin to grow it… and the world is that little bit different because of your presence. Even this, that I speak now, makes that one nanosecond of difference in your journey. It has grown, and you are conjoined more fully. You are part of the cult.

Waking came easy. They were glad to move on. The ground was damp and the wetness had soaked through to their clothes. A light summery dew had formed and was felt on the horses' tough backs. The camp was packed away and the box was strapped on to Stranger's horse once again.

"We should get there today," he announced.

Moses was packing his bag.

"The paths get better from now on..." he continued.

In the dips of the Moor was a light mist; enough to make you think the ground had disappeared. The horses and riders jingled on. Above the tors the dawn parted and let bright air though. During the morning, the ride was fairly easy, if tedious. Stretches of the Moor appeared very much alike. There was a word for this madness. You could become "pixie-led", but not this pair. Not with Stranger. Besides, like the hamlet dwellers, the pixies would have kept their distance from him.

They rode on, until some half a mile away, they observed figures. They were standing in marshland up to their ankles. These were the Fox Tor mires. Coming closer, the two riders observed that all of them were women, except one. He was a man in his forties, of bald head and big belly. Out of the marsh, they pulled a yellowish-green substance. They collected the substance in great woven baskets on top of the women's heads, and their foreheads and faces were stained from it. When they approached, the women stopped their work for a while, but unlike elsewhere on the Moor, they were not worried by Stranger and Moses' presence. They knew the type of men they were. They had seen them when they took the six-monthly supplies down to the naval stores at Plymouth.

"What is this substance you search for?" asked Moses.

"Do y'not know, and you being a sea-faring man?"

The bald-headed man moved towards them. He grunted something and then opened his mouth. His teeth were rotten, and his breath stank.

"Sphagnum moss," he spitted.

"Moss?"

"Sirs. That is what we do here. It d'mend wounds they tell us. I have not seen it myself, but I believe it true enough, or else I should not be here a-working."

Stranger was unaware of its healing quality, but he asked if he might have some.

"Aye sir… Take what you will. There's plenty for all."

The man squelched towards him, dug into the marshy ground beneath him, and pulled out a greenish slime.

"Hold out your hand sir."

Stranger did, and he slipped the moss into his hand, intending purposefully to make him squirm.

"Take it, and use it," the man said. "You might find it useful one day."

As Strange squeezed the water out and placed the moss into a satchel, the man tried to find out about their business upon the Moor, but Stranger told him nothing, and so, when they rode on, the people did not start working again, because they had to talk about them.

Two more hours long journeying brought them up the valley that Stranger had wanted. He became more relaxed, confident now that he had achieved his goal. A track was present, but it was poor-going for the horses. They tethered them and made the rest on slow feet. The valley was wide, and thick with vegetation. A small river cut through the bracken at the bottom. Westwards, the scars of tin-streaming of a couple of centuries before swung down the valley sides, the delta wash fans still black and shimmering at the bottom. They were in bright sunshine now. Stranger's steps became more lengthy and powerful.

He led Moses up an overgrown spur which cut into the main valley. Two tiny clapper-bridges stood over the stream. Few had come here recently. Locals would know it, but had been there so many times as children, that they never thought to go back again now. At the brow of the spur, Stranger breathed a sigh of relief. He turned back to Moses.

"It's here," he said.

"This is the place then?" Moses confirmed.

Ahead, between Hameldown and Hookney Tor, stood the ancient remnants of a village. Bracken shot up from the centre. Around it ran an outer wall, now around three or four stones in height, though once it had obviously been much higher, and had crumbled over the centuries. It was a Pound, an enclosed settlement, typical of many found across the Moor, but bigger than all the others. Inside the outer wall, were the remaining stones of the huts which had once been so alive, and had bristled with sound, the way the Barbican did now. He cut through the undergrowth, singing one of Moses' highest-quality ballads. This was the place. They would bury it now.

"Here," said Stranger pointing to the ground, and Moses took his shovel, and began to dig.

It would not be found. See, this was a time before archaeologists and anyone else who had an interest in things old. Antiquarians weren't born yet. Old things were thrown away or were ignored, the same way people passed the withered, blind old beggars on North Quay. Such things had no value, and were left alone, especially after the Reformation, where the whole of the past was dismissed as superstition. It was the same reason this place disappeared amongst the profuse undergrowth.

After the soil was patted and stamped down, they left and the place found peace again. The trodden bracken recovered, and the rain watered the bare patch of earth.

Soon, no trace at all.

Longer, and nothing.

There was time now to shorten some of the way back. The sun was still high enough. The horses were rested and had lost their sweat. Saddles were re-adjusted. They smiled to one another. Moses touched his nose lightly. Yes. They had a secret. No-one need ever know.

I believe the journey back home felt shorter and less arduous, even though they spent an extra night on the Moor. This time, there was gold at the end of the rainbow. Fewer people met them. One solitary shepherd turned his back to them. Shaggy ponies, coats swirling, watched the duo being pushed by the wind. Occasionally, they caught sight of a bird hovering. So, them, and age-old things up there: animals, birds, grasses, tors and streams. As evening came the tors' stacked fragments let wedges of light through, reflected in the streams in the valley bottoms.

On the Friday, return came. Familiar sights. The Plym in the distance. Sentimental pats on the horses to thank them. A change of clothing. Familiar holes in the floorboards. Familiar stale bread in the corner. Two blackjack leather jugs on the closet. The pleasure of luxury. Come evening time, all that had again become tedious, and they strolled down rocking slabs and dingy side streets to the front.

There was the smell of tobacco in the air. Yes. It was the leaf they had sold. Now, to track the old man down. On the north side of the harbour were the lodging houses where the Separatists stayed *en masse*. That was where they were heading. In order to avoid the helmsman's wrath they took a detour past a netter's lodging which they knew the helmsman rented out, then stepped back onto the quay. The place was still, only a few gulls stamping on the decks of the ships. The sea was calm.

Impatience had got to them now. A jobber's life was ruled by coins, by that chink of metal. To have them, he would do whatever it took. A Separatist stepped out of lodging house, but they could not ask the gentlemen where Carver might be staying. Questions would be asked: the wrong kind of questions, and the secret out. No, subtlety was required. Many of these more expensive houses knew Moses. He was often around their doors, procuring custom through fish or ballad. Stranger, they would not know. He would assume an identity, and ask to speak urgently with Carver. He could be a good mimic if needed.

Three lodging houses were tried. A fourth also resulted in failure. No, Carver had kept his secret for long enough. He was cleverer than this. He was no ordinary fool. He knew how wet the wind would be. An older, rougher place came into view. He questioned the double-chinned mistress at the door, and she confirmed he was staying there.

She called for Carver, and he came quickly to the top of the stair well. He walked down the steps without his stick, almost falling to reach them.

"Done?" he asked softly.

"Buried," came the answer, and Stranger passed him a roughly-drawn map of the place where it had been buried. Carver eyed the parchment, noting the precision of Stranger's sketch.

"Money?"

"Yes—the money…"

Carver climbed the stairs again, his chest heaving. Stranger and Moses could hear noises from above. There was the grind of a drawer opening. When he again reached the bottom of the stairs, Carver passed Stranger a bag of coins. They felt weighty and good.

"No questions from either of you?" asked Carver, as if now expecting some.

"Sir, we do or die. We question no-man for his whims."

"Then let that be the end of it. Good night. May God bless you both."

No hands were shaken. No smiles were exchanged. In the darkness of the house, Stranger peered at Carver's beautiful daughter. She glanced back; a quick look of intrigue, a dash of desire. He saw sea-grey eyes, with a story in there somewhere. No matter. The latch clicked. Inside the house, a candle was blown out. Fleetingly they thought of what the box held, but that did not last long. The coins clinked nicely. Then, the pair skipped up the candle-lit street with enough noise to wake the dead.

Listening to Moses' grotesque grunts and fantasies whilst he was asleep, Stranger felt a new warmth. Something had yawned, and showed its teeth. He had been awakened. He tried hard, but he could not repress it. The vacuum had filled him on the trip across the Moor, and had grown wider tonight. He thought of her sea-grey eyes; those beautiful story eyes. He wanted to read them, tell them and pull them out of the darkness. He always got his gullet, they said of him, on the quay, and he resolved to have her as well. Suddenly, he was becoming the familiar.

They sat on their riches like Kings of the Orient. Whole days passed. The stale bread hit the other Jobber who lived above them as he left for work. He had been given an easy job now by the helmsman, but revenge has been achieved. They had not ventured down to the quay for several days, but word told them that the *Speedwell* was in too poor a state to be crossing. Stories about her being rebuilt filtered through to him. It was just as they had thought: a transfer to the *Mayflower* was in progress.

At this time, Moses felt his companion has been distanced from him since the moor journey. One evening, he has even gone out selling, so strange had his companion's mood been. His friend was restless, and slept badly the night before. Normally, this was a sign that it was time for him to move on, but these were not his thoughts, for indeed, he had already asked him that the night before. When he returned, however, things became clearer, and were moving. He could tell from the expression on Stranger's face, before he even looked at the table. Stranger had divided the gold: a sixty/forty share. Moses had done well from this. The share was a good deal better than usual, and he was grateful. It might set him up if he spent it well. It might ruin him if he spent it badly. Time would tell.

"This is yours. I'm leaving," Stranger said solemnly, after he pushed the coins across the knotted table.

"But…"

"But not by land. I can do nothing more here now. I have a new ambition Moses. I must leave."

He understood. Reasoning was more difficult.

"I'm leaving with them."

Moses was incredulous.

"What—with the Saints?"

"Aye. With them. I have a mind to try this New World. I once thought it fickle… but now, well, I think there might be a future there for a man o' my nature. I can gain passage as a Jobber. Her crew know me, and they need a worthy hand. We sail the 'morrow."

In fact, Stranger's take on the parting was incorrect. The ship was delayed a further day. Her mid-sails were also thought to need repair, and so were taken down and re-stitched. Then, on the sixth of September came the departure. Stranger, shrouded by a hood, stepped into a gundalow. In a Hessian sack were his few possessions and money. He'd even packed the Sphagnum moss, in case. There was little time for goodbyes. Down the algae-green steps the rest of the Saints were boarding. Nearer Moses on the quay, Carver and his daughter climbed aboard a boat laden with fruit. Moses watched them intently, but their eyes showed no sign of recognition. Prayers were said. Psalms quoted. One Separatist preached to the quayside from the ship, his white hair and triangular beard ruffled in the wind from the Sound. Stranger swung out of the boat, and waited, bouncing in the lull at the side-port of the ship. A last look to Moses was given. This was a sworn friendship which now had to be broken. A secret or two though. Moses felt few tears. His life had always been here. Women teased and pushed him. They pinched his bum. He told them to clear off, but they giggled and did it some more. Despite this, he watched closely the events unfolding.

The fruit-carrying gundalow made it to the side-port of the *Mayflower* where Stranger stood. On climbed Carver, who did not for one moment see Stranger—and perhaps even if he did, on that fateful day, he would never have acknowledged their connection. But then, as the final prayer was said, Moses pushed to the front of the crowd. The girl stepped up, out of the boat. He stared. Stranger held out his hand, and she pulled herself up onto the mid-deck. Her smile told him everything. Moses had no more fears.

"The bugger!" he said, under his breath. "So that was his plan, all along…"

So, the Stranger might finally have become the familiar. Moses did not wait for the final departure. He had seen the like a thousand times sail out of Sutton. Besides, he had another task; one that Stranger had asked him to complete the day before. He had told him what he wanted written, and had given him the money in order to pay for it. He said this would be a better explanation. He still owed money to a few people. With "death" nothing could be taken from him. His disappearance would be convenient. Stranger was like the wind people knew, and his death would not be that much of a surprise. Besides, there was always a certain greyish pallor to his skin.

And this, this is where I come into this indulgence of mine… And that's what happened…

Moses found the fat undertaker on the north side, near the graveyard, and bought a coffin.

"May I ask who has died?" the fellow asked.

"Stranger," said Moses. "My companion…"

"Never?"

"It's true," offered Moses. "This very morning. I woke up and found him dead in his bed."

"Stranger you say?"

Moses handed him the fee.

"Aye."

The undertaker looked into the bag. His eyes widened and bulged. He smiled.

"With this, I take it you will be wanting something special?"

Moses nodded.

But before the actual burial—Stranger's expensive and untimely burial—Moses had to do something. He could not bury Stranger without it. He needed a disclaimer. He hated the thought of God looking down upon him and seeing him falsify the dead. And so, he set to work…

This was a job well done, for on the day after the funeral, which only he, a few more of the Jobbers he knew, and a couple of snivelling bawds from Eastgate attended, two men rode into Sutton. The word was that they were looking for Stranger. Some debts he owed them, no doubt. And so Moses kept low… and word came to the two men that Stranger was dead.

Ah—but I run before I can walk. Stop a little and rest. I ask you now to remember only one thing. It is something that I used to believe could never be true: fact holds our senses more than fiction ever could. Let me prove that to be true. Let me shape your mind's eye, the way mystics bend spoons, and how fakirs complete rope tricks.

Jude

We are walking through a damp, moss-filled mire, close to where we have camped. We can hardly speak for laughing. Our feet get stuck in the boggy suction, and every time we squelch, we laugh uncontrollably. Through our giggling, Pete is talking to me about peat on the Moor, and how it was once used for everything: for building, for heat, for roofing, alongside gathered heather. I am telling him how wood fascinates me. We have been scavenging for any branches that have been damaged in storms during the winter. Peter had tried lifting this one heavy log, but dropped it fairly quickly when a mass of wood lice swarmed out from underneath it, like the start of some crustacean marathon.

I am thinking back to school. You know, you do all those projects in school don't you? Well, we did this thing once, if I remember it correctly, about petrified forests and coal. How it was actually wood that has been turned to rock. I liked that, Magical isn't it? Like alchemy. I suppose that it the attraction my father saw in fossils (I will tell you more of that soon enough). I like the way it can be preserved. Kept. If only everything could be like that—turned to stone—and kept. Things would last then. If only we had the Medusa touch, eh?

I speak of wood because it is an ancient thing, a Pagan thing. It is right for us to be using it. I like the knots inside. I like the way the lines of the wood have to swerve around them. The knots are bastions of another angle; a different approach. They are a natural, organic growth and are more like what we demand. Others things on this Moor do not grow, yet they remind me of the wood. The tors are the knots of Dartmoor, poking through the surface. Come back in one hundred years' time, and that tor will still look the same. This is us then: wood and stone.

But I can hear you laughing. You are saying how, then, can we progress? How can we take on the modern era? Easy. Think not about the end, what is produced, but think about process. See the tough bark on the outside. See the growth rings in the middle. Then, see our rise.

Eddie

Sure, I'm in the wrong place. I shouldn't be here. I've kinda made a bad decision; a poor calculation. I have taken the wrong route. Convincing yourself of that is perhaps the most difficult thing of all. It's like the time you go away for a while, and all the time you are away, you look forward to going back to that place, or people, or atmosphere that you left. But then, when you return, you find that it has irrevocably changed, and that everyone has, like you, moved on. Suddenly, the right place becomes the wrong place and you are frightened of life missing you.

My comparison with that is all of my twenties. I mean, tell anyone in a bar about what I did, and sure, they think I have seen it all. But then, they know very little. See, I shouldn't be like this, jumping around the world. Though that part of my soul which told me I had to do it my twenties is still here, the homing, settling-tendencies in me are rising, so that is why I feel misplaced. Ever had that did you?

I should be at home now in the States with a family. With kids. With a home. Going bowling over *Len's Lanes* every week. Going to *K-Mart* or the Mall. Normal shit yeah? *Walgreens* drugstore at every junction. *J. C. Penneys* for clothes for school. Cook-outs. Memorial Day. Taking the kids to that Dinner Theatre for a Christmas treat. I need a job that doesn't make my heart beat faster and faster, and an easy life. I should own a store in the suburbs. That'd be good. I should do a little overtime at weekends, and go on vacation each summer to the lakes. Yes—the Wisconsin Lakes. It's good there, they say. Photography should be my hobby. I should not be lying in some hotel, living out of a travel bag and finding the nearest thing to homeliness, the house maid who tidies while I step out of her way, and lift my hard-soled feet up while she forcibly vacuums around me, and chat about how poor the weather is again.

My camera equipment needs to be checked over this morning, to make sure all of it works properly, and that I have what I need. I gotta remember to take that blue filter and clean all the telescopic lenses. I had a parcel of film arrive yesterday morning which I must go though. I also need to plan my route around the rest of the country. I looked at Devon and Cornwall, and a map of Dartmoor last night, while sitting on the toilet.

But I have all these negative thoughts you see. At least it feels like summer today, and I feel more alive than usual. I stretch and grow in the morning light. I am still in bed. The sheets are cool, but not sharp, like some hotel linen. It is nearly half-past nine. Here, I can feel at ease. So maybe, just maybe, I am wrong. Perhaps it is not the place, and just the individual.

I have had breakfast in bed today, and there are crumbs from my toast, on the bedside table. There is a knock on the door. It is the house maid. I tell her to come in, and make a naked lunge, just before the door opens, into the shower, out of her way. She is talking in a monotone about how surprisingly sunny it is today. I am grunting back amongst the gasps of hot water on my back. We don't communicate very well. This is one price paid for travel.

She is Polish and talks in a kind of broken English. I know she will be out in the room, wiping away my crumbs. We cleanse each other of our sins.

VI
The Pilgrim's Vow

Robert

I suppose I am some kind of relic as well; a piece that no-one has really wanted. You might think that this gives me sorrow, but then, are not relics the most interesting bits of existence? They are the parts that do survive. They are the parts of the whole that will last and remain, sometimes forever and forever. Relics are at once the bones of the dead, and the reminder of the living. They are still organic, still crumbling, still existing, still falling, to re-assemble somewhere else. But they are somehow still with us. Just there, see, in the air.

When I think of myself, and what I do, I have often thought of a round tea table, an old Victorian one, with a daintily-creased linen table cloth, and snow-flake doilies and an aspidistra plant in the window. And stacked on plates, are iced-cakes and currant buns and biscuits. I watch the tea. I watch what happens. When they are gone, all that is left are the crumbs. Nothing else. Tiny crumbs on the tablecloth, itchy-don't-get-them-in-the-bedclothes crumbs, little pieces of Garibaldi, a minute sphere of Madeira cake, breadcrumbs, cheesecake crumbs. They are the tiny reminders of what has been and gone.

Then, I come down from the ceiling, go in low, so the crumbs appear as targets, as I am on some German bomber—a *Heinkel He 111* (more of these and their friends later)—attacking Plymouth during the War. I circle them, touch them. The crumbs of existence are what I am after, and the older, the staler, the mouldier, the blacker, the more rancid, then the better.

I have a recollection of childhood here. That uncle of mine—Jack Bolitho from over Lelant—is pushing a collection of cigarette cards at me. Beauteous things they are. I still have them somewhere. I meant to pass them, but haven't. It wasn't the Household tips that thrilled me (I name "Keeping Milk Fresh" and "Cleaning the Lavatory" as two of the most exciting!), it was their detail, their smell, their individuality, their being from the past.

Even more so, I liked to think of them first being taken out of the Woodbine packet. Who by? And why did he or she save it? Why didn't that person just scrunch up the packet, and let it fall, fall away to decay like most things do? Why keep them? Was that individual thinking of the future? Why did they then pass them on to my Uncle Jack? Did uncle think things might change? Did he see me looking back on his collection from the future I now stand in? I have a wish that he did, but a heart which tells me that he did not.

But do you know what interests me further, what interests me more than anything else, are those crumbs that are never found, those parts which are lost, those pieces which would have finished the puzzles of existence? Where do they go to? What becomes of them? They lie back there in time like all those unmarked graves and the undiscoverable. The untranslatable. The unpreserved. All those riddles I couldn't damn well solve. That's where the real stories are. I told my son that countless times. Yeah, in one ear, and out the other—probably.

But there is worse to come. See, to many, it is better to have no relics, than parts of the whole. It is the whole or nothing at all with them. My dear wife is one of these. She is a better the devil you know than the one you don't. I am the opposite, although my life might have been easier and undoubtedly less strained, if instead, all relics disappeared or vanished overnight. So we could wake up and the only things with us were the present and the future. Think how simple life might be then. No jarring memories. No reminders. No red wine stains on that white shirt. No scars. Yes, that would be something. But then, I am old. Change comes with difficulty to me. I could not live without it. I need the past. I need objects to remind me of it. I need the certain past, I believe, for the uncertain future.

I have said that I am some kind of relic. I am a mishmash of eras long since gone. I knew undergraduates laughed at my old suits. But then, they were my trademark, my blot on their memory. They will take that with them, if not geophysics, or luminescence dating or the intricate field systems of West Penwith. I am a magpie, you see. A collector. People have introduced me by saying that I have an interest in antiquities. That is true, but it is not that which I seek. It is the process of the past reflecting off the object. That is more it. Like the tramps and winos that I watch in the city. Most are younger than me now. In their wild eyes, I see a power. Their cheap bottles are a symbols of an unhealthy world before "awareness", before the idea of alcohol abuse.

They are lovely. They are tokens dropped out of the sky: metaphysical remnants. They are wizened and they beg and shout at you, or like one I knew in Bristol, who kung-fu'ed cars in the centre of the dual carriageway near Temple Meads railway station. Mad bastard. They are alive. They are animals. They talk and breathe, and one day, I must come to know them better. They are outsiders, but then are not all things that have passed, outsiders? Not of this earth? Aren't they just encumbrances upon our existence? Drivel? You may think this, but let me show you. Let me demonstrate how wrong you may be.

Again, come closer, and watch my hands. Hear my words strung out, like washing on a line. I want to tell you a story…

Let me make something completely clear to you. I do not, for one moment, think I am the only person on this journey. There must be others. There must be travellers in similar orbits, or people on a parallel path. I am convinced there are some in the same special dimension. Yet I don't see them. They are truly either not there, or I am blinded. Maybe I am just blinkered, plodding the way of a heavy horse, the pads of polished leather blocking out the modern way. I search for a logic in this, a meaning, a reason. Sometimes, it is graspable, but then as swiftly as it comes into my hands, it vanishes. It is as slippery as the tar soap father would give me to bathe with, after he'd come back from a shout. My orbit's path is shaky and elliptical, and not really the way I want to go.

I have more in common with medieval man. There is a picture I know. I used it regularly in my lectures: a transparency of it on an overhead projector. Let me explain. It is a work called *L'Image du monde* by Gautier de Metz (1246). A poem about creation, the earth and the universe, later art and illustrations illuminating the writing showed that circumnavigating the round earth makes one's starting point one's destination. Yes. This is me. Back in Devonport. It tells me that a circuitous journey is therefore combined with the one way pilgrimage which is a symbol of our existence, the search for paradise, for heaven, for the dream, most of all—for love. Yes, this is the orbit I am in. This is the journey I make. I believe then, I must travel to worship more than I travel to learn.

Ah, but what is worship?

Not that old question again, says modern man. See, we all worship different things. I have known men who worshipped tobacco, more who adored women, others who worshipped at the temples of Union Street. I know another who worships technology.

I worship…

Hang on. You tell me.

Fewer I know now who worship anything older. A god maybe? By now then, you know my meaning. I talk of idols. There are many orbits with many different idols within them. But you know this. And very soon, the idol shall become the myth. Eventually, the idol will become the myth it never intended to be. It is the way.

True pilgrimage has died you know. It was that old vagrant Samuel Purchas who came up with the phrase "of pilgrimage" as an image of travel. So then, if you have travelled; pat yourself on the back, for you are a pilgrim, but kick yourself hard, for not realizing it earlier.

What do you worship then, friend?

Who is your idol?

What shall be your myth?

What relic do you want to survive?

What keepsakes will you hold onto?

Will it be postcards?

Will it be antiques?

Will it be photographs?

Paintings?

Stamps?

Toys?

There are too many to list, and at least, these are easy. With stories, it gets a little harder.

Then let me tell you the ultimate. The ultimate art here then, is to die at your destination, so that the journey parallels life itself. Then art and reality can walk hand in hand into Paradise, or Oblivion. And here my mind wanders. Yes, you can see this coming. I am thinking of Stranger migrating; a transferral of luck from one Plymouth to another. Oh yes. This is some pilgrimage: a one way trip to Paradise. A get away from it free for all. And he was on there.

But you and I are born between times. Let's be honest here. We are in a tragic age. I am on the pivot of the see-saw. We have discovered our entire world, and then destroyed it in the process, and yet we have only dipped our toes into the chilly water of Space. And I am born too late.

Previous to this, as the discovery of the New World drove out interest in the Holy Land, men flocked to see the new reality. So powerful was this that it even turned my friend Stranger into a pilgrim. Yes, this is the truth. I cannot be he, and neither will I be the he who takes his chances and sets out into the black void that is Space. Surely, that then, is where we must go next. They will leave for the Martian pilgrimage when men are bored of worship here, or perhaps when our Earth finally collapses from environmental disaster. And yes, of course, they will take relics with them: old compact discs, that video, maybe still that old teddy bear, maybe real relics, just for old time's sake. Ah, but I dream. I am indulging again. I am making mythologies that I do not actually care for.

I make them the same way my wife used to bake yeast buns every Thursday. She picked the recipe off her mother-in-law in St Ives. She made them the same way: my son and I always returned from playing, or shall I say "simulating play" in our garden, to smell that yeasty, thick kitchen air.

I make them now, the way… the way we shape our own destinies, the way we follow our intellectual paths. Making them then, the same way I find myself back in Plymouth.

I am old. That is why I told you about the ultimate art.

I tell you once again, that it slithers through my fingers.

See, I need to talk with you.

To be honest, I had a weary childhood. I can never remember being young. I can never remember a freedom, that childish freedom of no worry. I see myself unromantically as a snobbish, sailor-suited schoolboy, trapped in a very adult world. I was their plaything. I told you that I had literature forced down my throat—for medicine. The Bible, Bunyan, Fables. Later, Wordsworth, Shakespeare and Dickens. Then the archaeologists: William Borlase and William Stukeley. Father said he didn't want me ending up like him—out fishing for a living. Besides, "there wudn' the pilchards like there used to be". Education was my way out then. The Grammar School in Penzance. Then to Liverpool University. Like father then, like son they say. Where then, did I go wrong?

I never rebelled against my father. I did everything he said.

But my son rebelled against me. He found his own path—his own story.

He had it all I suppose. Christmas was my wife and I cutting across a room swimming with ripped wrapping paper. Underneath it all, was a boy with eyes as wide as saucers. This was a Golden Christmas—a Christmas card Christmas. Snow outside, even.

His room as well. I decked it out in blue for him. It took me a whole week. I even got a sponge and dabbed on white paint for clouds. I shut the door, so he wouldn't see. This made it more of a surprise. We let him pin all his *Airfix* models to the ceiling. Spitfires and Messerschmitts hanging down. 1:72 scale. Moon-lit war silhouettes. He knew them all inside out. Wing-spans. Engines. Crew sizes. Brainy as well. The best one we ever made? The *Heinkel He 111*: the so-called "wolf in sheep's clothing". Centre-place, yes—above his bed.

We had high hopes. And do you know, I hated it at first?

"Dad," he would ask—and I would be thoughtlessly engrossed in some research work—"Can you join this tail section for me?"

He would have clingy polystyrene cement all over his hands with an apologetic look. I would always do it with an obligatory moan. He knew the procedure. He played the game. We both did. I only wish now that I had played it more. Really played I mean. But I was always there. I am certain. And my wife. We were strongest then. He made us close. Blood-bonded in him, like liquid cement.

Then, after the bonding, the delicate decals. RAF livery and Germans crosses. Letters and numbers. Place them on with a steady hand and tweezers.

Good schools as well. A string of results followed. Ten "O" levels at Grade A. Captain of the rugby squad. He was my idol—the everything I could never have been. Then, I found meaning. I had found a passion.

The strangeness came after school. He had wanted a year out before University. Travelling abroad was the idea. We agreed. We thought it would broaden his horizons. Give him a chance to think about which direction he wanted to move in. There was so much to choose from. The world was laid out in front of him. It was then that it happened. Looking back, I think it was because we sheltered him too much. With us, it was always the good; never the bad. He wound up guilty. There was a thought, a point on the time line, when we though he might have entered the army. A commission was in the offing. Perhaps being bombed or strafed somewhere might have done him some good.

It didn't seem like that. First, he stopped writing. It was too much of an effort. Then there was the phone call: the bail at customs. Drugs. Not much really. Only a bit of cannabis resin, but it made its mark. A sordid story for the local newspaper. Only a column, but enough. His father—a professor no less—was asked to make a comment. Of course, we talked. I mean, you will know by now, I am no prude. He knows it, but he won't come back. We grow separately. Our veins do not join. There is no longer a root connection. He makes his own story; by now, his own children perhaps.

"We need to talk," I seemed to say so many times, but there was no forgiveness, no reconciliation. Next was the hair: firstly grown long, then dyed and shaved, then in dreadlocks, then the tattoos and then... nothing. I was paying for earlier happiness. I suppose I still am. I am my own Faust. Where did I make my pact with the devil? I am trying to remember.

You might find all of this shocking. Maybe not. You will have your own dislocations and dissociations.

He is officially a missing person—a name on a list. The police have him on file. All he is now, is a statistic. I have not seen him for several years now. I lie, like the best storytellers. When I think, it is a decade... It is ten years. He is a survivor though. I know he is alive. Vaguely, ever so vaguely, I search for him still at bus-stops and train stations. I picture him sleeping in squats or in layers of cardboard in shop entrances. Early on, I took a train east and flung myself around Paddington Station. A friend of ours told us that he was certain he had seen him there. I even paid for a private detective for a while.

But no, love avoids me, and irony hits me hard. My grim odyssey is the father's search for his son.

Jude

In the search, some things survive don't they? You take them with you forever. They are there as a continual ghostly presence. I have memories, and I have objects that I will never dispose of. I cannot. They are too precious. I could not live my paltry life without them. I name the memory of my first meeting with Pete as one; the earrings my mother gave me as another. Both catches have broken on the earrings, heaven knows how many times, but I still have them repaired, still wear them. There are some who are not like me in this respect. They disregard their objects and their pasts, their memories, as if they are an unwanted haunting that has no place now. They live for the new. I believe then, that I am special. I feel part of something; part of a "whole", though I have no idea what the "whole" is. There may be more like me. I do not know. I may never know completely.

We have a veggie stew on. It smells good. The kids are up on the horizon making The Beatles "Help" silhouettes with their bodies. Behind them is a cool, creamy moon. The moor-land before us is now yellow. There is no cloud. I am thinking of my mother and the way she used to cook stew. It is 1975. I am five years old and I am watching her cook. She always used the same pot. There was always the same order of vegetables going in. Then, the same seasoning. The same rich smell in the back kitchen. Now, I do the same. I think also of her, for it was when I was five years old, on such a moonlit night, that she first took me to London. We went up overnight on the sleeper train, and the milky moon followed us. I told her I thought it was beautiful. I woke her up to show her the moon. The trip was a brave thing for her to do. See, it had not been long since my father had died. I have only a few recollections of him. I was too young to understand cancer. There are only photographs of him on the sideboard back home. Black and white images in hardwood frames. Everything else went out in the jumble. My mother is not the same as me.

I do have one lasting memory of him though; his face in the darkness of the attic, calling my name.

"Judith Fox. Up here. Come and take a look at this…"

And so I would climb the attic ladder into this prehistoric world and he would let me set out his fossils, touch them, play with them, hold them up in the beam of my torch, and it's there, in that darkness, that stumbling, stony darkness that perhaps I found my desire for things old, and not for dollies or teddy bear tea parties in the Wendy House they bought for me.

So I am still a Fox, but I have, over the years, lost part of my name. See my name is broken, a fragment, a left-over. The "-ith" part of my name went when I left home, as though it were surplus to requirements.

But my mother tried. She took me around the National History Museum, as though it were her sworn duty. Father had apparently wanted me to go. You see, even though it was his interest in those fossils, she's still got them all home there. So, when we went to the Museum, it was the Dinosaur section she dragged me into. I can picture her sighing. She had accomplished his last wish. And, the five-year old me beneath the weighty monsters, breathed in my mother's love for him, the him who I believe might have preferred me to be a boy.

But it was never the huge Diplodocus that interested me. It was the smaller finds, those delicate chips of time I had played with in the attic; the delicate sea creatures, the trilobites and ammonites. Tiny pieces of organic antiquity turned to stone. That's what I always used to look at. Father gathered them but he was always after that big find. He was always pursuing the ultimate. But he never found it. It always evaded him. The past somehow tricked him and gave him cancer.

Mother loved him so much she kept them all, as if they were parts of him. They seemed to her to be his bones. They are all up in the attic, waiting to fall out on the future.

I never go back there, of course. We lived on the outskirts of Bridport. Not far from Lyme Regis and the Jurassic Coast. You might have guessed. My mother and I have, shall we say, moved in different ways. I still write to her, but I am not the sweet thing she took with her to London. I tried showing Pete to her once, but she locked the door. His hair and tattoos scared her. She saw a lost past, one whose prophecy had not fulfilled itself. Yet still I know, she cooks her stew, only enough for one now, and I cook mine. It is her age-old recipe I stir. We cannot help keep something of others.

The kids are coming back down now. They have been playing rolly-polies and their woollens are barbed with bracken. Sarah is with her youngest child Ally but she calls her "Baby". I hear little giggles and mothering noises. Pete is working on the bus. I hear clanking noises coming from underneath it; the occasional curse. When I call that the food is ready, we unite; the kids' bracken, Pete's grease, Sarah's silkiness.

For the rest of the evening, we sit, and talk. We make our own music. We play games. We listen. They all go to bed early. I am always the last. Tonight though, I am restless. I am thinking of too many other things: mother and fossils, earrings, moons, to listen as well as I normally do, to the children's stories. I just make the right noises, the way we all do sometimes. Eventually, I take a torch, and head up the road to where the huts are. We have been here a while now, and the police have made their first visit. The National Park are bound to be preparing an injunction to evict us. It will soon be time to go. I want to see this circle though, before we leave. See what is there. See, shall we say, if the Pound is as grim as time says it is.

The path up to the Round is worn and slippery. There is a slight dew. In winter, a stream flows down and crosses the road, but now, it is a mere trickle. Two small stone clapper bridges cross the channel as you walk up the line of the spur. It is still. The moon is high and clear. This is what I have come for. This is why I am me. My blood is not thicker than water. I can take the pain for this. The shadows where the huts sit are so magical that my breath becomes dew. The Moor seems to lull and sway like the ocean. The stone walls talk to me, like old sailors. They tell me their stories. I listen hard. I hear chattering, farming, loving, crying, listening and digging.

Below, I hear the children finally settling down. I see our fire. I want to keep this; close it in a box and lock it. Keep it for the future, just a bit of it, and open it on a rainy day. No-one else will ever have seen this, not in a thousand years. It is this; this sensation, and others like it that I live and crave for. I refuse to let it crumble. I have found it and I clutch it tight. I am the discoverer and the believer. So be it. It is here then, that I make my vow.

Eddie

There is little that is dangerous in our lives now. We have beaten most things, or at least, have held them down. Really, we have just kept them under. We once got the whip out, but now, well now, we use more subtle methods. We once retreated into dripping caves. We now love flinging things out into the open. Our individual problems become everyone's problem. At the same time, we are more calculated. We, each of us, have more of the ways of the hunter than the hunted. Some things however, will never be safe. Like flying. Like nuclear power. Like condoms. Like politics. There can never be that certainty, that one-hundred-percent assurance. So yes, they are still dangerous if you like. But then, we actually like danger don't we? We like living on the edge. We like walking slippery tight ropes. We like chance. And if you think about history, yes, the whole damn waffle stack of it, then it is the one percent we look at. It is that once chance, that iota of difference that strays from the norm. That is what is remembered. That is what is kept and preserved, and looked after. So we learn about the dangerous. We learn about the difference. And, in a strange kind of way, I find that comforting. Does if follow then that normality is discomforting? I think so…

You think for a moment, as well…

You think of all the things you have kept. Not only objects, but in your mind as well. They are there, because they are dangerous, or used to be. You have it lodged there now, because either the now or the then makes or made your heart race. It altered your life. It meant something. So, stop now, and see red. Observe the danger signs. Note the warning.

I say there is this danger. I have already put up a few risky areas off the top of my head.

There is another danger-seeker.

If you are clever, you will have spotted it already. You will have seen through me. Words are not dangerous on their own, but stories are. You can say what you want here. You can raise your voice. You can tell Mr President to fuck right off. You can conjure images. You can stand on your own soapbox. You can sit around fires and listen.

In some places, you can't do that. Do that, and you walk on the edge. You put yourself down the barrel of a loaded machine gun. Say things that people remember, and keep... and well, consider yourself extinct. Yes. There is danger in narrative. It can kill. Tell-tales in Iraq were shot, instantly. People closed their mouths. To be illiterate was an asset. Have no tongue, no vocal cords, and you were perfect: the ideal citizen in Saddam's regime. But then, you know me. You know I mess up. I come in on the fringe and alter things. It was hard to break the habit. I got into sealing my lips. I confess, it was harder than hell to give up. I swore I would never tell (you know how some people are), but I'm too far in now to let it go.

So, I'm going to be dangerous. There are some of us out there making up the one percent. That is one promise I am going to have to break. And boy, I can already feel the withdrawal symptoms.

VII

The Mortification of the Flesh

Robert

Here's one for you. Before my wife, before my son, before Stranger, I had an encounter. I return to it now again. It is as clear as a bell in my head. Years ago, when it rang, it used to give me so much pain. Now, it gives me pleasure the same way that bells peel on a Sunday morning. A kind of bliss you see. But this was no Sunday, nor is it any fairy tale. It is here, if anywhere, that I nearly "had" religion. But, in the end it was like everything, and just a fad. We had docked back in Guz. The ship has been around the Bay of Biscay and we were glad to be home after the gales there. I was a gunner. It was my birthday—8 June 1952. There was only one place to go. There is only one place to go to celebrate a naval birthday in Plymouth. You know where I speak of: The Street. Union Street. We got a Daimler taxi up from Devonport, across crumbling, grey Stonehouse, to where the action was. I was already half-cut. We had been drinking since tea time in The Ark Royal.

That Friday we did all the pubs. Half of them still had broken roofs and collapsed ceilings from the Blitz, but that didn't stop them from opening. Yes, we'll take a pint in each. People criticize the youth of today, but I can't, for I know we were as bad, if not worse. We drank until we virtually pissed our pants. Later, when the pubs had closed, I could hardly walk. It was then that she crossed the road, up the Palace Theatre end. We whistled like tom cats, throwing our hats in the air.

"Who's that?" I asked the others.

We had to find out. She strutted across the road. She had power. We had been every where that night: *The Antelope*, *The Phoenix*, *The Clipper*, the whole damn lot, and not seen her. No-one knew who she was.

It was they who did it. They gave her the money. And I became part of it, like a slave. She led me through the darkness of the night. I remember her nails digging into my hand. The lads were far away now.

She led me to a room, somewhere. I was intoxicated by her femininity. I hadn't expected the pad to smell so fresh and clean, and yet it was.

"What's you name again?" she asked.

"Robert."

"Bob then?"

"Yes. Bob."

There was a porcelain sink in the corner. She leant over it, and cleaned her teeth. It seemed like she always did this before working on a client. I stood silent. Her body was the ultimate. I wanted her. I moved closer.

"What's your name?"

"Sal," she answered, between brush strokes; her accent Plymouthian sexy.

"If you want me again, just ask for Sal."

I felt myself hardening. She dried her face with a towel, then turned towards me, taking out the pins in her hair.

"How do you want it then?"

She moved closer. I put my hands out, palms vertical, to hold her waist. She kissed me, but I broke. Though her kiss was the sweetest I have ever tasted, I could feel the drink wearing off. I was as hard as ever, and she tempted me, but I couldn't do it. She noticed my reluctance. She began to take her clothes off, carefully peeling down her girdle and stockings. I stopped her. I just wanted to be next to her. That was enough. There was no need of sex. When I looked closer into her gaudily-painted face, I saw an incredible beauty that I just wanted to release, and not hurt any more. She told me she'd been on the game since she was a girl. I sat still, appalled. Her mother had been one, and her mother before her. She was the end result of a history of squalor.

I left her in the small hours a new man. The next day I went to church in hope, and in pity, but there was no change in me. No great conversion.

I called back at the end of my stint in the service, but she had gone, disappeared when Britain become modern, as though her softness was no longer needed. I think of her now, nearly every day. I think of her fallen beauty. I think of a missed opportunity.

Back in the hotel, she knows nothing of this moment in my life. But I have been able to tell you. It must be the kindness of strangers, eh?

Jude

I push my feet into the slimy moor mud and wiggle my toes, the way I used to as a child. Tomorrow, when the sun shines again, the mud will bake hard, and I will have left my print. My mark might still be here at the end of summer, the way actors' hands are in the pavement outside Grauman's Chinese cinema in Hollywood. Mine, unlike theirs, will eventually vanish, but then that does not matter. If it remains for one day, then I will be pleased. Normally, the ponies come to this pool to drink. Around it is a pattern of hooves and hooves upon hooves. Those ponies have seen it all—generations of them—pounding the Moor; here when the world was still young. Today though, they have moved further downstream as we are here. When they become used to us though, they will move nearer, and make us feel better about ourselves. That's what nature does.

The pool is small, a slight deepening of a river flowing southwards. Trace it further, and I imagine the water here, flows into the Dart and then into the Channel. It is cool and fresh, and we come here to bathe. The evening is still; still enough for us to feel alive. The moon is climbing into a white sky, and small, warm swirls of air fan our bodies. Other creatures share the pool with us. I have seen frogs and water-boatmen. Peter is in there with them, floating steadily. Occasionally, I see the rise of his hairy belly and wrinkled penis as he regains his buoyancy.

We took our clothes off earlier, while the sun was still out. Then we fell onto a wet patch between two sloping stones, and did it there. A soft moss lay under us. I still have the green under my fingernails, and Pete's back is still stained. It was beautiful in ways I cannot tell you.

So now, we are washing; washing away our sins. Let our passion and evil flow down over the Moor. Let it pollute. Let it mingle. And let it say, passion and evil like blood brothers. It is a craving. Later, because of that craving for each other, we will do it again. The ponies will watch and the frogs will croak and we will make love.

Pete comes out of the water on his knees, walking like a comic Toulouse Lautrec. I pull him over and let dribbles of wetness slide down my sides. I pull his beard. I take dry grass stems and tattoo his back with them. Our feet splash in the water. We kiss, like you are supposed to in such moments. He rolls over and we gaze at the moon. I hold his hand. His other hand lies beneath my stomach, his little finger teasing my sex. I smile.

"Soak it up," he says. "We won't he here much longer…"

I pour the atmosphere into my body. I become brim full. If I move, I will spill it. So, I sit still. The breeze stops. The moon is high now.

I shiver. I have goose-bumps like barbs pushing out from beneath my skin; each a splinter of sensation. I look at my flesh. It is white. Deadly white.

"What's wrong?"

I cannot answer Pete. It is as if I hear voices. They are not far away. They are not over the hill, but the voices are tired and there are two of them. Two men, dressed in garb of the past. I look up. A westerly cloud is above us.

"I feel…"

I listen again. The old trails open up again, but I decide not to tell Pete. I choose to cover up my shiver.

"I feel cold."

He wraps his warmth around me.

I look to the moon for answers, but she is dumb. We wash for the last time then having dressed, we walk back to the bender for supper, without hearing the frogs' croaking again.

I forget, then remember this incident. I forget, then I remember it again. I had forgotten it, but remember it once more now. Memory weaves a curious magic, don't you think? Time likes to play tricks on us. It also likes to press replay. This is how the past and present blend.

Eddie

I have sat through a comedy. I have watched the myth. I have laughed. The bawdy comedy is Iraq, and the actors are Saddam's government and the people who live there. They play their parts well, but this is a shifting form. The whole thing is stage-managed by the good old U. S. of A. In the interval, when the lights are up, it changes. One minute it is comedy; the next it is classical tragedy. I watch more closely the myth. I listen more carefully to reality. I cry.

Visiting Iraq is like stepping into original chaos. It is that bad. A regime change might alter things, but I have my doubts. They certainly didn't before. There are nodding revolutionaries telling the Shi'ites to take control. Then, there's the two young Syrians I knew, who found Allah again, and decide Iraq might be the place to make a buck in the aftermath of the Gulf War. There are sweaty businessmen and oil millionaires who say Saddam's government is stopping their free enterprise. There are orphaned children who don't know a fuck what is going on. Oh yes, and a world that doesn't give an honest fuck. There was a report on the place by the Human Rights Watch. It said that Iraq shows no sign of evolving in the direction of a democratic society in which freedom is respected. The truth? Maybe. I cannot say. All I know is that there are so many paradoxes and contradictions that it is incredible the people stay sane. The problem I feel, is that Iraq does not know where she wants to be. Half of her still lives in primitive huts, worshipping sun-gods, while the other half carries machine guns and lives in Armored Personnel Carriers.

Then, if you had been through the history of Iraq, then you might have gone the same way. Remember, once this was Mesopotamia—great Mesopotamia—land where the West meets the East. It is the land between the great rivers: the Tigris and the Euphrates. It is the cradle of civilization don't you know? Oh yes, first, there was the Sumerians, then in the south, Babylonia; in the north Assyria. Then the territory came under control of the Persians, until the Islamic conquest of the seventh century. A lot of imposed "rule" followed. First, the Turco-Mongols stamped their imprint. Then the Ottoman Empire, and then in the twentieth century, more "rule": the British

Mandate of Mesopotamia and then the creation of the Kingdom of Iraq. Yes—know that do you? The Brits created Iraq in their own image. Later, came the 1958 revolution, then the 1968 revolution, and then, in 1979, young Saddam. And that's where we are now.

So in the present, we have Iraq almost penniless in 1988. Then we have claims of Kuwait being part of the Ottoman Empire's province of Basra. So come July 1990, we have 30,000 Iraqi troops assembling by the Iraq-Kuwait border, and then by August, we have an invasion, with its warplanes bombing Kuwait's capital, Kuwait City. Saddam neatly installs his cousin, Ali Hassan al-Majid as the governor of Kuwait.

Then, on state television, Saddam is with some Western hostages whom he refuses exit visas. He's ruffling the hair of a young boy named Stuart Lockwood, looking all like a benevolent storyteller and friendly father figure. So the threat to Saudi Arabia is on, and so begins the "wholly defensive" mission of Operation Desert Shield. So you know the next part of the tale. It is 543,000 coalition troops ready to go, co-ordinated by the United States. It is a propaganda machine in operation. It is human rights and Congress tipping in favor of action. It is "Stormin' Norman" Schwarzkopf, Dick Cheney and Colin Powell marching up to the fisticuffs with smiles on their faces.

The response begins at 2:38 a.m. Baghdad time, January 17th, 1991, when eight Apache helicopters destroy Iraqi radar sites near the Iraqi-Saudi Arabian border. Then throw in the Nighthawk stealth bombers, the Tomahawk Cruise Missiles, the cluster bombs and the daisy cutters. So the USA bombs the infrastructure. I mean it's aiming for the military sites, but then there a lot of civilian stuff that's taken out—you know, dams, bridges, power stations, telecommunications, railroads and sewage treatment plants, so the place is— you know—completely fucked. And get this, they are using aerial photography, real advanced stuff: GPS co-ordinates to the Pentagon.

It doesn't matter, because I saw the results on the ground. I saw the casualties. I went in there and photographed it all. Obviously, they didn't like it. Bad PR. Not the right kind of propaganda for back home. Yeah—the helpful military at the border "disposed" of my film. It doesn't matter. Some survived. You'd be amazed at what you can get out when you have the right friends in the right places. So, what was the total again: nearly 6,000 wounded. Oh yes, 2,278 civilians killed. 10,000 combat deaths in the air campaign. 26,000 Iraqi military personnel "neutralized". Is that enough for you yet? Now do you understand why Iraq doesn't know herself any more?

Let me tell you about one report I covered. I did a hospital in the north that had been damaged by an earthquake the same time as the war was going on in the south. The colors were horrific. When people who'd been crushed came into hospital for treatment, they were bled into transparent bags. That made it worse. See-though bags. These bags were transported south, seemingly as one of the few raw materials the north produces. So this blood is for the benefit of Saddam's Republican Guard at war in the south. Sacrifice. You're still at the comedy stage when you see them go in, but then, I got this one shot of several crates being loaded into a van bound for airport; Chaldean nuns protesting pushed out the way. It's then that an earthquake splits the head. Tragedy is given the stage, and I am the lamenting Chorus, hidden behind a mask—a convenient photographic veil. I could say more, but I do not need to. You knew the truth before I even began, before you got comfortable, before the lights went down. Iraq is the story of past against present—of relics against the brutal face of modern humanity.

VIII
The Journey

Robert

They say it took nine and a half weeks, which is not that long to start a nation, but much too long to be in a cramped, child's toy of a ship, travelling across a grey Atlantic, with all thoughts back to Britain, and memories of those last few days in Plymouth. See, this was not just travel. This was leaving. Travel indicates that one day you will return. Leaving does not. It is for good. By our standards, you might say the *Mayflower* was ill-proportioned to cross an ocean. It was a stout bucket of a ship with tall masting and a high superstructure, so she would have lulled with every single plankton filled wave. Stranger felt them all. It had been a while. He has been as sick as a dog initially, but now, his body had become accustomed to the motion. Elsewhere on board, people still heaved. Faces were olive green, and the place stank of sweet sick, with several buckets a day thrown overboard. The crew went around scrubbing and salting the decks. Amongst this stench of bile, he tried to keep himself sane. He tried to rationalize what he had actually done. He had got on a ship going to Hell for all he knew. He had given up his lucrative tobacco business and European travel. He had left behind a good friend. In Sutton, he had now become the dead. He felt like a nobody yet all of this was pushed out by his other thoughts. He felt the confusions of attraction. Carver's daughter he discovered was called Alice. His aim was to pursue her. He would fish for her love. Fortunately, the line would not have to be cast very far for a bite.

His task on board was no different. He was one of the ship's jobbers. He made any repairs needed. Constantly, his days were made up of sealing any holes in the rickety ship. Sometimes, on calmer days, he threw a rope ladder overboard, tied himself to the masting, and went down, working his way around the hulk. Other days, he checked the sealing on the inside, banging the wood, and listening for hollows or rotting.

On the whole, the *Mayflower* was wet, and in the hold, constant streams of salty water ran in, and constant, spilling buckets were carried up and tipped overboard on the sides of the foredeck. The children used to help him bale out the water. They liked Stranger. He used to make them laugh. When they ate, he would tell them about scary monsters from the sea, all of which he defeated, with only a bucket and mop.

On the decks, conditions were filthy, though perhaps no worse than any other ship that Stranger had previously served upon. Though there was a reek of vomit, and rotten food, it was the smoke from the passengers' warming braziers that caused most problems. The smoke blackened the whole place. Sometimes, they had to go on deck simply to fill their lungs with clean air. Stranger was a part of all of this, though he never let it affect him. He was too cunning. He just got on with his job, and forgot about the real reason for the voyage. It was awkward to make moves on board ship. One of the more important Separatists—the Yorkshire man, William Bradford—had asked Stranger how he withstood the conditions so well. Stranger gave him some cock and bull answer, but ultimately, it was because Stranger was a survivor. Bradford saw that as well.

Oddly, there were other strangers on board. These were what the Separatists called the other non-believers present. These people were not of the Leiden congregation or their families. Instead, they were the planters recruited by London merchants, and then men and servants hired to stay for one year. Stranger was just stranger than the rest of this group. He ate on his own, and always stayed in the male quarters. He would never be out whistling for the wind, like the others. He would laugh at such notions, tie back his jet black hair, and casually light a pipe of tobacco. He sat calm in the storms, when water rushed across the main-deck, making the wood slippery and mossy; his pipe lighting up his face in the blackness, while the seas thrashed the ship about. He always kept his gold around his waist in a leather belt purse. He was one of the richest men on board, but few knew that. Only the two dogs on board, a mastiff and a springer spaniel, seemed to warm to him.

For a while, the Separatists did not take to him. He was mysterious and dangerous they felt. He did not sing with them. He had, however, lashed out on a young man named Turner who had made life obnoxious for the other passengers. The youth made fun of the sick—not the sea-sick—but the diseased. He cursed them. Stranger could not care less for profanity, but then came one day, when the young man spoke to Alice, and pulled her hair as she was sick over the vessel's side. He had already seemed to accept his fate, and told her they would never make it to the Americas. Then, Turner punched her. From the rigging Stranger watched. He monkeyed his way down assuredly, and grabbed the youth. He hit him hard on the jaw, making him stagger around the deck. The youth came back for more. He would not be beaten by jobber scum.

An audience gathered. This was the entertainment they so wanted after weeks of boredom and routine. But no, working the weary, pirated Spanish lanes had left Stranger a tough man. The youth tried again, but Stranger thumped him harder. He lay unconscious on the main-deck. Stranger's presence became manifest. The Separatists knew his power. He would keep order it would seem, and after three weeks of the voyage, that suited them well enough, religion or no religion.

Carver remained aloof and apart. He was sliced off, as always, and made of a different cloth. He stayed in the male deck most of the time, at the opposite end to Stranger, reading the Bible, and in some kind of silent meditation. His eyes always recognized Stranger, though—showed that knowledge—but he would not speak, even when Stranger felt they had lived close enough to one another anyway that no-one on board would suspect anything. But others were more talkative. They told him about Carver. He was well thought of. Apparently, he was something of a big-wig in the church, born in Nottingham. It was he who worked as the Separatists' agent. But there was some mystery in his past. He had not, of course, always been a Separatist, and sometimes, he believed the others felt him false. They said there was another religion under his exterior. Carver was an older religious man. He still had some of the old ways: the old faith. And then someone must have told Stranger.

"He has riches and holy things. From overseas... from the East."
And Stranger made a connection. Now he understood.

"Men and women go to see him if..."

But they would say no more, or was it because they could not say anymore? Whatever, Stranger knew he might not ever find the reason. Carver kept his secrets. He could tell. There was one day though—a calm one upon the ocean—when the ship was making little progress. The crew were out whistling, full of hope. Carver was on deck. Stranger felt that Carver wanted to speak to him. He was on the aft deck, repairing sailcloth. He saw Carver's figure move towards him. Yes, he had a secret to tell. Stranger turned, but Carver was quicker. He could not face him, and ran down the steps. By now, Stranger had realized that what he wanted to say was something important, though by telling him, his position as a Separatist might be jeopardized. After all, he was down to be Governor of the new settlement. But Stranger did not push him. It would only have damned him more. And Stranger knew that the box was well-hidden, and that Carver would never return to the place where it was buried. So, the matter would have no consequences, not in his lifetime, or anybody's lifetime. So, when it came down to it, such anxiety was unproductive in the first place.

There were days, and nights, when navigation proper became impossible. Even Stranger could not use his equipment. The stars and sun were obscured by clouds and bad weather. Visibility was down to less than quarter of a mile. Fixing an exact position was difficult normally. Now, it was impossible. At this time, the wind was also at its worst, howling and terrifying all. The children were screaming on board, and nuzzled into their mothers' breasts. Few remained on deck. They were mid-Atlantic now, and the figure of despair walked amongst everyone. The wind took away some of the smell of shit, sick and body odour, but it outstayed its welcome. With some of the passengers developing infections, Stranger saved the day once again, with his curious methods. I see him reaching for the dried moss given to him by the gatherers of the Moor. He is wise man and Shaman.

And it is here, at this very point, between continents, amongst the shit and sick that I picture Stranger smelling something else: a fragrance. He pushed back the long strands of his hair, and placed a blanket around his shoulders. The wind shouted again. Waves chopped. A baby screamed. A dull prayer is spoken at the other end of the deck. Through the angled port-hole, spray could be observed, spitting into the sails. He climbed the worn steps onto the main deck. It was not bare. There was not enough room for everyone to be below. Carver watched him, but Stranger still could not fathom his mind, and if he was totally honest, he had no wish to know. He followed the fragrance.

Alice was sat on the aft deck, shivering. Thin strands of hair fell upon her face. He would not see her legs. They were tucked under a rush of rough blanket. He startled her initially, but then she welcomed him. She had asked him before why he had come on this journey. Stranger had told her a lie; how he felt he was making a new start. Then there was getting away from that fool Moses. Perhaps he told her about his debts. I do not know.

"You're wearing a perfume," he said.

She smiled.

"Yes. I wanted to save it, but I had to use it to feel good. I wanted to smell something different... That's why I come up here. I don't mind the cold."

Stranger breathed her in. She looked out into the blackness of the Atlantic. She finally thanked him for ridding the abusive young man from her company. Stranger explained how it was nothing, and that the lad had deserved his physical reprimand. He steered the conversation in another direction.

"Your father... he—"

"He wants to tell you something."

"Yes."

"I know he can't though. Just be happy with the money he gave you. He wishes you no harm."

She was nervous.

"It's Alice isn't it?" he said in a slow manner.

Stranger felt foolish. He had to ask this question. All the time he had known her, and he had only found out her name from other people on board the *Mayflower*: a chance question to the children in fact.

"Yes. I'm named after my mother."

Stranger was about to ask what had happened to her, but Alice had already anticipated his request.

"She died. In Leiden. When we first went out there… when we ran the press, and looked after the—"

A wave cracked against the wooden hull, and her words seemed to sink below the surface again. Timbers ground together, and smoke wound its way through the deck planks from the braziers below. The smeech was staining Alice's dress.

"She was persecuted. They gave her trouble. Gave us all trouble. I must go. I have work to do for my father."

"No. Don't go…" Stranger insisted.

"Please. I must," she stated.

The situation offered to him was now, was one where he could not duck or dive, the way he ran the tobacco business. No. A meeting like this would not happen again. It was unique. Momentarily, he looked more intently at her. He breathed her in once more. He wanted to keep her, preserve her forever. It had to come. She made a move to stand, but Stranger touched her shoulder and pressed it gently back down. She did not resist, and instead, smiled like the devil himself.

"Don't go."

He was helpless. He was a Stranger to himself. A door opened, and he walked through. He grabbed her near him. There was no more speech. Their mouths slid together and they became land-locked. Tongues darted in and out. She caressed his beard. They fell onto the slippery deck, sliding about like landed fish. The smell did not matter, not anymore. His breeches slid off like discarded scales, and she hitched up her dress in gilled layers. When his breathing became heavy, she silenced him. They must not be found out. He took deeper, slower breaths, not daring to let them become audible. She reeled him in. He felt a new man, and a new life beginning. The *Mayflower* lulled, as the two made love.

It began to rain. Droplets fell from her breasts onto his hard stomach. The wind changed direction and spray tickled their feet. The journey would soon come to an end. There was to be no looking back into the blackness, now only a peer into their future happiness. He withdrew and she buttoned herself up, her bodice once again encasing her white breasts. She watched him ease back into his trousers. She had tamed him. When she left, in a whisper, she said, "I don't have religion the way my father does."

And now, not only her father had a secret.

There was no more monthly bleeding. She knew what this meant. The storms ended. The smell of the air changed subtly. New species of bird circled overheard, and begged and cawed for food upon the decks. The passengers heaved themselves up from the damp interior and their lice-ridden beds. Possessions were packed up. Men and boys fished. Women and girls washed and cleaned. Relief eased over their tired faces, like a new tide.

There had been two who had not made it. One was the young man, Boy Turner, who had teased Alice and whom Stranger had sorted. He had contracted hypothermia, and little more could be done for him, despite the company's prayers. Poetic justice many felt. Another old man had gone on. He was found dead in his sleep. The sphagnum moss had help heal a wound he had gained from a misplaced chisel, but in truth, he had been on borrowed time since the start of the voyage. Now, time had caught up with him on the other side of the world.

Stranger went below deck to get some peace. The interior now felt strangely secure, perhaps because it had survived the Atlantic's full force. He slept a great deal. He saw Alice only a couple more times on her own, and then they had only been brief exchanges, disguised as random observations. He had asked her for marriage, and she had accepted. It was what she wanted. It was what they must do—and quickly. His face changed colour. The old grey pallor went. He stopped his pipe-smoking. He threw his tobacco supplies and clay pipe overboard into the deep. He'd stopped drinking too.

It was November. The first sight of land came at dawn; the air chilly and brisk. It was unspectacular; just a dull black on the horizon. It almost didn't seem to matter anymore to Stranger. The atmosphere on board, however, changed instantly. The New World had been reached. A new start. Paradise. Bibles were quoted and recited. The ocean had been beaten.

Accuse me of heresy. It doesn't matter. I know the truth; my truth, at least. It is just that here, the truth becomes vague. I reach the edge of the world; the waterfall into nothingness. Voids. Here be dragons. My research tells me nothing more. My story is near an end. I have followed Stranger from one continent to another. I have walked up and down the centuries. I have trod in his shoes. He was there. He was one of the "Fathers"—the pilgrims who set out to find the Promised Land.

I can tell you this though. The actual landfall cannot have been easy. Explorations are made. I am certain that Stranger goes with them. His curiosity is too great. Ah, but hold on. Stranger is a new man now. No. I see him on board still with Alice. And so the others return with juniper, maize and fresh water. A site is chosen. You know it. You have known it all along. They name it Plymouth. New Plymouth. It was on the tenth of November 1620 that Stranger and Alice went ashore.

Carver rowed alongside them. He knows now of Stranger's intentions, but I believe he still will not tell the secrets of the box. No matter. They have arrived. Their pilgrimage is over. Their destination is reached.

Surely I do not need to fill in details for you here. You know the first huts were made of wattle and mud, brown windows out of oiled parchment. You can picture the energy of building the settlement along the banks of an unnamed river. You see the *Mayflower* in the calm waters of the harbour. See Stranger working on her baulking. The last sails are lowered. An anchor has been dropped. They admire a new view. They are on the other side of the glass that is the Atlantic.

Stranger must have married Alice. I cannot imagine an existence otherwise in such a steadfastly Christian community. They, I have a feeling, survive, surpassing the great mortality of that first winter. Carver is old, and though he makes it through the first winter, dies the next spring. Stranger searched for the keys on him, but could not find them. Alice believed her father had simply dropped them overboard. Oceans hold secrets see, better than people. She saw him go up on deck one night. There is no last minute request for Stranger in the Common House. There is only the slightest twinkle in his eyes as the candle burns low. A dull prayer is spoken. When he leaves this earth, he believes his daughter is in good hands. And by now, Alice knows who Stranger really is. I will come to that matter soon enough as well. But just maybe, in the chink of the door opening to everlasting peace, Carver had plans for the growth of the new community. Maybe, just maybe, his secret was passed on.

When, one day, a Native American walks into New Plymouth, I feel it in my bones that it is Stranger who first greets him. He alone can see past skin and costume. They are perfect strangers. They are history. They both come in peace. They belong together.

In the early summer of 1621, Alice gives birth to a baby boy. A future is assured, and the past is forgotten, or tries to be. William Bradford becomes governor, and modern America is born.

Now, what was that about Plymouth giving its name to more towns across the world than any other?

Jude

You are hearing my story, my chronicles, my recital, my yarn. I have not realized it before, but so much of our tiny lives are composed of stories, of listening to anecdotes. You may hear them on buses, in shops, in your homes, in pubs, in your dreams, and in the strangest of places. There is a human need to tell, to offer experience, to offer advice. We tell stories to make sense of our confusing lives. We all have stories to tell. It might be the "everyone has a novel inside them", but I believe stories are more important than that. They are older and the art of telling is lovelier and more satisfying somehow. See, before anything else, stories were being told. I picture them being told here on Dartmoor, before Holy men had even been seen. Yes. Tales of the Bards of Wistman's Wood, the Wrath of Taranis, the Nymph Tamara, the Golden Maze, and the Vengeance of Belus. All of them are waiting to be heard again. They are there in America too with the Native Americans, in Australia with the Aborigines, in New Zealand with the Māori. Perhaps then, once, there was a time when stories were more important; and time when people just listened and learned, and maybe never questioned the world so much.

Telling is what first attracted me to Pete. He has made it his art. He enthrals us with the soft, collected tones of his voice. Telling was why I first wanted to know him better. It was at a free festival in Somerset, just outside of Taunton, a few summers ago. He sat outside his Volkswagon camper, and was just telling stories. And people listened. When he had finished, they swapped tales. One leading to another, and then another, and another again. So, the story of the Little Cook, became the story of the Little Tailor. And Pete wished them to take the stories away and tell others. That's the way he likes to think of it: a kind of underground spread of wonder, from traveller to traveller, teller to teller. And yes, all those wonder stories of Dartmoor, fell out of his tongue, and dazzled me.

When I first spoke to him, I didn't really have much of a story to tell. He was well-spoken and confident. Such confidence. I was nervous and curious. I'd been on protest at RAF Mildenhall. You know, American bombers, the fuckers that eventually trashed Iraq. Yeah— what did it become? 100,000 sorties, and 88,500 tons of bombs. He asked me to stay though. I asked him to tell me some more; this was when the others drifted back to their glowing campsites. I stayed until the fire went out. Then, and can you believe this, he asked me to leave. No more tales, he said. He was tired, and though now, he prefers not to recall it, his voice ached. But I ached for him. It's often the case isn't it? Chance makes so much of a difference. Stories can be made upon chance. The chance that it was his camp I had wandered across to that evening, the chance that he was there, the chance that it was not someone else's camper.

I knew I had not been travelling long, but there was something about him. A difference. A hope. I felt union, togetherness in his old world.

When I left, he stamped out the fire. I thought the story was going to end there, and that it was just another meaningless collision— you know, the ones that make up most of our lives. But no—I slept late the next morning. I woke to the sound of Ozric Tentacles playing in the arena nearby. A heavy dub bass was filtering across the field. There were strange smells in the air—the smells of takers.

Sarah was cooking. She must have seen him first of all. Pete's long figure was determinedly walking towards us. He had a wispy beard then, deliberately forked, and though he was already thinning on top, he kept his hair long, in dreadlocks. He wore a single earring, shaped like a sickle moon, and a waistcoat of blue and red. Do you see? Do you see how I am storytelling now?

"Is... ah... Jude about?" he had said softly to Sarah.

Sarah was defensive at first.

"What do you want her for?"

"I wondered if she was in. I'd like to speak to her. I was a bit rude to her last night..."

I poked my heard out of the bender. Sarah looked at me.

"Do you know him?"

I nodded.

Pete greeted me. His words were now clumsy; not the clear orality of the previous night.

"I wondered... Do you fancy a walk?"

I asked him to wait. I needed to clean my teeth, and so, between a foaming mouth-full of paste, I said I would like to.

That afternoon, we walked away from the festival, up into some ancient woodland, a couple of miles away. He told me his true story. Rich parents. The usual rebellion. And when I told my story, for what seemed like the first time in my life, somebody listened. He listened. But I could have kicked myself that day, because even then, I lied to him. I told him untruths, the way it is unstoppable for us to do so. I put forward the same relics; the same lies. I told myself I was merely embellishing the truth—what all storytellers do—but really, it was lies.

After I had spoken, we remained silent for about five minutes. Then Pete said, "You're a romantic I think... in the old tradition..."

Then he kissed me.

Those fucking evil, lying bastard stories.

See, words are powerful things. They can kill.

Stories even more so. Genocide. Think of history. Remember all those fucking lies told by the governments about the bombing of Iraq.

They can enchant you. That's what makes them dangerous.

I don't care if Pete is a trickster, or a magician even, but when he spoke to me that day, I felt several stories having happy endings. And so that when he touched me as we lay in the leaves, I felt a new story beginning.

And our story has continued.

It seems that we have had our "regulation" three days stoppage. There is an official standing in our camp, reading legislation at us. The language is familiar to us: the same old thing. This time it is a Dartmoor National Park Warden. There are a couple of other men standing next to him from Devon County Council. What is remarkable is that no-one loses their temper. This is because they have given it a thousand times, and we have heard it a thousand times. Simple. I stand outside of us, and peer in. The picture I see is so odd sometimes, that I barely believe it myself. The pin-striped council officers are all standing there with clip boards, M&S suits and legal documents. Then there is us. There is no emotion in their voice. They have been trained well. We are advised to move on within the next twenty-four hours, or else they will be forced to use eviction orders and stronger methods. "Stronger methods", incidentally, means the police. This is normal. The order is pinned onto a nearby post, presumably for us to read. We have no complaints though. Nor can we moan at the police. They uphold the law, and we break it. But then, we demand a different kind of society, fucking anarchists that we are. You know that already.

It rains while they speak to us. The children are shivering, and dog is barking. It doesn't look good. They can have us for deprivation and maltreatment of the kids. Child abuse. I call them over to me and cuddle them.

Pete does not lie. He just, embellishes a little, just like I did. In fact, this time, he lays it on with a trowel. It is the only way. This is a survival game and a battle of wits; a war of epigrams and hyperbole. He works with the flair of an accomplished practitioner. He knows how to operate. He is also educated, but knowing that makes little difference to the suited men wandering around our camp. To them, he is the worst kind—not just a traveller—but an intelligent traveller. He represents more paper-work for the secretaries back in Exeter to process and photocopy.

"Do you wish to say anything?" the Warden asks, after he had read the National Park Act to Pete.

"No."

Pete turns his back and walks towards me, his neck taut and proud. The men leave. It takes a while for them to start their car, and while we talk, their damp starter motor can be heard clicking across the chilly moor.

"I'm not moving yet," Pete says. "This is a good site. We need to make it through the week here. We'll move on then... when we're ready."

As always, I ask what will happen. He is uncertain and won't answer me. The police will probably arrive tomorrow: a softly-softly approach at first. Then it gets harder. In some places they remove people like us during the night. One place, up north, the entire village came into the camp and started packing up the equipment for some travellers we know. It gets violent then.

"I want to take the kids inside."

The Warden's car finally starts, its window are steamy with rage. Angrily, he spins away.

Pete follows me inside the tents. They have had no schooling this morning. Pete will now sit before them, and make their eyes unblinking, and their mouths open with wonder. He will make them laugh, then cry. He will lead them among all the emotions. He will let them join in. He will sing and he will shout. And they will come out as better human beings than National Curriculum creations.

By now, I expect my whole existence seems completely alien to you. I care little. Your existence does not seem odd to me. You tell your story the way you want. What seems odd to me is the some of you who do desire more; perhaps some of you listening now; who look for a better way, perhaps our way, but who are afraid, afraid to make the jump. You are afraid that the gap is too wide and you will fall, and plunge. Have a leap of faith I say.

There was a policeman once; the only one who ever really spoke to me. He told me he understood. He told me he was caught between two worlds. He had his house and wife and family, and what he did, paid for that and allowed them to exist. But he knew he wanted more and he hated what he might have to do with us. He didn't think we were committing a crime. You meet so few like him, but they are the people with a second vision; a kind of split personality. Look closely out there, and you will discover them. They are around you, and sometimes, I think they are braver than we are. We do not stick with the system. We simply reject. But to stick with the system, and challenge it from within? Now there's a story…

The police who eventually arrive at the camp are friendly enough too. They make jokes with us. They ask us politely to leave. They look around the camp. They ask us a few questions. Where might we heading next? What are our plans? Where have we come from? See, they like to pin us down; keep tabs on us. They read the same piece of legislation to us. We listen as always. Keep it polite see.

They seem tired. But then, it is nearly dawn. This is their last call of the night. A fresh shift can sort this lot out tomorrow. They yawn and rub their dull eyes. Humanity wakens beneath their uniforms when I make them cups of tea. They've still arrived earlier than Pete anticipated though. There is an inevitability about it all which neither of us want to discuss.

The darkness fades. A delicate, sugary coating of mist settles on the Moor. The twisting heather is damp. It will stay so for most of the morning. Sunshine comes late up here. And it is here, that very morning after the police had come, that my story takes a very different turn, and somewhere along the line, becomes integrated with that of another. And not just with another storyteller, but with a different time as well.

You see, I wanted to take a last look at the hut circle above us. I like the feeling I get when I am alone on the Moor. Time stops. You hear people speak such clichés, but there's something in it.

I'm feeling rough; a kind of roughness of mind and body brought on by the stress of others. The breaking sun is the only thing that takes the edge off my body. I shiver a warm shiver and climb the worn path up to the huts. Hameldown and Hookney Tor peer down upon them. I've read a little about the hut circle now. They're late Bronze Age. Twenty-four huts in total, surrounded by a low stone wall. The name of the site was first recorded by a Cornishman: Richard Polwhele in 1797. He reckoned it was probably from the Anglo-Saxon God of War, Grim. You'll know Grim as Odin, or Woden. The wall made the place a haven. Archaeologists reckoned that wall ran to around 1.7 metres tall. Polwhele reasoned it was "a seat of judicature" or a "principal temple of the druids".

Certainly, it was densely populated and sophisticated. The whole site consists of four acres, with many of the huts having L-shaped porches. All these porches face downhill away from the prevailing wind. You can still see the hearths and cooking holes. In the rear of each, is a kind of raised level area, where the people slept. I lie down there, and pretend. It is an earlier time, and I am not longer Jude. Instead, I live in this seat of judicature, warm and comforted by the fire. Here, I come close to everything I have ever sought. All I need now is a child to nurture, and Pete to come home from outside of the wall and I will be complete.

There is a slight fog this morning, compounding the mist. It is not a damp one, but one that swirls and dances in the morning's light. In the huts, I begin to feel alive again. Sleep wears off me and I forget about the cold-eyed police and our imminent problem. I climb to the top, where the northernmost outer wall of the circle lies. I am alone, completely. It is here that I first see it: another life-changer.

The sunlight reflects off it. The grains of quartz in the wall stones shine brightly, but this, this dazzles. I look at it for a moment or two, firstly dismissing it as a beer can or a discarded glass bottle. But it is neither. I move closer to check. My heart is calm.

Only a corner of it is uncovered. I find it hard to believe—very hard—as I imagine this place to have been excavated by archaeologists, but then, this is on the periphery, just outside the main enclosure. Any excavations may not have reached this far out. I yank at it for a minute or so, tugging the peat loose. I pull harder. I lift a stone above it, to gain it more freedom. I can tell the object is fairly large. I pull again. Gradually, it works free. A rectangular-shape is left in the black soil. I have the box in my hands. The carvings on it are dramatic; obviously holy, but depict couples making love. All of it is beautiful; with a Christian-style cross on the lid of the container, and on four sides. I shake it carefully. I hear nothing. I try to prise open the lid, but it is locked and sealed, tight as hell.

At first, temptation tells me to throw the box against a stone and break it open, but instantly I know I have found something valuable—something ancient. I trace the intricate carvings with my fingers. I feel the tips of them, and the whole of my body becomes energized at the find. I shiver some more. The fog is getting thicker, blocking out the sun's heat. Now, this, is a stumble. This, is a find. This, is a story, and it seems, it is one that I alone, must tell.

I knew instantly the box was holy, and that it contained something of great value. It was the same knowing as when as a child you rummage through your parents' wardrobe to find out what your Christmas presents are. You see it there. Your breath becomes sticky, but you will not dig any further. It is enough to know it is there. That is just what this was like. And I obviously knew it to be of a different time than the circle. I longed for a date on it, but there was nothing. Close up, it smelt disgusting. You could taste time, mildew and dread. Copulating figures stood carved on the sides of the box. I presumed the others to be either saints or apostles, and this, a kind of primitive reliquary. On each end were two figures; one male and one female, but the figures were too tarnished and muddy to see exactly what they were doing. The whole box was difficult to decipher, but as I held it, there was definitely a warmth that exuded from it, that came through me, into my body. Size-wise, it was about the proportion of the bread-bin we had back in the bender. The walls were thick; whatever was inside, was cushioned perfectly.

That morning, I made a mistake. I became selfish. I went against our way, our code. I didn't share. But then, I wanted this to be mine. My story. My child. What I had always dreamed about. I thought of money and prestige, the first time I had done so for a very long time. I wanted to be the discoverer and scholar. I wanted, for an instant, to be my father. I wanted to be his girl again. For my mother to be proud of me. And… and… and…

In the stillness, I heard a car stop down below. I slipped the box back into its hole. The earthy walls had now crumbled and it sat in there awkwardly. I hurried. I used my hands to cover over the earth. I took dead ferns and heather, and disguised the find as best I could.

I prayed that this would stay my story, and that no-one else would find it. It had been there a long time; only recent washout water wearing away several layers of soil, and exposing it. Why now should anyone else find it? Most people who came here did not venture up this far anyway. To stare at the fossilized huts was enough.

I ran back down the lower slopes. A figure was walking towards me. I was gleeful about what I had found (too gleeful I believe now). My face must have been gleaming. But I would not tell, not yet, at least. Lower down, I crossed the stone bridge over the West Webburn River and the fog became thinner. I was still being selfish. A man was struggling up the slope—a tourist. He had sunglasses draped around his neck; a compass and an OS map in his hand. Silly shit, I said to myself.

"Morning," he said.

I nodded, mouthing a silent hello that showed all too well my desire for control, for secrecy. I felt him turn around behind me, and watch me; my behaviour was clearly odd. But nothing mattered now. I was no longer without direction. I was the discoverer, and it felt good.

When I got back to the site, I saw a white and red transit van with wire mesh stretched across its windscreen. A blue light was flashing. There was shouting going on, and I could hear Pete's angry voice. I stopped for a second or two, and watched as the fog pulled back and revealed the scene. Reality hit me finally. It was the police, and they were moving in hard.

Eddie

Shrines interest me. Places of worship fascinate me. In Iraq, they had mosques for everything, idols, prophets and shrines for every whim, vice and deed. In Britain, they are Christian (or at least, Christian overlaying the Pagan). I am unsure of the reason why I like these places of worship. Perhaps it is because of their age, and only that. I go to their shrines, rather than those of my own culture, because they have age. That is what counts. Time counts see.

For a small archipelago, a lot has happened in Britain. It is a land riding on its past, galloping in history. And still the mare is not tired. So I have tried to ride as well, and I have searched for shrines. I have plans to go to Lindisfarne and Iona. To Canterbury as well. Earlier this week, I visited Glastonbury, shrine of Arthur and centre-point of British mysticism. Avalonians and hippies. Up the tor and into the Abbey. I drank from the Chalice Well. I shot about ten reels of film there. I know that some of those shots will be for the magazine.

Now I have come further west. Gone the way of my land's forefathers I suppose. My eventual aim is to reach Cornwall, and perhaps the Isles of Scilly. Get some of those quaint little fishing harbours. But I've been advised to go to Dartmoor first. So far, I have been impressed with this place. There is nowhere in the States like it. We have canyons, forests, deserts and lakes, but we do not really have moors. I see an incredible beauty here; a more ancient beauty. I don't attempt to explain it. To feel it, is enough for the photographer. I leave explanations to poets, painters and storytellers.

I'm down here in a rental car: a Ford Sierra, a top of the range model. It's paid for by the magazine, of course. Money is no object so it seems.. I spent yesterday doing the granite tors: Hart Tor and Leather Tor, Hameldown and Hookney. Windy places. Then I went to some of the mires and bogs. I travelled out to Whiteworks, an old tin-mining place, and on to Fox Tor. People back will love all this stuff. I took some marvelous shots up on Fox Tor. I always go for the unusual angles you might say. There's a fairly famous one of a blind Iraqi beggar I took from a window above him. Just as I took, he looked up. His black eyes were as deep as a deer's. It made the cover of *Time* magazine. It then went on to win a photographic award back home. So I'm always on the take, seeking angles, perspectives, light and shade. Does that sound mathematical? Calculated even? It shouldn't. I rarely use light meters or anything now. I just take, and what's good, I use.

I love the tors though. I think of the mesas and buttes of Arizona when I see them. If I was a kid growing up here, I would have climbed each one.

The clapper bridges fascinate as well. Snap. There's one at Post-bridge. I got a shot of it, with a pony nestling beside it. The mist makes the whole place mysterious. It can be difficult though. You want it but not in such quantities that it ruins the shot. It can change in a second. You set up, ready to shoot, and then it rolls in thicker, just to deceive you.

Last night was good. I dropped into *The Plume of Feathers* inn at Princetown. I guess I was as much of a curiosity to them, as the reg-ulars were to me. I bought them drinks and took photographs. I explained and they told me about their lives. What the Moor meant to them? They talked until the cows came home. I buy them more drinks and we put the world to right. We talk some more. An old timer gets singing and I photograph the staccato of his song:

"Oh—I am—a right—unlucky—old chap."

His dog is sat next to him. His four sons are at the bar. There are tales of losing boots in the mire, ghosts, hairy hands, beasts, pixies and saints. Then come stories about the stories. I listen intently. This is a lot to ask of these men, to let their secrets go across an ocean. I will be parading them in a magazine. It is a kind of ancient pornog-raphy. Still here, I can ask permission. I speak the language. In Iraq, there are so many variations, you give up. You don't bother. Odd isn't it? Here, I care. And after they have told me all they know, and I have captured them in mid-existence they want to know more of me. As is always the case, when we are strangers, we give little away. I do not tell of me running away from the diner back home. I don't speak of me smoking dope in high school. I give them a hillbilly story of my youth and they love it. I tell them the same stories my grandfather delighted me with.

I walk back to where I have camped, drunk as a lord. I sing. I feel at home. These are real people who don't care about appearances. There are men in the pub who have never set foot off the Moor; never knowing what it is like to find a landscape of verticals instead of rolling horizontals. They are men who never wanted to go up in the world. They are men who only know one way of life. This is what I come for. I hear their voices as they depart. They will be late rising and their wives will shout at them, but at least they will remember me. I will be talked about in that pub when I am long gone. Surely then, one part of our lives is worth something. I will send them some prints. Mementos.

My head is murky in the morning. In the black box of my mind, I have a dull recollection of the quantity of beer consumed the previous night. It is still early. When I first came to, my head was spinning. Now, it is not much better.

I give it a while, and then drive to a place they recommended me to visit. The road to it is old and had many pot-holes. I worry about the vehicle's suspension. My lights are on full beam as the fog is thick this morning. I may have to wait a while before I can take anything. There is no other life up here. I am alone.

After checking my location once again, I park the car at the bottom of a slope next to a bridge named Firth on the map. I take out the ignition key and open the driver's door. I leave the car in park. Outside, a sticky coldness grabs me. My kit is in the trunk. Once I have removed it, I lock the vehicle and begin the climb. The path up the slope is well worn and slippery. I have taken the lightest equipment I have, as I am uncertain how far it is. I've my head down, making me ergonomic in the slight wind. Right here, right now, I am wondering why the hell I decided to come on this assignment. Thoughts of the girl at the gas station suddenly come into my mind. I am wishing that she were with me, the way we do when new situations confront us. I want her warmth again.

I am shocked when from out of the fog a figure suddenly crosses before me. It is a woman. She walks with an ancient, considered step, but hurriedly. Her eyes are wide open. She sees me first, but I am the one to speak. I greet her, but she merely nods, as shocked as I am to see someone out here. She looks eccentric; mad even, vaguely hippified but with a kind of punk mentality. A black T-shirt enclosed her large breasts, and they wobbled as she stepped down through the stones. Her eyes seem to focus onto my sunglasses on my forehead. I stop to rest, to catch my breath, and turned to see which direction she went. But in the time it had taken me to turn, she had disappeared into the mist.

I laugh to myself. It seems to me that Britain is one of the few places in the world where such events happen. It is where two people in the same place at the same time can ignore one another so precisely. Britain seems the only place where they can chide the other person for disrupting their peace and quiet. Anywhere else and we might have chatted, and passed the time of day, but it is not the way here. Independence and solitude seem to be what is wanted. Too many people on too small an island I think to myself.

When I arrive at the top of the slope at the plateau, where the huts are, it takes a while to orientate myself. I cannot see the full extent of the circle. What was its name again? Grimspound. They told me about it last night. Well, it is certainly grim here. I resolve to start my circumnavigation at a distinctive gorse bush, and work my way around the outer wall. It takes me around fifteen minutes to come back to the bush again. I don't have the equipment for wide angle work, so I elect for close-up shots which will deny the presence of the mist. When I hear a noise, coming from somewhere close by, I turn around and search for the woman. She is nowhere in sight.

But it does make me re-evaluate her again. I noticed that her hands were dirty. She had been digging in the ground, kneeling, because there were wet earthy patches on her knees. She had been excavating or burying something. I have a vague thought of trying to discover the location of her work, but the pound is vast. Had she stopped and spoken, of course, I might have found out more. I certainly would have asked. I'd have yearned for her story.

The actual photographs I take, come from the mid morning, when the sun is that much higher, and when the mist had begun to clear. The light is right. Once I've finished, I pack everything up, including the lightweight tripod. Now that the mist has cleared, the day feels fresh and open. There is a light drizzle. It seems that there is always a light drizzle in the west. It doesn't soak me though, so I am grateful for that. Climbing down, I look further along the valley towards Challacombe Down. I see a blue light flashing. I hear anger. I run. I am like this. Any action magnetizes me towards it. The woman begins to slowly fill my viewfinder, and in cynical anticipation, I load another film.

IX

The Heretics and the Cynics

Robert

On the heavy, imitation teak desk in my study, sits an object at odds with the rest of the room. It is why I keep it there. I like discontinuity see. I like contrast, almost, you might say, as much as I like the dead. I like things to speak to me in a different way, in another language almost. Other symbols, then. Other markers. The object is very grey. It has many shades to it, and two textures. One texture was formerly its outer edge, and it smooth, hammered by hard years of wind and rain. The other sides are rough. If you juggled it all day long in your hands, it would cause builders' blisters on the tips of your fingers, like those working at the *Drake's Lodge* site. They would burn and sting. Grains of sand in it shimmer when the morning sunshine enters the window, just as they did before they were sealed away. But for the most part, it just sits. I don't use it as a paperweight. It seems too valuable for that. I will endeavour to explain why. My object is made of concrete. Where it once sat, you see the rusty marks of steel reinforcement rods—fingers of imprinted orange corrosion. It's odd, but very few people have asked me about it. Perhaps they think I've just left a lump of decaying concrete in my study on purpose. I suppose it is not that old really, not in comparison. See, relics are all around us, and are being created constantly. Most of us do not even notice them. I live to make them explicit whenever possible. Open them right up and expose them. This way they are *momento mori*; this concrete lump, a kind of vague skull. It is a reminder, yet it also gives me a power. Like history and all its vagaries. You know how the roads of pilgrimage go far back, and they come down to me in the present.

I have told you of Plymouth. I have explained why I need to tell. It is the urge to exorcize I know. One cannot keep secrets forever, so objects have a continuing appeal to me. That is why it sits there. But for me not holy cloth, or bones, or flesh. No, my reliquary is more recent. It is the physical and the tangible that I can hold which is important.

I keep it because of the future. I want it to remind them, the *them* who will inherit this tiny, silly sphere in space. I thought the pursuit of one relic was enough, but here I am, walking around another. I view it from eye level, the way my son (he who is supposed to inherit my relics) used to view his *Airfix* model aeroplane kits. I tap it. I stare at it. Picture then, where it once sat, in times when it had no ambitions of becoming a relic. Shall I spin you the yarn of the Cold War? Shall I tell you about desperate families crossing in balloons at night? Men shouting. Guns crackling. Barbed wire. Graffiti. Checkpoint Charlie. Michael Caine. Shall I tell you about a split nation, and the entrepreneurs who took the broken shards away?

Some friends brought me mine back from a holiday. They said they knew I would appreciate it. My type of thing, they said. I cannot think of anything more holy. If I were to choose a relic of the twentieth century myself, I may well have chosen this. On the desk in my study then, sits a tiny fragment of the Berlin Wall.

Jude

I need you near me, the way, when we are children we need love after grazing a knee. Forget the TCP and the wash under the stinging cold tap to take out the gravel. It is the love we crave. Every story needs a listener, as much as a teller, and you are mine. Listen—I need love right now… I want to be safe, inside that protective wall, higher up the valley.

It is raining. We have started to pack, but the police have moved in hard. Scare tactics. They don't want any more like us to follow, and this is preventative medicine. They hope the traveller grapevine is working. People like us make the countryside look untidy. We are human litter. I've heard people say it. We are filth apparently. We turn visitors away. I am saddened, and I am bitter. They have said that unless we move on in the next hour, they will move us on themselves. Pete is bartering hard for time. He says it will take at least three hours to pack up. I arrive back from my find. The police want to know who I am and where I have been. I tell them. They give us two hours. It's fairer than usual.

Pete struts around the Vale, playing the territorial male, in charge of his pride. The police are non-believers. Stories do not work on them. They have no regard for antiquity. Pete is now shouting chaotically, collecting up our belongings, throwing in the occasional whispered curse at the police. I go to the children and try to calm them. Ally is crying. Adam is aggressive and confused. Cari's gone silent. The police want a social worker brought in to visit them—an assessment of their mental and physical health. They are already on the radio to County Hall. I lie and tell them I am their mother, and there is not a problem. Sarah is already in tears, and for some reason is sat in the rear of one of the police cars, crying uncontrollably. At least she distracts them from us—probably part of her plan.

We meet in the same tent. It feels better—the warmth of one another. We talk about our next move. Pete is worried about the lapsed road tax on the bus. When they see it—and they always check—they will fine us. We have no choice though. The fine for camping here is large. We take the lesser of two evils. The police put more pressure on, by bringing in another Transit van, and make a big deal of kitting up in riot control gear. Young constables move through the site. They take out truncheons, which we are meant to see.

I go outside to take down the washing. The packing is hurried and difficult for us. I have little time to think of the buried box. Even if we do move on, I will want us to come back. The young constables sneer at us. They think of their semi-detached wonder, and of a comfortable warm shower, when their duty is done.

Pete gets angrier when a reporter from the *Western Morning News* arrives. He speaks to the police first, and not to us. They are still laughing and joking like this is just another job. Our life is being destroyed and all they can do is laugh. Fucking wankers. When the reporter comes to speak to us, Pete tells him where to go. This is one story he does not wish to tell. His dream of a promised way of living is one he believes in totally. He won't stand for some obnoxious journalist who had no real interest in what we are about. The reporter is persistent though.

"Sir, a word or two about your situation perhaps?"

Pete ignores him.

In the end, I speak to the reporter, to at least ensure he departs, and leaves us alone.

"Look," I say, "we don't interfere with your way of life… We don't need anybody to interfere with ours…"

But he is there with the challenge.

"You know that it's against the law to camp like this, don't you?"

"We do no harm. We take and we give. We shan't leave any rubbish. The site will be left exactly as we found it."

"Would you describe yourself as 'New Age' travellers?"

I knew that phrase was coming. He said New Age, like we were from another planet. Like we were off on one, like we were on drugs.

"Yes, we travel, and that is all that we do…"

The reporter wanted more, but Pete would not let me say anything else. At this point, I noticed that one of the police cars had moved further up the track to the hut circle. He had stopped next to the tourist I had seen earlier. No doubt, the constable would give the tourist the low-down on things. That's the thing that most annoys me. Perhaps I should have spoken to him earlier. He might have been a sympathizer. He looked the type at least.

For the rest of the morning, the police keep their distance, and Pete managed to control his anger. Fortunately, no social workers were available. At noon, Sarah turned the ignition key, and the bus heaved its way out of the site. I checked the ground for anything we had left. It was unharmed, apart from a few tyre tracks. I slid back the door and climbed on. We drive on. The police, had, for once, turned a blind eye to the road tax, but this did stop Pete yelling a final piece of abuse at them. I tried to keep him calm, but it was my mind that was racing. Something else now gripped my mind entirely. It seemed to ignite the mitochondria of every cell.

Eddie

"They're scum you know. Real low-lifes…"

"What are they? Dead Heads? Druggies?" I asked.

"They call themselves 'travellers'. Kind of gypsies—only much worse…"

The policeman had asked me if I had taken any photographs. I knew what he was thinking. One journalist was enough. I said I was just a tourist. From the crest of the hill, I had watched activities unfold for most of the morning. I had actually taken some photographs as well. I had seen the woman wash her hands. I had seen the way the police operated. It was a non-violent approach—just hard pressure. All the while I was thinking of the Native Americans back home. They once lived a similar way, and were now forced into the degradation of modern living. Like this lot, they were often forced to move on, and not to choose. It was on a smaller scale here, yes, but the same thing; the same unhappiness.

So when the policeman spoke to me, I felt guilty, because I was not down there defending them.

"I suppose it's the Moor you're most concerned about?" I had said.

I was a hypocrite.

"Well, yes, but we're more worried about where they're heading next. Bleddy crowd."

The policeman left me watching their bus pull up the steep hill at the other end of the valley. I felt an injustice, but could do nothing. I had seen injustice ten times worse in Iraq, interfered, and nearly got my head shot off. You live to tell the tale, but you learn as well. I watch the slow bus until it disappeared, and saw the police move on. They would, of course, follow the coach, hoping that it would go out of their patch, and onto somebody else's. They are juggled by the authorities, but those authorities cannot be bothered to sort out a real solution for them. So they remain suspended mid-air.

I took one last look at the hut circle, and somewhere, I could see, or rather feel a connection: the travellers and the Native Americans. I felt the North Atlantic Ocean grow smaller. I felt the Moor transpose itself to the States, and the tors become mesas and buttes. I saw humanity unchanged. I saw love, and yet I also saw real hatred. I had made a connection, and a bell rang loudly inside of me. Here, on this mist-bounded hell was a parallel, a direct parallel to what was going on back home. Sometimes you feel places attract you to them, as if in another existence you have been here before. You know you have not, but still you feel it. Like the very huts themselves, you sense more fossils from the past, and a taste of the present in the old air.

X
The False Relics

Robert

Let me throw some philosophy at you. I'm going to fling it at you hard, like a frozen, packed ice snowball. There is, I believe, an ancient human desire to clothe beliefs in form and substance. This notion has grown as if from a magical soil in the human conscious-ness, yet it is also possible to see that it is a simple step from discov-ering miraculous properties in an object handled by some Saint or someone, to going on to see the person and to benefit from his or her powers; perhaps to bring objects back. Somewhere though, somewhere along our journeys (I do not know precisely when) that, I fear, has gone wrong. The direction is misplaced. The desire to clothe beliefs in form and substance is there, but the form and sub-stance of these beliefs have changed. We read different signals. We have beliefs, yet they are manifested in the wrong ways. Our Age moves towards duplicity, where values no longer have one defini-tion. Substance and form have changed irrevocably. Unlike my piece of Berlin Wall, nothing is concrete. We are in a precarious state, still believing in some sense, but trusting in the wrong representation of our beliefs.

So, for religion—and tell me if you don't agree—we substitute television and credit card transactions. For our children, instead of sitting and reading, and listening, we slam in the video, and leave them to stew. For love, translate this as "What can I get out of this?" or just plain, old sex. We pursue the miraculous as part of some ulti-mate consumer dream. We indulge. Our venerations have changed before our very eyes, yet we do not see, or rather, we ignore. And to ignore, is worse, horribly and despicably so, than to be blind.

Our beliefs lie in money and in gain, greed and reward, products and property. The aperture is closing quickly. Only a few of the right believers scramble through—those whose form and substance are not so tangible—not so malleable; more magical. And as we go on, fewer relics are left behind.

Remember, this is the consumer era, the throwaway age. It is the age of knocking them down, and then building them up. This is an age where form and substance have no time for age. No respect. Our beliefs are reflected in the shiny, perfect faces of cloned model pop stars, and the way we pretend to recycle. So, you can laugh off fundamentalism, but you can see its reasoning as well. And because humans are humans, we demand substance and form. Belief is not good enough now. Belief is the air and the wind, and is of no use. We like to touch and stroke. We like to feel good. For belief then, perhaps you may read "self". And for relics, well, don't even think of them, for no-one will have the time, or the inclination. Now, that is when the shit will really hit the fan.

You have stuck with me all this time. You have heard me philosophizing. But there must be a question on your lips. You want to know why, don't you? I would, in your shoes. I would want to know "Why?" Some of you might even feel that what I tell you is simply some mad notion from the mind of a deranged old fool. Just a story. A fiction. But then, that is the thing with all stories—when does the fiction stop? And how do you know? The scary thing is: You don't. You have to trust me.

You question is "Why do I tell?" Why don't I just keep this inside me? I ask you that. Are you not human? Have you not experienced the desire to tell? Or rather, I confess then. I cannot keep a secret. I leak. I am a mole to my soul. I want to broadcast it. I have had few stories to tell—not real stories see—so this one had to come out. I had to birth it, let it breathe fresh air. Give it is slap on the bum to gulp the first breath.

I tell you, because you are somebody. You have taken this time to listen, to indulge me.

My life, as you know by now, has been an absurdity. When I married, I had nobody left to tell. When my son became estranged from me, I had absolutely no-one left. When the others in the department thought me an eccentric and an irrelevance, no-one would listen. I stop you then, because you are somebody, and I can tell you. I care little if you think me crazed. That feeling has passed. I tell to check. We all do. Only this one comes as a rush. Death is right beneath me see, binding my feet together. See, now, I really do fear it, and I don't want to go without someone else's knowing.

So, stay a while longer. This is my soliloquy; my greatest hour upon the stage of life. Call me a tell-tale if you want. You think I jest with what I say. I can tell. That I make up stories. I mean, Stranger. How do I know? What certainty do I have? Isn't this just stories for the sake of stories? Stories for boys, and stories for girls. No. I tell this story because I need to. It is a story you know well by now. It crosses the world, and falls down through the years, and wallops me while I am not looking. It is a knockout punch of a narrative.

I hand this to you, so you may take it away and tell it to someone else, or write it down even. Store it. Put it on a computer disc. Keep it for the future the same way I keep my lump of concrete. I don't care what you do with it, as long as you preserve it. Write it if you wish. If you will, then I shall be happy. I shall feel a weight lift off, not only my shoulders, but my whole eggshell body. I shall see a shadow fading. I will have victory over those who distance me. I am able to tell you then.

You have heard.

I will go back to her. I will tell her how lovely it has been. And I will say to her, I will say, "I must tell you this story some time."

"Yes," she will say, "You must, some time…"

I have a puzzler for you. Now, after all this, what would you say if I told you I do make up stories the way I did when my son was small, and that I merely cast them out of the air? After all you have heard, you must now make up your own mind. Believe me, this is the best way—the way the world always has…

Jude

There are other stories you know. These stories are different. When they break, they are not nice. It is not only the subject matter, but the way they are told, the way they drip off some people's lips like fatty gravy; a bloody juice. They are stories that squat in corners, bruised and broken. They are stories without endings or beginnings; stories with no tellers. They are the stories about the crumbs, and the fragments, the pieces that we never find, nor, I would suggest, if we are honest, that we ever want to. These are the things that time had decided will not last and will not be worshipped and revered. These items do not reveal themselves. They are stories that lie in the dark.

All this, when…

Heavens, I could spout you a list of the things we do not need to worship. I could give you a long and painful injection of horror. Sing you a song of it perhaps, but I know I do not need to. You know the score. You know where they lie. They lie in the same places in society that woodlice lurk in dark forests. They are places where you do not want to put your hands. With that in mind, we'll put these down as the stories which do not need to be told.

Ever.

Never ever.

Eddie

Hell, I must admit to falsifying a few things in the past. You do it, to get on. To leave your trace, too. Your heat trail. Your etching, or in my case, my prints. I mean, you focus it on what you want, don't you? You make the print smaller in the red light of the dark room. You cut out other action. You snip. You juggle. That is the way to make a photograph. This isn't going to be here long. Soon, the computer will store everything, and one touch of a mouse, can shape an image exactly the way you want it. Manipulate *ad infinitum*. When I am retired, I will have a box full of curling photographs. Then I will be able to pick out the true ones, and confess my sin of manipulation to the world. Talk to a priest Eddie. You'll need it if you want redemption. Now, though, I'll let sleeping dogs lie.

People hang on to the strangest things don't they? I'm thinking right now of the Mosque of the Prophet in Ziqar Province, destroyed by the 1981 earthquake. There are still bits of it left, even now. Other sections of it were lifted by scavengers and used in the construction of the shanty towns to the north. But they won't let go. It is as if there were a hologram of the real thing in front of them. Even after all this time, it still haunts them. And the Marshes—a place where anything can become an idol. I met Shi'ite tribes there who had seen plenty of westerners, plenty of nattily-dressed "Ameri-kan", but who had never had anything materialist. I've seen some oil workers out there take the piss. Gave them a set of joke-shop chattering false teeth to worship, with a wind-up mechanism. Praise of the clock-work. Reverence of the plastic. Still, that makes you think. Put our civilization back a few hundred years. Flick the hands of the clock back and we'd feel the same way. We would certainly have worshipped anything abnormal, anything different. So we all act so god-damn superior and laugh behind their bent backs and bulbous stomachs, but we were there as well once, scratching around in the darkness. We have made the same mistakes, and some of us are still there now, worshipping the trash of humanity's past. Step into the future, and we will be there still—the whole fucking lot of us. Nothing will have been solved. We shall still have game shows where thousands can be won for a trivial answer, and where afterwards, pictures of starving, flies-in-their-eyes children in Ethiopia can be seen on CNN. Mark my words. We will all be there, worshipping this time, this present, saying just how good it was.

XI

The Evidence

Robert

Replay. Let me find the rewind button... inside... It was about a fortnight that passed between the time when the bare coffin was recovered, and when Bill asked for me. None of the find had been particularly interesting, up until the time I went up. The other two coffins had two relatively normal bodies inside them, facilitating the usual dating processes. One skeleton had a poorly-healed leg that had once been broken—probably a fall from height—and dating showed that the coffin had been buried later, as was confirmed by the plaques themselves. The large coffin had obviously been for someone with, or in power, or else for someone with a lot of money to spend. It was also made for the proportions of a man.

I arrived at the laboratory mid-morning. The three coffins sat covered in plastic sheeting in the artefacts depository. An effort has been made to preserve them, although a lot of work still had to be completed. They were kept in a damp atmosphere. There was talk that although they were not that interesting, they were rather well-preserved coffins from that period. They had potential, at least.

"Ah, Robert," Bill said, eyes poking upwards, as he leant over a data sheet. He held out his hand to greet me. His hair went in several directions, and was not helped by his rummaging right hand, which he seemed to draw through his coiffure every minute or so. Grey hairs spray from his nostrils and a few more had leapt into his ears. But this was Bill. He cared little for appearances. He loved his work, and that was all. He never married. He had lived in the same flat for as long as I had known him, close to the church at Redcliffe.

I knew what was coming. We'd written a book a few years back on archaeological techniques. Bill had a habit of blinding those he met, with the latest methodologies. The latest was amino acid racemization—work he'd been pioneering for a number of years now.

But I knew what he'd be up to. There would be the usual absolute dating techniques: atomic absorption spectrometry, the beta-ray back-scaling and diffraction analysis. By lunch we'd usually move onto isotopic replacements and wonder if hydration dating might be a good move on the latest artefact. No doubt it would be no different today.

"Good trip?" he asked me nonchalantly. "Thought you might like to look at these cumulative graphs of the readings…"

I nodded, scanning the material he presented.

"Come with me."

Bill was originally from Pontypridd, and the Welsh valleys' ring still sounded in his voice. He could be authoritarian when he wished. We wound around a series of Formica-topped desks, with various artefacts covering their surfaces. A few students there at work, looked up at me and nodded. My reputation was still intact, at least. Now and then, Bill would say a few praising words as he passed them. He led me into the depository, and once inside, he threw back the plastic sheeting as if shaking a set of gritty bedclothes. It was then that he pointed out the piece of bone on the side cabinet, and revealed the carbon-dating figures.

"This one," he said, "and there's some kind of grouping. A connection…"

We walked around the rotting, wooden lozenges.

"I have a question for you Robert," he said. It was the obvious one; the one that everyone had already asked a hundred times.

"Why bury a coffin without a body inside of it?"

It was a question I had asked myself nearly every waking minute since they had first been found. You simply cannot contemplate it, or even comprehend it. I only had one answer, though there could be infinitely others. I leant down and touched the cold wood, reaching for feeling.

"Because someone wanted other people to think he was dead."

Bill sighed.

"Yes. Now," he said, "remember the date... on the side of the tomb itself?"

"1620. The sixth of September..."

"Yes. The same day the Pilgrim Fathers left."

"Now," continued Bill. "I would lay any money at all, that the man whose body was supposed to be here, was in fact, on that ship."

I laughed. At first, the notion seemed ridiculous.

"Mock me. Go on," he said, "but I've seen it before. People pretending to die... and turning up elsewhere. And this character—the Limper—I'll bet he had a notion of this. That's why he's here too. The man would have given his money to bury him falsely, and money enough for his body eventually as well."

Bill's voice became mesmerized, and it began to enchant me all the more than usual. He continued.

"Our man here had reasons to leave Plymouth. Must have owed money or something, but he made sure no bugger would find him. Perhaps even to fool people like ourselves, eh?"

"Or left his wife and gone off with another."

"It happens," Bill said stoically. Bill knew a little of my wife and her affairs.

I turned and looked out of the eye-level window in the laboratory. I tried to suspend all other thoughts; clear my mind.

"No," I said after a moment. "The skeleton's just turned to dust. It happens sometimes Bill. Atmospheric conditions... you know... weak bones or something."

I realized I was telling Bill his job.

He looked at me with his usual mixture of love and hate.

"No," he said assuredly. "No evidence of decay. We've tested. Besides... the others; they didn't decay did they? It shouldn't have made that much difference."

I tried to reason.

"All right then. Grave robbing. Someone took the body out."

"Impossible. The seals weren't broken remember. You simply couldn't have done it."

I looked at the skull of the limping man. The eye sockets were empty and black. The jaw was silent. We both wished for a tongue in him.

"Okay then. So they put the body in there after he's died and then take him out before it's sealed."

"That's more likely," said Bill. "But somehow I don't think so."

When Bill thought something, you knew how it was close to the truth. Archaeologists, at their best, were excellent scientists.

He sighed again.

I turned back to face him.

"There's a mystery here… Could be a bit of a tale this. Good paper for you, Robert? Perhaps a new book eh?"

All I saw then was an empty box.

"Did you bring the stone plaques up with you?" I asked.

"Yes. They're in the store downstairs. We'll take a look shall we?"

I remembered reading the names at the time, but they had just been a blur. Brimicombe was one that I thought I could recall. Yes. Definitely Brimicombe.

"I'm going to dismantle the larger coffin tomorrow. I'll have finished the tests by then. We might find something else. You never know. Man always leave his clues you know. Always."

He closed the depository, sliding a bolt across, then locking it. We walked out again, though the maze of broken pottery and bone. Above, a fluorescent light buzzed.

"Tomorrow then…"

"What time?"

"About ten."

"Fine."

Bill went back to his data, and I left.

That afternoon, I racked my mind for answers, but only more serious questions came. Here was I, a supposed expert on graves, on epitaphs, on tombs, without a clue. I couldn't even put time into perspective. There were certain facts, certain dates, but then, that was always the case with the dead. Apart from those, there was nothing. Only a story remained with the facts for a fiction at my fingertips. Pure invention then perhaps?

Sometime that night, when it grew dark, when I lay in bed in my hotel room, with the lights out, I felt frightened. A body that had not rested properly, or the image of a man that had two graves flickered before me again and again. This was a man whose story went beyond a single tomb. A second chance. I thought of all the other burial places in the world. I wondered where his bones were actually laid to rest. After an hour of wondering, I had to switch the radio on to tell his ghost to go away, and put my body to sleep.

Very often, light comes in the strangest places. Street-lights prod their orange glare into our bedroom. Dawn trickles in under the curtains. Sometimes, we see in the darkness. Fresh light is thrown upon something. The light-bulb zings. Bill has a technique. He zings. He, in fact, has many techniques. He continues to remind me of his innovative techniques even when we have lunch together, or talk on the phone. This time though, it is more interesting. We are in darkness in the depository. A crack lets in some light from the laboratory outside, but we are, for the most part, faceless. I fumble. Bill is more sure-stepped in his own environment. He wears his old, red-tinged brogues, which had been soled and heeled so many times that the shoes must feel a constant rebirth every year. I see them first when he switches his torch on. This is the technique then. He shines it towards me. He must see the reds of my eyes. We are crouched.

"I like to do it this way," he reveals.

I stay silent. Bill looks like he is in pursuit of original chaos.

"More feeling somehow," he states. "Looking at it all in the darkness. Things pop out as well; things you don't always see in normal light."

The technicians have brought up the covers to the tombs earlier on in the morning. They now stand like gravestones against the rear wall. We crouch over to them. Bill pushes the torch closer to the stone. He touches the words as he reads them, as if they are some kind of inverted Braille. He shivers occasionally, for dramatic effect I think. He likes to scare me. (No wonder I couldn't sleep.) I have noticed he does the same thing with his students.

I knew the inscriptions well enough by now, but then... Then, it was just another epitaph until Bill droned out the words reverently.

"Sacred to the memory of Samuel Hopkins. Died 5th September 1620... aged 35 years."

He continued to read the rest in a lower tone.

"We meekly beseche thee O Father to rayse vs from the death of synne to the lyfe of righteousness that when we shal depart this lyfe, we maye rest in him as hope is this our brother doth, and that at the general resurrection in the last day, we maye be founde acceptable in thy sights, and receive that blessing whiche thy well beloved sonne shall then pronounce, to all that love and feare thee, saying come ye blessed children of my father, receive the Kingdome prepared fore you, from the beginning of the World. Grant this, beseech thee O mercyfull Father through Jesus Chryste our mediator and redeemer. Amen."

Bill faces the torch on the floor, so that the light splinters out in a web.

"It's wrong," I say.

"Wrong?"

"The prayer. It's an elegy, but it would never have been used. It's worded wrongly."

"Where exactly?"

"I can't quite say. All of it really. It's inappropriate. That kind of wording wouldn't have been used on a tomb. In the service maybe, but not on the tomb itself."

Bill is quick.

"Slap-dash job then?"

"Possibly. It's done by someone who knew little about the correct inscription to put on a memorial of this sort. Must have picked up some prayer, and have copied the first thing they saw out of it."

We read it again.

"I'm certain."

Bill believes me. He understands the awkwardness in the language. There are subtle mistakes in the phraseology.

We waddle along further, still crouched, to the second tablet. Bill remarks on the crafting of it. It is simpler, and also more delicate. The torch comes up and the stone talks through Bill.

"In memory of Moses Brimicombe, beloved husband of Louisa Brimicombe, who was taken from us the 3rd day of April 1639, aged 62 years."

We remark on its simplicity and the Devonian name. Moses strikes us because of its dislocation. The Old Testament and the Devonian somehow jumbled together and left in stone. I continue to stare at the stone. I look at the skeleton's smashed leg. Bill is at the third coffin.

"His wife then," he says. "Her size. Smaller skull. Pelvis is a woman's."

"No inscription for her?"

"Probably no more money. Just enough for the tomb I expect. Threw her in with the husband. Her teeth are rotten as hell. Look at the bones too... the pox or something..."

Bill is talking to me. He is telling me what he plans to do. I am in a daze and just hear noise. I ask him to put the lights on. No. He likes to work in the dark. It is his way. He is going to take the coffin apart.

I stand there, watching all morning. He is in his element. I am merely an appendage. This is his show. He treats objects with love. He strokes and caresses the coffin sides, the way a craftsman might treat a piece of newly sawn wood; only here, he is not carving or joining, he is stripping apart, and searching. He journeys back.

The air inside the room is now musty and feels deprived of oxygen. I ask to open the door, but my request is ignored. What I didn't know, was how Bill's rapture would later come to affect me. It was almost as if the force of what he was doing, had jumped there and then, into me.

Bill is now piece by piece, carefully disassembling sections of the coffin. It is like my son's *Airfix* models in reverse. The structure is complicated. Within the outer coffin, is an inner lining where there may have been some material. It is when he lifts the bottom out that he finds some rather rough flaxen-style material. Satisfied, he sits back and switches off the torch.

"Lights," he orders.

I quickly rush to the switches, and turn them back on.

For a moment, we both adjust our eyes. Sections of coffin are neatly spread around the room. The foreboding disappears.

"Coffee?" he asks. "There should be a pot on outside…"

"I'll get some."

When I return with two Styrofoam cups full of a brown-black liquid, burning my hands, Bill is standing. His feet are at ease, in a military fashion.

"Treasure bleddy Island, this crowd," he says.

"What?"

He ignores my attempts to hand him his coffee, so I place it on a cabinet near the door. He holds a slip of parchment.

"Listen…"

I move closer.

"I found it, look, at the bottom… Someone who couldn't come to terms with what they'd done. Had to put it here to justify it in the eyes of the Lord."

"What's it say?"

"You're the bleddy expert. You read it."

He handed it to me. The script was faint and written in a scrawling hand. I took my magnifying glass from my jacket pocket. I read aloud.

"Lucky, or a deville be thee who dost read this. Reason beguiles he, who is suppos'd to lie here. He will lie in other land. This fellow and I buried vpon ye moor Carver's box o' wonder gi'un by those in black. Grim is ye place. M.B."

I cannot wholly describe to you the feeling of elation we both had, when Bill found those words. They wrapped themselves around us, constricting us, and ordering every move. What we loved was Brimicombe himself. And what the hell was a "box of wonder" given to him by a Separatist?

But wait.

I lie. I have told you untruths. There is more. See, upon the empty tomb's cover was another word. A word you now know well. It slips off my lips. Then, I could not even picture him. Now, I know the very lines on his face and his gait. See, just after the words Samuel and Hopkins sits another word. It is a naming word. You have never known this man as Samuel Hopkins. No, the word that follows them is "Stranger". Now, does the fact fall stranger than the fiction, or is the tale as strange as you first thought? You tell me.

Jude

The others and I are oddities. We look strange to you. We know it. We know we reek of many dislocations. We are a huge wart on the face of sanitized, late twentieth-century society. But we will not be eradicated. See, we are a different breed—a cross of cultures and histories: Romany, Hippy, Nomad, Tribal. We are not interested in placement. We are shifting. We don't just accept the human condition. No, we explore, and travel its spectrum from end to end. That is perhaps, how we get our kicks. That is not, however, to say we are alone. We are far from alone. There are many of us, as many as there are of others. Perhaps we should be more forceful, but then, that is not our way. And if you think our way started in the late 1960s with kaftans and joss-sticks, then you would be wrong. I have met many who took our path long before all that. People would probably have called them tramps, or vagrants, or gypsies maybe. But then, it was more difficult than now, to break out of the world, to snatch what you wanted. We have it easier. So yes, there are others. Many more. And we meet. You may not know it, but in some ways, our year is complex. We are now in summer, and this is our time of getting together at fayres and festivals. Oh yeah, I know how it's reported: one hundred and fifty drug-related offences at Glastonbury, or Stonehenge. But there are the smaller ones too. We are heading to one in Cornwall, called Skinner's Bottom. See, there are those who do understand, who appreciate what we do. In doing that, they too, risk harassment, fines and legal battles. They are on the fringe, and yes, I know we need them. I mean, things are not ideal. I wish we could have even fewer connections with the rest of the world, but that is impossible I now know. At least, only pockets of modernity push into our antiquity.

There was a time when I was more rebellious. I mean, the whole of my twenties was filled up with hunt sabotages, camps outside American military bases, protest about vivisection and environmental destruction, *Amnesty International* and rights for people like us. I had so much anger in me; still tinged with the agony of Punk. If you had seen me in the '80s, you would not have recognized me. So, yes, I have mellowed. Maybe we all have. Maybe we should have carried on the fight. But now… well now, it is hard enough fighting for our own lifestyle, let alone anyone else's. All this despite the New Right clamping down on us, and anyone who doesn't fit or isn't a banker or investor.

Pete agrees. He holds me that way I used to hold dad's fossils when I was a child, with respect and wonder. I lay my boots over his legs and feel good. We have stopped again; ground to a halt off a side track onto the Moor.

To the north, is the squat form of a another tor. On the granite clitter, Sarah has laid out some of her washing, and is playing a game with the children. Pete has been working all morning to prepare the bus for the next step of the journey into Cornwall. Dog—yes, just that, sits beside us, yawning, his ears floppy.

A *Rizla* paper sits in Pete's hand. It isn't what you think. It isn't cannabis. None of us touch drugs. Well, that isn't strictly true. Tobacco's a drug, but you know what I mean. That's the picture though isn't it? People want us to do stuff: heroin, crack, acid, and cannabis. I've asked Pete to stop smoking—for the kids' sake. He blames those who first brought it back from America. I tell him what it is doing to his lungs, but the storyteller in him, will not listen. But he did do drugs once. I know this, but he won't say much more about it; only that he won't become involved with it all again.

Things like this are how we have survived and grown. I have had other relationships, where everything was pinned down. It was controlling: where you came from, what you'd done, what colour romper-suit you wore when you were three, who you first slept with, what your story is. That kind of history is futile in the end, and only leads to resentment and anger. I try to merely be grateful for what there is, and stick by it. But then, old habits die hard don't they? Do I not tell you my history here—my story? So, then, conventions are not quite dead yet. I take consolation from the fact that it takes many years before we turn into myth. So I have prepared the way. Let me take you right to the heart of the matter now. You are ready...

I have a problem with my ovaries. I make it common knowledge. I wanted it that way. I didn't want any underhanded comments against me, as to why I have no children. I wanted it out. I didn't want sympathy. I just wanted acceptance. Yes—unlike others, for all my ideals, for all my radicalism, I still wanted children. I wanted conception. I wanted pregnancy and a nuzzling child. I know of fertile women, who cannot stand the actual thought of bringing children into the world. It is because they fear the world their children will inherit. That's always the same though isn't it? You always want something you know you cannot have. So at first, you go through it all. The reasons. Whatever you say, whatever philosophy you drown me in, women are the bearers of children, and have that responsibility. They are built that way. The female gives life. When you come to know that a part of you can give no life, then your own life stops short. I used to think my emotions would be stunted, and I would end up a knotted, bitter old woman, with a hooked nose. Yes—a character in a fairy tale that you never want to become.

That passes now. I think now, it may have taken most of my twenties to deal with it, to give it the real space it deserved, and not to push it deeper down inside. I can see it now. That's maybe what all the protest was about; nothing to do with my father dying, as my poor mother thought. Then, you think about children. You want them, but you cannot touch. You see children crying and babies in the street, and you want to touch, but no, you can only look. I would sit and stare at the walls of my room, crying out a lifelessness within.

You travel down many avenues. You follow a number of paths. You track many lines. You kick though thousands of scrunchy, red and brown leaves. You come to dead ends always though. You never find the green leaf you so seek. We've been to the clinics see. I've had IVF. Sometimes, when I was in there, I've just wanted to get out. Them, touching me, commenting, concluding. But nothing comes. Nothing bears fruit. The exception is for my deeper love of children. I have inexhaustible patience with them, so Sarah says at least. So then, you come to realize that you may have another purpose, and that's where I find myself right now.

Pete is good. He cares. He knows my agony. Childhood means little to him though. He has told me vague snippets, but more often, he just tells me that he was unhappy. His father always busy with work, and his mother disengaged.

And so we end up here, on this day, on a heather-strewn moor, beginning mythologies. He knows I am thinking about this. It is not hard to fathom. I am always thinking about this.

But there is something else now: that box at Grimspound. I look at him. In a moment, we will make love, and all will be temporarily beautiful. The Moor watches and raises a smile.

"Pete..." I say, but it is too late, as we are drowning in kissing.

He is listening, but it will have to wait.

Eddie

Wait. I should speak to you in hushed tones, in a whisper. This is because language is dead. My very words rot as you hear them. Yes—they are dead as a dodo, and more dead by the minute. Language is a graveyard, and the words are but headstones. We seem to spend our lives keeping dead languages artificially alive. We hook it up to life support systems and respirators. You wonder whether it is all worth it. Language is at the point of death with the words politicians use, but we are all just as bad. We all say the wrong thing at the wrong time; that, or we use some platitude, not the real thing we want to say. In so doing, we make language extinct. We fail to communicate. It is because dead language is more comfortable. It feels right. It makes us feel snug and secure. So, rarely then, does language really progress. Its journey is slow, and it walks with weary steps. Your grandfather used the same plodding language as you. Of course, there is life after death. There are words that suddenly slip into our speech. There are culled from urban legends, arrangements and abbreviations which create new markers. Derivations walk in and out like the living dead. It is only then that language can drag itself forward.

But speak to me of photographs, and that is a different matter. Photographs cause discomfort. You know this. They are never relieving. Do they not show every line, every mark? The camera never lies—and all that. Photography is no graveyard. It is a rich orchard of life, and the pictures are in bloom, pretty or not. Photographs do not merely represent the world. They notice it. They speak for themselves. This is how I get my kicks.

But you know, it is not really as simple as that. Oh no.

We notice those parts of a picture which speak to us. They say something beyond words. It is the hole in the photograph that we see. We find the meaning there; that part which pricks us, and makes us jump. It is maybe the only member of a family group whose arms are unhappily folded. It is the figure who wears no shoes. We take in the whole, but we see the prick. It is here we notice, and here we learn anew. So then, I aim for the pin prick, that part of the photograph that hurts—the part that draws blood. The hurt can be good or bad, but what counts is that it is there. I mean, I came back from Iraq with so many pricks, it felt as if I had slept on a bed of cacti for a year. But you do not have to go that far to feel these spines and spikes.

I have a copy of the regional newspaper in the car—the *Western Morning News*—looking for the story on the travellers. I like the title—a straight-off-the-press, ride 'em cowboy sort of thing. I rest it on the steering wheel and read. So when I see an article on *Shopmobility*—a presentation on free wheelchairs for disabled shoppers—I don't see the smiling face, I see the slight twist of foot. And when there's some story on a new housing development (*Drake's Lodge*—how's that for kitsch?) being built, I don't see the interested face of some academic from Bristol University, I see the pissed-off builders in the background, because their chance of making a buck is screwed.

Look closer then, and notice

Be wary though. The photograph is not infallible. I mean, you've see them: images of Frisbees and hub-caps above the Sierra Nevada, meant to be UFOs. I used to do that as a kid. Took them into a teacher once, and she thought I was a new Arthur C. Clarke. Then, there are those Victorian slides of fairies at the bottom of the garden, which only come to light after they were developed.

You know what I am saying then. Sometimes, the desire for notice is so great that people will stoop to art, to artificiality. So beware. Cast aside those impostors, these false relics. Treat your viewing, and I must also say, your listening... even to the dead... with care. Engagement will follow. You notice the world, and the world notices you. The spirit of the true photograph burns brighter, and language... well, languages, reaches around the hearth to grab the brush and shovel, to clear up its own still-born, warm ashes.

XII

The Sanctuary

Robert

So, my course is set. Brimicombe's words give me the clues and the solution. Yet this time, my route is not to any cathedral, abbey or church. Now, I'm not seeking etchings made on alabaster tombs or certificates of indulgence. No, this time, I speak of something far less tangible, but inevitably something much more valuable. If it is a holy relic—a real one—and I feel some sense of trust in this man Carver, who is mentioned, then we have a bit of a find. Of course, already, all kinds of journeys are travelling through my mind. First of all, I am wondering how did this relic come to be in Carver's hands? Was he given it whilst a member of the church in Britain, or did he stumble across it in Leiden? Did the old faith still have a power in him? Sometimes of course, we acquire items we do not want. They find their ways to us, despite belief, change, force or time. But he knew he could not be found with it. Disgrace would be part of his punishment, but depending on his persecutors, more serious prosecution might follow. In the close confines of the *Mayflower*, it was sure to be discovered. You could not keep something like that secret. He knew it must have had something significant inside. Some magic. Some superstitious power. He must have. After all, we only keep what is valuable don't we? The rest, you can chuck.

I have returned to Plymouth to learn more. Down the M5 and the A38. The cars following me are filled with Pilgrims—the collective noun for Plymouth Argyle fans—returning from some victorious match up the line. Scarves float out of back windows. White and green shirts fill up Astras and Volvos. Modern pilgrims then, making their collective ways back home from the cult of the penalty area. I wanted to come down earlier, but instead, knew I needed to complete some more research. I spent a couple of days in the university library reading about relic cults. So now, I have flicked through several hundred pages of pilgrim badges, prayer cards, martyrs, mystics and illustrations. Looking for clues was less my purpose; but more ideas as to where such an object could have come from. Obviously, to have survived to the early seventeenth century, it was already highly thought of. Was it British or Continental in origin? Brittany was still Catholic. The links between there and the west of Britain were age old. But Leiden. Some obscure piece of Continental Catholicism perhaps? Or from even further to the East? In my mind, I am back to the Holy Land itself. I am plotting passages. I am figuring out trading routes, examining the Crusades. Was there a Leiden connection? I recreate how relics were passed on. I ask where and when. I discuss it with Bill again. I dream up possibilities. You see, in Stranger and Moses, we have only a tiny portion of the puzzle. One corner is complete—but only that. There is so much of this box of wonder's story that is untold, unquestioned and intriguing. Bill and I came to the conclusion the box of wonder was a reliquary very early on. Many sources refer to them as such. We still, however, had only a notion of why it came to be buried on an ancient track of moor. Odder, because Grimspound itself was already an interesting site for archaeologists. Stranger and Moses must have known the site was old; somewhere they felt it fitted. So, you see me, casting things out of the air, like the very saints themselves. Only this felt like a very small needle, in an enormous haystack.

I am now back in the hotel room on the Hoe. There are books and maps scattered on the floor. I have been through everything once again. Indeed, so it seems, there are very many relics missing. Hundreds of British ones made it to mainland Europe after the Reformation. Only a few have ever been found. I am too excited these days even to sleep. It both frightens and delights me that somewhere out on Dartmoor there sits something incredibly valuable, perhaps even more important than the proliferation of standing stones which coat its crust. Imagine: something so holy, something so powerful, it could not be allowed to cross an ocean.

She comes back from one of her walks. I know who with. She doesn't say anything about the mess, but chooses instead to just ignore me. She must have had a bit of a row with her Major. I pack away the books, but leave a map out for the morning. I have it open at Grimspound. An X marks the spot. See how this is a fairy tale? I know I am about to solve a word-search—a centuries-old word-search.

When I am packed away, I change into a collar and tie for dinner. We present a polite, united front for diner. It is unsaid, but I pretend to forget about the Major, and she will forget about my treasure. We talk, but neither of us listens.

Jude

To listen is the ultimate skill. We, none of us, listen enough. Our lives are too full, too busy, obviously too interesting, to stop and listen. By listening, you learn. Think of history. Humanity had to listen to make the wheel. We had to listen to save lives. We listen to progress—and learn. But then again, much of humanity's history has been spent in ignorance, in a dumb refusal of not turning its ear to the right source. We do not listen when it comes to religion. We do not listen to the bombs being dropped. We still do not listen when famine-stricken bulbous-bellied children cry.

Just as you listen to me, we want our children to listen. We want them to know. We want them to learn, to not make the same mistakes. We want them to break down barriers, cross oceans and skip aside time. They must find meaning, and oh yes, progression. They listen now. Pete is wringing out a story into their heads. It is scary one, about Dartmoor spriggans and death; one he has learnt down here. Their minds are riveted to his oracy. The smaller children grip me tightly. I cannot transcribe his stories. They are not for writing down; that is the root of it. They are the educational and the religious institutions of the culture we have chosen. Pete still speaks a primordial language. There is spirit in the way his words are woven. They are released out of his mouth like sparks from a fire. Tonight though, the words would be interrupted, and we would have to listen to the words of another.

We are camped at Whiteworks. The site is not that good. "No camping" notices litter the location, but we are forced to ignore them for a while. I have spent the evening running around the small tin holes, in circles of death, chasing the little ones. I am tired, and so Pete's tale, lulls me to sleep. My eyelids flicker and close. But here comes another story; another that will pass into our culture, and be told down the line.

I believe that I was the one who saw him first. I didn't say anything, not for what seemed a long time. Even in the darkness, I recognized his form. I hadn't taken that much notice of him first of all at Grimspound, but now I would soon come to understand that he was no simple tourist. He was more than that. One of the children spots him. He felt my form go rigid.

"Who's that?" asks Adam.

Pete has stopped. He has not yet seen the man, but notices the unease in my eyes.

"What d'you want?" asks Pete, warily.

The figure introduces himself. He's called Hopkins. Eddie, I think he said. American. His voice feels like an echoey drawl, breathless and enthusiastic.

"I saw what happened to you with the police a few days ago."

Pete maintains our territory.

"What's it to you then?"

He tells us he thinks we were being bullied by the police. In the conversation, Pete tests him out. He tries to find out his angle. The fire spits and crackles. I see a cold breath coming from his silhouette. He is staring into me. He knows me from the Pound. What did he see? Is he in on my secret? Is that why he is there? The box. My box. I hold on tight to the children. I have no choice but to invite him closer. I offer him some soup.

"I know this might sound odd, but I'm a professional photographer… I work for a magazine back home. We're running a feature on contemporary Britain. You look interesting…"

This is spoken like he is a drone, like it has been rehearsed many times. False. Not genuine.

He asks if we are travellers. We are obliged to laugh again. I relax more, but my body is still tense. He wonders if we are a cult. I have to speak, and put him right. I tell him about our lifestyle. There is a flicker of understanding I think, but more worryingly, I feel he wants me to tell him what I was doing up at Grimspound. He wants to know, I think, but says, "I'd like to take some more photographs. Would that be okay?"

Eventually, Pete reacts better to him that I do. I believe he can see some glory here. This American has noted some radical side of Britain that he wants to show. This is what Britain is really like; not just mortgage repayments or Ford Escort XR3is. They talk late. Only occasionally does he look at me. He doesn't fancy me—you can tell when that happens normally. No, he still scares me. I try to listen to their conversation, but my mind is slipping and sliding. When he comes to leave, I am cold. The children are in bed. Then comes the punch, and I realize I am Judy.

"I'd like to come back tomorrow. We could talk more about Grimspound…"

I nodded, and said some platitude back to him.

Pete shook his hand. He has a victory. Publicity. Someone sympathetic at last. He had even told him the spriggan and death story. Hopkins told him one back as well. Something about the Water Clan—from the Native American tradition. It was the first time Pete had been told as good a story as that for a long time. I don't watch him walk away. Instead, I turn into Pete.

"What's wrong?" he asks.

"Him."

"Him. What's wrong?"

I don't answer. I stamp on the fire.

"I want to leave," I say, "in the morning…"

So when the dawn comes, we trail off again, a nomadic mishmash again.

In the early morning, the tors and hut circles keep telling their stories, and because we are who we are…

… part of some fad…

… some cult…

… we listen.

Eddie

I'm fearful. I'm scared. We are gullible—all of us. We swallow anything others throw at us. I swallowed the United States of America's

Foreign Policy until I went to Iraq. Lies have been told. Lies seem to have always been told. Fear follows.

I make a confession then.

I haven't been straight with you.

I have covered up my own insecurities.

Other motives bring me here. I didn't just take this assignment by chance. There was competition for it. I had to prove that I was the one who could handle it. It meant pushing for it, but now I'm here, and that is all that matters. I'm here to take photographs, to find the barbs and pricks of British society, but I'm also here to chase my own tail, to see where I sprang from. Zip told me a lot you see. He had a lifetime of tellings: tellings off from grandma too, but telling Indians, telling, telling. Couldn't read or write that old boy, but he told me things the way his grandfather told things. There's been a line of us, see. Same songs. Same tales. I'm the only one to jump though. I'm the one who hasn't devoted his life to carrying on the old ways. I can see it now. The farm back there, with the windpump creaking, parts of agricultural machinery lying rusting in the barn, never to be used again. There's now talk back home of the land being bought up for some real-estate development.

I feel pleased now though. I've told the truth. Owned up. But I can't help asking myself, even if I hadn't bothered to own up, would you have known I was telling a lie? A half-truth, or a half-lie even? What if I knew more than you thought? What if I released secrets? What if you'd swallowed the party line, but all was not what it seemed? What if my "foreign policy" was just as manipulative as that coming out of the Pentagon?

Listen more carefully people.

Such things as this come easy in this country. Britain is a land of contradictions and ironies, of recollections and unknowing. It is a land of mystery and disbelief. It is a place of tall stories, folktales and folklore. You may think the States is where anything can happen: "Only in America" and all. Yes, that's true—to an extent. We start crazes, and by the time the rest of the world has caught up with us, we've managed to launch a new one. American homage is much more cut-and-dried. There is no mystery. There is one right and one wrong.

Britain holds so many things up in the air. It juggles with many areas of existence and still retains some sanity. No-more so than in this western peninsula.

And now, I am resolved to catch those balls which fall from the juggler's hands. For posterity, as they say. And for new encounters.

Those odd, travelling people have intrigued me since I first saw them. I can't help but think of them as kind of quasi-medieval minstrels or traders dropped down into the twentieth century. Kind of like a State Renaissance Fayre with a good dose of reality. They appall me and attract me. They refresh my ideals. I have come to speak to them. Actually, I followed them from their original site at Grimspound. They managed to waddle haphazardly across the Moor. I had to be careful, and stop often to ensure that they felt I was not following. I have camped. I have even been so naughty, so supremely nosey, as to have driven close to their camp though, and walk around its periphery at night. Call this photographic license, or downright intrusion into their privacy, I do not care. It is part of my art; what I do.

They have camped at this place called Whiteworks, not far from Princetown. I have been here before. Here, once, lay a tin-mining works. Small cones point into the Moor, and rough stone buildings surround where they have positioned themselves. Southwards, heads the Abbot's Way across the marshland and mires to Buckfastleigh Abbey. This is an ancient place. I am resolved to make contact with them. I have been here before you see: making contact. I am skilled in it from Iraq. There are ways. You lull them first of all. You give them gifts. I did some pictures of them at distance, silhouetted against the Moor the other night. They will do. They are those kind of pictures which are irresistible.

It is late now—around twelve—but their fire is still a sunburst orange against the black of the Moor. Smoke drifts thickly up into the air from their camp. There is a man telling the rest of the group something. I can tell it is a story—a fantastical story—because his hands made wonderful gestures and shapes. The children's faces are alive and I can see the pleasure of the teller. The two women are there as well. I move closer. I wait to take the natural shot. A step more. The teller's voice is suddenly interrupted by the boy.

"Who's that?"

He points to my shadowy movement. The teller stands up, and stops the story, appalled, I feel, at the intrusion. The group joins him and they turn towards me. His eyes show a primitiveness; almost the fear of a wild animal being disturbed. I have invaded their privacy at the very worst moment. He speaks.

"What d'you want?"

My mind is shaken. Almost the same greetings as the Indians might have said to the Water Clan in the large canoe, with sails: The Pilgrims and Chief Massasoit. I am silent. I step forward into the camp-fire light.

"Eddie Hopkins…"

I extend my cold hand, but it is not shaken. It feels cold, like the stumps of rock on the Moor.

"I saw what happened to you with the police a few days ago."

"What's it to you?"

"I'd like to talk to you about it. I felt you were treated unfairly."

By now, the man had gained a sense of the sympathetic in my voice.

"You an American?"

"Yes."

I wanted to tell him what I was doing, but that could wait for now. It was then that I saw a familiar form: the half-crazed woman whom I had encountered at Grimspound. The same yes, but now the children gripped her, as if she were some huge mother figure. She acknowledged me.

"Come in closer," she says. "I saw you, didn't I? Before…"

I walked into the circle, a circle of innocent, dark eyes.

"Yes… at Grimspound."

"Some soup?" she asks.

I nod.

"I know this will sound odd, but I'm a professional photographer… I work for a magazine back home. We're running a feature on contemporary Britain. You look interesting…"

When I say this, the group laughs. I finally break the ice. She passes me a warm vegetable soup.

"I'd like to feature you in it. The policeman I spoke to, he told me you are Travellers… Is that right?"

They laugh again.

"Or are you some kind of cult or something?" I joke.

They become more serious.

The woman speaks rehearsed words.

"We pursue a lifestyle that suits us. We seek an older, more peaceful way of life. Call us a cult if you like... but we aren't really... we're just normal, people, honest..."

"I see... so..."

"So... it's really not the best way to put people at ease just to sneak up on them, taking photographs," says the male, still not quite warming to me.

"I know... I know... It's just... if people know they are being photographed, it's not the same... Do you understand?"

"I was mid-story..." says the male.

I wanted to say, yes, I understood, yes, we are all mid-story—all of us not through yet, but I didn't. Instead, I apologized.

"Sorry."

The male thawed a little then, and told me his name—Pete. He introduced Jude, and Sarah, and the children: Adam, Cari and Ally.

I supped at the soup.

"I'd like to take some more photographs. Would that be okay?"

I watched them look at each other for confirmation. They agreed.

I stayed at the site until around three in the morning, and then made my way back to my own lonely camp.

"I'd like to come back tomorrow," I said to the woman named Jude, as I was leaving. "We could talk more about Grimspound..."

At that, I noticed a slight panic in her eyes—like I had discovered some kind of secret, but she responded with a dull, "fine" as I waved goodbye.

At least, I had made contact.

In the morning, I again made the journey down the winding road to the old tin works. A few walkers were out, red rucksacks contrasting with the Moor's dullness. It was with shock then that I found them gone, lock, stock and barrel. My pursuit had reached a dead end. Now who was the gullible one?

XIII

The Pursuit of the Miraculous

Robert

So, now you know what lies behind my tale. Am I a liar or embellisher? Was my story one of fact or fiction? You say. You must decide. Are you gullible or not? No matter, really, not now. You know why I am back here. Oh yes, I was back here to relive those National Service Navy days, but now I have a journey to make, a task to complete. A quest. I have to find Brimicombe's "box of wonder". Those three words have dominated my life since Bill first found that decaying scrap of parchment. Sounds the kind of thing children's stories are made of: boxes of wonder, Kings and Queens, tinkers and tailors, fairies and pixies. I find it hard to contemplate, to be honest with you. Here I am, at my age, off on a miraculous journey. It isn't a long one, but it fills me with as much excitement as those long medieval journeys to Canterbury (bugger the Chaucer conference now!), to Santiago de Compostela, or even Jerusalem itself. See, it didn't take us long to work out where "Grim" was. In fact, you already know. In the tale I related to you, I called it Grimspound, the place where Moses and Stranger (I cannot yet call him Samuel) trekked, and now, I am heading there to revisit it. I will travel along the same lines. I will follow their way; their song.

We do that anyway I think. We spend our lives following in the footsteps of others. None of us is that original, except for the prophets, the saints and possibly, the poets. This, however, is special and certain. I know names. I have the past pinned down. Everything is clear; clearer I suppose than anything in my own lifetime. See, things are very calm in my mind now. See, though I tricked you and embellished the tale somewhat, I did have facts. Check them with me. Stranger did live in Plymouth at the time of the Pilgrim Fathers. Moses was buried after Stranger. Moses did need to explain a false death. One of the Pilgrim Fathers had such a fear of God put into him that whatever was in that box, had to go. It had to be kept in the one sense, but in the other, it had to go. He trusted Stranger.

Oh yes, there are pieces of the puzzle missing all over the place, and I dare say that you can pull my theory to pieces, but the frame is complete. It gets easier after that—so forgive me if the names have been wrong or if other inaccuracies were present. I have embellished, because this is not any simple tale. Besides, all tellers embellish. I tell now, because the story burns me from the inside, chafing my innards. It is a spontaneous combustion of narrative you see. I need to give it voice, let it out, or I will explode. My years grow smaller as well, so if you hear it now, then you may tell it again—albeit in a Chinese whisper—across the globe.

There is another reason, just as important, as to why I tell. It is because I want to leave behind something positive. Though it is only oral, it will make up for the other area in my life in which I have failed. Here, of course, I think of her, and my son. So, if I have used these events as my sparkling touchstone for contentment, then forgive me. I have confessed my past. I have done my penance. I hope I have now found true reason. Now, I must begin the final task. I have to find the box of wonder, and become amazed all over again.

All this comes to me as I doze in the early morning sunlight.

She wakes me and I step out of the bed, and get dressed.

"Where are you going today?" she asks, as I pull on one of the jumpers she knitted for me.

I look at her though the holes in the light wool.

"Dartmoor," I say.

"Anything… exciting?"

Her form of exciting is different to mine.

"Not really," I lie. "Just a look around."

We achieve silence again. Our salient pause is perfected once more.

I tie my shoe laces. She watches. I comb my hair back. She lifts her own body out of the bed. She is clad in a silk nightie but nothing of it or her excites me. I know she will say something, but when she does speak, it is not the normal chiding about my dandruff, the state of the knot of my tie, or some such trivial matter.

"I didn't sleep well last night."

"Oh? How come?"

"I had a letter…"

I know what she is going to say.

It is from our son.

This has been the first letter we have had from him for some time. You see, he does write, but there is no address included. Apparently, he is fine. It has come via our neighbours, who are looking after our place while we are away.

"It's been forwarded. The first postmark was Exeter."

She moves to hand it to me, but I am hard, and I do not hold out my hand. The guardedness is for survival; to help me not to cry.

"I'll read it later," I say.

My delay gives my wife a little taste of agony. I am no longer sure if it is intentional, or just natural for me to do so. She stares at me harshly. I take the car keys from the bedside cabinet. I close the door softly. I do not say goodbye. I am leaving. I am journeying. I am in pursuit of a box of wonder—what I know I believe to be the miraculous. No, not the miraculous, but the real thing: the Miraculous. Biblical. The Beginnings-of-Time-kind-of-Miraculous.

I am waving goodbye to the sea. Goodbye to naval days then too. I am journeying past the city's hubbub. Up though Drake's Circus, past the university, through Mutley Plain, and onto the Tavistock Road. I am passing signatures of humanity, signs of life, signals of the late twentieth century. There is no time for that anymore. I am following instinct, a holy instinct. For once, I am journeying higher. I will feel my ears pop when I come down again. I am amongst stone and space. Elementals exist here. I am with the Moor now. I head north east, turning onto the Moor road at Yelverton. I am entering a story. I am a new character: part-pilgrim, half-traveller, wholly a discoverer.

Jude

I told Pete about the discovery of the box at Grimspound. The image of where I found it is unrelenting. I have told him why I wanted to leave, and why I didn't want to see the photographer again. I leave, because I fear he knows something. I don't want him to find out anything more. He is not part of us, just a random entry point in our lives. He is of no significance; no connection. Pete is open-minded, but he didn't like it when that photographer called us a cult. Cults are for weirdos right?—and I have told you already, we do not belong to anything like that. We took down the bender in under a couple of hours. We left just as dawn was breaking. We hadn't done anything like that, not for a long time. The Moor is cold this morning, almost biting, and the heater in the bus is broken. We shiver. I hold Pete's hand. Sarah is driving. The kids are still sleepy. They lie with dreamy eye movements. As we move up the slope, the first devious sunlight of the day filters through the bus's dusty windows. We grimace and shut our still sleepy eyes. We let the warmth enter us.

Although cold, my body feels good this morning; energized and alive. It feels new almost, as if the fear of him knowing had somehow shaken every cell into life again. Pete places a tattooed arm around my chest. My breasts tingle. If I could choose a time to make love with him, then it would be now. We only break our clasp, when Sarah pipes up.

"Where are we going then?"

"Grimspound," I answer plainly.

Sarah's tone becomes annoyed.

"Come on… Not there. You know all we get there is hassle…"

"I know," I say. "Only one night… That's all. I promise."

I cannot explain everything to her, not yet.

"But I thought we were heading for Cornwall…"

"Eventually yes, but I need to go back there…"

Sarah argues the toss for most of the journey back across the Moor, but things are too complex for me to explain to her at the moment. Eventually, Pete placates her. He tells her we might have found something valuable. She increases her speed, and puts her foot down. We pass Princetown and Dartmoor Prison—the latter a relic of another time—cold, grey walls facing a colder, even greyer landscape. We sing songs as we travel, though it is not that far: just a morning's travel. We watched the faces of both puzzled local people and tourists as we go by. Our rainbow-painted bus stops them in their tracks. We alter their lives that one little bit.

I have half a notion that the photographer will show himself before we know it. Hopkins wasn't it? I fear he will have thought about us and have already gone back to Grimspound in anticipation of our return. We don't need his sort. He seems one of those who swears he is with us, but really isn't. He is a Taker. I am certain.

I continue to picture the box. I can feel the texture of it; the delicate carvings in the pewter casing. The symbols. Something holy. I can't tell exactly, but I am drawn to it.

On the pot-holed road down to Grimspound, we are held up. A farmer is crossing some sheep from one open stretch of moor-land to another. I want to ask him, why now? Why, out of all the times he could have crossed, why this exact moment? You know these questions. You ask them every day. He stands by the verge and waves us through. He is old. I want to touch his face, feel the lines of his forehead—as many as the Moor itself. Momentarily, I feel like sitting down with him, a pint of ale in one hand, and hearing about his life. But no… we must push on. I must push on.

The bus chugs noisily through the countryside. Grimspound is not that far now. A rain is beginning to fall. At first, it is light, but we are in the rain shadow here. When the westerlies finally lock in, a little further on, a torrent begins. The air turns blacker, and large globules of water slip down the windscreen. Pete is watching me I can tell. He now knows something of this box; knows its importance. Suddenly, the bus shudders and comes to a stop. A rivulet of water flows down the spur and into the stream under the clapper bridge. I say nothing except for Sarah and Pete to go down to the previous campsite and wait for me there. I slide open the door. Rain bangs inside onto the steps. I don't bother with a coat, but I no longer feel the wetness. Pete shouts something after me. He is probably telling me to be careful, but this is my race now. When I get the box, I will hold it up to the rain, like an Olympic torch. I will ignite.

In my haste, I slip a little. The bracken smells earthy. The clouds above are black and heavy. I turn back. The bus has gone, snaking its way to the bottom of the valley, to where the police had originally moved us on. I am tired from all the panic and haste. I pant. My breathing is erratic.

"There's time," I tell myself, but not believing it.

I try convincing myself that if it has been there for that long, it will still be there now. I curse. I dream. I still tingle. I feel cleansed.

When I am finally inside the hut-circle itself, I slow down to a walking pace. I try to catch my breath. I am now oblivious to anything around me. It is near now. I creep up to it. Slow steps, the kind of steps you take as a tumbling, inquisitive infant.

I slump down. My body collapses. The place. I dig. I uncover. It shows itself to me. I wrench at it. Before I finally pull it out again, I look around, just to check. No-one there. Hopkins? No. Not this time.

When I have it in my grasp, I do not hold it up. No, instead, I clasp it right to my chest. I will not let it go this time. It's finders-keepers, losers-weepers. I walk back slowly. I do not want to drop it. I don't shake it this time around. I have found the truly ancient here. I know. I have found what I am looking for.

In the rain, a voice.

I see the form of a man on the ridge. It is an old voice, full of dignity and presence. It makes me stop.

"Hey! You! You can't take that box. It's of enormous value!"

There was an impartialness intended in the voice, but a betraying undercurrent of personal longing for it. I stopped briefly. I did not say anything in response. Before me was an old man. He was distinguished; obviously an academic. In some ways, he was an older vision of my father; in other ways, from a memory created elsewhere.

"There is something of immense archaeological value in there," he said.

"I know."

He came closer.

"Please…"

Momentarily, I realized that this box had other contenders. Mine was not the only connection with it. I was part of a collective, a group all after the same thing. This came as something of a shock to me. I had thought it was my secret alone. It was already breaking my heart.

"My dear, where did you find it?" he asked, moving closer. His tone was now less aggressive, and more considered—almost loving.

I thought for a moment. He really longed to know. I could see his eyebrows arch pleadingly. I had to tell him.

"There," I pointed. "Beside that hut. The northern-most one. Between that and the wall…'"

Mud dripped off the box. Hairs fell down my face. The wind tinkled my earrings.

"What's in it then?"

"Well, we think it's a casket. Seventeenth century—but probably from much earlier. A reliquary..."

He seemed unsure whether to continue.

There was a pause, to check if I understood. I nodded.

"There's probably a holy relic in it. I've been searching for it for some time. It is... very old..."

His eyes demonstrated a long wait, longer even than my father's search for that one large fossil. There was a teller in him too—the same eyes as Pete.

"You'll be recognized for finding it..." he said, neck stretching forward.

I wanted to give it to him. I wanted to hold out the box, the way Oliver Twist did his bowl.

"Have it," I wanted to say.

I couldn't though. Not this.

I was selfish here, for the first time. This was mine. It was too precious to give away to this strange old man.

So, I ran, dodging him.

"Don't!" I heard him shout, but he was not going to stop me. I was crying. I called for Pete. He was following. He was old, but not as old as I had first thought. I scrambled down the slope. I ran through the stream. The rain was coming down harder now. He had reasoned with me but I had nothing left inside of me. He was gaining. I could go no faster. The ground was wet and muddy. A misplaced foot and I would tumble. He began to climb again, following the arc of the ridge. I saw the pain in his eyes as he ran. I fancied he might collapse with the strain. He shouted at me. I came to the road. I screamed again for Pete. I ran down through the valley, but he got to the corner before me.

He tackled my legs. The box fell instantly, grating against the tarmac. I shouted abuse at him. He was seemingly ruthless, any loving completely gone. I kicked him in the groin as he reached for the box. He said nothing, only taking the blows as if he himself were some kind of hardened martyr. Something snapped then though. He stood up and punched me. I never thought he would do it. Not him. He just didn't look the type at all. I toppled over like a skittle. I saw him grab the box. He ran toward his car. When I had recovered from the blow, I headed up to where the car was parked. He was fumbling with his keys at the door. He pushed me away again.

"Bastard!" I shouted. "Piss off…"

Once inside his car, he slammed the door locks down. I ranted outside. As if he were in some other time zone, he slowly placed the box on the floor of the front passenger seat, packing it in with his coat. His car started the first time. The box was going. I had lost it. I was still volatile though. As he drove off, I picked up a weighty stone from the verge. I flung it at the back windscreen, and it shattered to resemble melting ice. He didn't look back. Tiny shards of broken glass coated the road. It was still raining. They glistened in the streams of water on the dirt road.

He was gone.

The box was gone.

Pete had come rushing to help.

"You're too late," I bawled.

"I'm sorry. Who was he?" he asked.

I mumbled to answer him with, "Some academic…"

The box was gone, and I had no idea where it was going, but that no longer mattered. No, what was important now, was who he was, and how he knew that here, at Grimspound, he might find it.

Eddie

I suppose they left for the same reasons I headed for New York City. They had that yearning in their hearts, which nothing would alter. Nothing can cause that desire to stop. It could be that, or it could be the fact that I'm a Yank, and they might not like me, even though they didn't say it to my face. It might be because they really don't like people prying. Do you often find yourself like this—plodding through the reasons? I can tell you—it's a mug's game. Well, you can slap down as many alternatives as you want, there is always the true reason, and if you are honest, or at least (like me), try to be honest, then you will know it. And with those Dartmoor travellers, well, I'm sure it had to be something to do with seeing her that first time. I actually went back there afterwards, to look around again. I couldn't see anything, but I could feel "it" oozing around me, playing with my hair and tickling my spine. Not a shiver, no; it was too powerful for that. It gave me an erection just standing there.

So, I head back to my tent, off the trail again. I believe I've lost them now. We collided once, but are now back on separate courses, plotting new routes, new lines, new ways. I arrive back at the camp-site around lunchtime. It is in Princetown itself, at the back of *The Plume of Feathers Inn*, not that far from Whiteworks. There is a car-avan near my pitch—a couple from Norfolk I have discovered, and further across, a family from Germany. Then there's myself. I sit alone in the tent, listening to the rain battering at the canvas. I flick through some photography magazines I brought at a gas station on the highway, and boil water for a cup of coffee. The blue gas coughs and splutters in the front awning.

Lying on my back I am thinking of another time, to take my mind off the present. I am remembering Stacey and me—up around the lakes—three years back now. Time flies. We were heading out to the islands, where the trout fishing was good. We walked back barefoot, because our new walking boots hurt. I carried her most of the way. When we got back, we lay in the same position I am in now. She told me she wanted to marry me. She wanted to have children with me. It never happened though. I was careful and always carried rub-bers with me. I didn't want the burden, right? Not in my line of work. It's a memory you wish you could erase, that you could just stamp out, but then, when someone says she would like to have chil-dren with you, and then the next minute, you're not together—somehow you lose a bit of yourself.

That was then. We made all the mistakes: the great love-of-your-life mistakes. We did it all, almost. We aimed too high I think, and demanded too much of ourselves.

If we'd kept it practical, then we might still be there, walking bare-foot around the shores of Lake Michigan, but no, we were too ambi-tious, always had to pursue it to the nth degree, to the ultimate. We demanded too much from each other. We sucked out each other's souls, and then spat them back at each other in gobs of hatred. Anec-dotes, eh? Who'd have them?

Over coffee, I contemplate my next move. I'm going to head for Plymouth, the big naval town. The road looks easy, sprawling down the south-western side of the Moor. I've reserved a room, at the new

Drake's Lodge hotel and apartment complex. Right now, a warm bed, with a bath and shower sounds wonderful.

Before I pack up, I put my hand into my rucksack and feel for an old bottle of Zip's tonic, I carry with me. I unscrew the bottle, and jam it into my mouth, taking a fulsome slurp of the liquid. Yes— venerable old Zip's Patented Vitamin and Life-Enhancing tonic. The taste took me home, and told me something that I already knew. It was time to stop travelling, and put down some roots.

XIV

The Object of Veneration

Robert

Life, the way I find it, and now tell it, is a continual barrage of discovery. Shots of knowledge hit you, the way shorts of whisky used to numb my National Service blues down in Union Street. Knowledge comes not only from facts, nor from the creation of fiction. Knowledge can also come with collisions. Such collisions can be of small significance (you will recall the one I had with the prostitute), or they can be more devastating. They open up a new set of doors for you to walk through. They can change your views fundamentally. I spoke a while ago of the notion that I believe there are others involved in this story. Here then, I will tell how another came to be involved, or rather involved herself. And I know so little of her story that I find it almost incredible to believe that she has now, somehow, stepped into things. It may have been a lucky find, of course, though I am unsure of that. I feel there is something more. There was something ancient about her, as though she had been thrown down in the wrong century.

My journey into Dartmoor's wilderness did not go entirely as I had hoped. I suppose at the back of my mind, I had the fear that it would be gone anyway—dug up before, or destroyed even. And really, I was just on a wild goose chase. In any sense I would need a whole excavation team to find it—a full undergraduate dig over the summer maybe. I didn't really even expect to find it. I just wanted to be close to it, to the denial of everything else. Having said that, I

175

had always kept a metal detector in the boot of my car in case just such an opportunity presented itself.

It was raining when I arrived, a dull, thudding on the tinted sun-roof of the car. The place was dark and shadowy. It's odd, but when I first arrived, I noticed this brightly-coloured coach winding down through the valley. It looked like the usual hippy trail to the south-west of Britain. No more than that though.

There was a small valley that led up to the hut circle at Grims-pound. A path wound carefully through the bracken. I locked the car, and walked slowly up the slope. At the top, I stopped dead. I could see a woman, kneeling down. At first, I thought she was pray-ing, but no, she was digging. She was finding, discovering. A pre-monition here. I knew it was what I was looking for: Brimicombe's "box of wonder". I wondered if I was in Stranger's actual footsteps. I looked across at the two tors between which Grimspound sits. I shivered a little, with excitement and fear. She looked from side to side, scared, as if she were stealing something, or trespassing. I couldn't but think she was trespassing. My find this. She was tres-passing on the past.

I am very still. She doesn't see me. I hear her laughing, talking to herself. Her hair is beaded and in dreadlocks. She holds an object close to her. I smile. I strain to see it. At last. I try to speak in an assured tone. I tell her that she cannot take the box with her. I inform her of its value, what it might contain. She walks towards me. Her clothes are dirty, ragged. She was wearing a ring in her nose. I cannot understand why she wants the box. What use will she have for it? I notice she is soaked. I cannot help but notice her breasts showing through her T-shirt, as dewy rings. I repeat what I said about its enormous value.

"I know," she says assuredly.

How the hell does she know?

I cannot understand this. I am dumbstruck. What is her interest? I have to be careful. She looks crazy. She could do anything with it. I alter my approach, even though I am still incredulous she is here. She explains where she found it. She brushes her drooping dread-locks over her forehead. I choose my words carefully. I tell her again about what might be inside it. The full story can wait for now. Then I understand her interest. I could suddenly see that in her rejection of the modern world, this might hold something for her. I could see her realization that here, in her hands, was something old, something precious. It didn't matter that it probably contained a Catholic relic. Something spiritual sang to her from it. Her tune was a different one to the rest of us; almost a higher frequency, inaudible to me.

Just as this realization came, she made a run for it, ignoring my reasoning. I had to catch her. I never thought I would ever have to do this, not at my time of life. My more frantic and irrational thoughts take over again. The box of wonder was more important. She made her way down the slope. I had to stop her. There were no options left. I gave chase. I was forced to climb the ridge, in an attempt to cut her off at the road. I hadn't run like this for years. Every joint ached like hell. I was unsure how long I could keep up the pace.

She was screaming, crying out for help. From where I was, I saw a male figure come running to help her. This worried me. I hadn't anticipated any kind of encounter like this.

I became more desperate. I almost fell down onto the road, and lunged at her, grabbing her legs. She kicked me hard in the bollocks. She was wearing hob-nailed boots. In the end, I had to punch her. The box fell onto the road. I was praying it hadn't been damaged. It had chinked against the road surface on impact, but nothing seemed smashed. I picked it up. Momentarily, amongst all this chaos, I fingered the delicate casing, feeling for the first time its sense of wonder. As she came to her senses, I ran up to the car. She was shouting abuse at me. I could understand why. I wanted to freeze it all, there and then. Stop everything. Sort it out. But I could not.

So, she was a part of this too—a pursuer, a tracer, a follower, a pilgrim—and I was selfish, but at least by taking it, I would be able to show it to more people, and solve the links in the story. Finish a tale or two. How's that for selfishness? See how I justify my own desires. But I was learning. There was another who had a like interest, and I had to deal with that. Hers might be equally valid.

She was crying now, sobbing deeply. She swore at me again. I got inside the car and placed the box on the floor of the passenger seat. I started the car and pulled away. I was just thinking I'd got away with it. That's when a stone came through the rear window. I wasn't surprised—not really. I looked around. Glass shards covered the back seats. In my mirror I saw a man comforting the woman. Rain poured in through the back window onto the parcel shelf. I drove for miles, even as far as Mortonhampstead, until I was sure they could not have followed me in any capacity. I had barely looked at the reliquary. It just sat there, full of wonder.

Jude

There was one certainty about the ground-borne box that I had found and then lost: others now knew of it beyond me. That made me angry beyond words. I was so angry that when I got back to the bus, I kicked things and scared the children with my sobbing and shouting. They saw another side of me, a side I hadn't seen since my twenties, and which I thought had gone. I saw their white, downy faces watching me, wondering what had scared and angered their plaything, and why their teacher, Pete, was so concerned about me.

We had walked back after the old man had snatched it. I kept shouting "Bastard!" at the box thief to let out my anger. Pete tried to calm me. He said how it could actually not contain anything at all, and that it could just be some imitation; part of a forgotten treasure trail or something. I nodded, but I disagreed with him. It was as if when I held the box, the rest of the world locked into my body, rays of energy tracking me, lining up the soul with earth and sun in one perfect constellation of spirit. I don't tell Pete this. Unlike me, he doesn't care for the superstitions. He wouldn't laugh, but he would be sceptical; too much of the scientist in him—something he got off his father I sometimes think. Certainly, he has less belief in the magical than me. He is a realist. Instead, he has poured me a glass of wine, and I sit in one of bus seats. The windows steam with my hot air, and with my forefinger I draw pictures. Water runs onto the rubber seal and wets my arm.

"What gets me," Pete says, "is why that bloke was up there the same time as you. Coincidence, or what?"

I explain to him, that it can't be. I explain about it being a relic, and that something must have drawn us both there. Some energy.

"If you'd shown it to me… I might've contacted…"

"Might've?"

"Never mind."

I know that thought bubbles erupt from earlier in his life, but he chooses not to release them.

"I thought he was just telling me about it... as though he knew it had always been there. He had a calming voice. It made me stop."

Once he is certain that I am settled, Pete goes out to find Sarah and her children. I try to look forward, to disconnect, and switch off. But the more I try to disassociate, the more I become dislocated, and my mind swings around to the two men I have met there now. I mentally thumb through them. The first, an American photographer, about ten years older than me. Rich I can tell. Doing the southwest for some magazine. Then, the academic. Bald, but with a swoosh of white hair combed over his head. A man who knows what the box is. Then me. A nobody. An outsider. A Pagan. A rebel.

Although both men scared and annoyed me, I realize I do really want to know them. I want to scrutinize their souls, analyse what makes them tick. They have no sexual interest in me. Therefore, in them, I am just another human being. As far as all this is concerned, I could be either man or woman; it would make no difference. I become less scared because of this, and then feel myself being pulled in. I am being added, as if some ingredient; some pinch of salt; only now it is too late to find out what the broth is. Puzzled beyond belief, I curl into a ball and drift...

I sleep soundly for a couple of hours. I wake with a crick in my neck, and my legs numb from being curled on the seat. Peter has come back from visiting some other travellers he knows, who are camped at Chagford. He has cycled there from our camp. Trading was the purpose of his visit: some engine parts for them, and bender materials for us. He has some news. Apparently, there is festival on at the Barbican in Plymouth. Des—Pete's mate—says that it will be our scene: street theatre, music, and stalls. Pete is already rooting around in the cupboards for face-paint. He has re-stitched his costume for his storytelling show. This is chance for us to show our face in public, to step out of the dark age of the Moor, and the shadow above me.

I am, of course, not into it as much as usual. The others realize this, and say nothing. It is more difficult for the children though. They wonder why I am not myself. I look into the driver's mirror and see, for an instant, the face of my mother, instead of my own.

We shall leave later this evening. If is often better for us to travel in the dark. We are, in that sense, nocturnal creatures. It is useful camouflage. Others may call us sneaky and under-handed for it, but then… for us, places in the dark are easier to find. People only find us when the rest of the world heaves itself out of bed, and they have nothing better to do than find trouble for us. But Plymouth. It's not exactly known for its sympathy for our type of people: Naval town and all. It is hardly New Age friendly; not like Totnes or Penzance. I have a feeling, it will be all right though. It is dark, but I see light at the end of this tunnel. I put on the earrings my mother gave me, and Sarah and I check the costumes for any more weak buttons or threads. I have come to a conclusion. There is no telling what I think anymore.

Eddie

Being on, or around water eases me. I find it relaxing. Water is life-giving. It is where life originally began. It is where water creatures, first heaved themselves out of the depths to breath upon land. Water is necessary for life. All creatures need it. It also holds sperm. Life begins in water.

All this is strange really, because my father could hardly take a bath without feeling sea-sick. He always had those same two and a half inches of soapy water that my mother used to joke about. Maybe that's why he never had many baths. He said most nights after work that a "bath in the sink" would do just as well. I relish water even more now. I mean, it was enough when there was a drought on the farm, but after I had been in Iraq, tapped water to me just seemed too wonderful: miraculous even. There, I would have to trek five miles one day just to fetch fresh water. That's when things really do get ancient, when you couldn't give a flying fuck about having a cool hairstyle or smelling sweet. It's for when you do give a damn about where your next meal is coming from, and when you can next have a cool drink, or just a drink even.

I'm on the water at the moment, on an afternoon's cruise, around Plymouth Sound and up the River Tamar. I'm drinking luxury water—a cool beer—on the rear deck. So I'm taking in the sights. I caught a boat at Sutton Pool in the Barbican, though I still want to spend a day nosing around there. We're now heading up past the dockyard, the origin of all those British ships out in the Gulf. We are dwarfed by the grey hulks of frigates and minesweepers. I note their missile launchers. So that's where they came from.

There's a guy up front, calling the toss, telling us all the history. I'm kind of half-listening, half-eyeing up a tall, dark-haired French tourist on the opposite side of the boat. She's leaning on the deck side taking a photograph of an estate called Mount Edgcumbe and I'm having a nice view of her ass.

I'm trying real hard now to forget those assholes up on the Moor. I don't know why they moved on. Maybe I scared them, or maybe they just didn't want me sniffing around them. I keep thinking of that woman's face though. Jude, yeah, Jude—that was her name. Maybe she thought I'd seen her doing something at Grimspound— something she didn't want me to know. But I guess it's nothing new—I've had a few times before—people saying they'll be there, and then they don't show. See, there's something scary about being caught on film. You feel you won't be able to change or alter it, or embellish it after the photographer has gone. You get what's there— the bare facts. Evidence as well; to be used in the future.

But then, I wonder if I should have gone back to Grimspound again—to try and find out the meaning behind it all. Then, you can't do it all.

When first, Brunel's railway bridge, and secondly, the Tamar Bridge come into view, we turn around, but I get some good, unusual shots of the bridge decks. As the boat lunges around, I can see the Moor in the distance, taunting me with its secrets. I have to put it out of my mind. Instead, on the way I am thinking of Zip. I think of him a lot here. He is my conductor into the past, like a terminal into a battery solution. He gives the actual power in my life. I hear him whispering over my shoulder, so I stop eying the French tourist. I think harder about what he used to say to me.

"Boy, when you go over to Britain one day on yer travels, you look out for Hopkins in Plymouth. He was the first to come out here. Our family say he came out here on that first Pilgrim boat. They always said he was a real sly character, and knew every trick in the goddamn book."

Then he would always deny it. Tell me he didn't think there was much truth in it, but he would always tell me the story all the same. And then, when he was dying, he told me a bit more.

"First man out here, y'know," he would say, "—who founded this place, was a man by the name of Samuel Hopkins. Never mind them other fools. Just you think about our man Samuel…"

As the cruise boat rounded its way back into Sutton harbour, I am resolved to find out a little more about my forefather. I mean, we like to know don't we? We judge present on the past, and future on the present. So I step off the cruise boat, amongst chattering American and Japanese tourists, with the intention of looking for him. First though, I am told jokingly by a talkative, rough, tobacco-smoking fisherman, standing outside *Cap'n Jasper's* food-stall that I ought to sample the delights of Union Street.

"'Tis like hell on earth of a Friday night," he jokes. "I'd rather be out Iraq fighting than be down there…"

"Just my kind of place then," I say.

XV

The Medicine of the Sicke

Robert

I know that what I tell you concerns pilgrims of various kinds, across previous centuries, and the one I stand in today, yet I do not want to be regarded as some kind of modern Petrarch, Boccaccio or Sercambi even. No, my interest in pilgrims comes from my interest in the dead and in relics. I want to tell you about relics, so that you may understand why I needed Brimicombe's "box of wonder". Relics do fascinate me. You will know that. It is why I pursue the dead. It is they who leave their relics. It is one reason why I have kept a lump of Berlin Wall on my desk, but it is so much more than that. Let me explain. I told the students this when I lectured on undergraduate Medieval archaeology.

In the second century, the Bishop of Smyrna describes his collection of holy relics or "remains" as "more valuable than precious stones and finer than refined gold". Relics then, are special. You know how they work. You go on pilgrimage to see them, and to benefit from their powers. If a figure died for this faith, then the body of such a martyr was kept in catacombs. Picture the early Pagans, where worship of images has lasted for thousands of years: the sun and the moon. Then, came the Word. The conversion to Christianity was easy enough by readily worshipping relics. History and relics then, walk hand in hand with superstition.

So, in medieval Europe, relics become evocative reminders, or holy souvenirs. True meaning perhaps lost on the way. Anything could be sold and people would readily buy. Like rock from Blackpool, only with "Salvation" written through it. The traveller William Way brought back a whole collection of rich relics from his mid-fifteenth-century excursions to the Holy Land, simply to flog. Gather round ladies and gentleman, I have here a genuine thorn from those placed upon our Saviour's head, or how about this: a certified piece of wood from the True Cross?

But then, everything passes doesn't it?

There were heretics, disbelievers, cynics who knew there was no place for superstition. Relics were mumbo-jumbo. The Reformation put paid to the pathetic relic cult. It has been dying for a long time. Abuse of the way would end. Villainous pardoners would become extinct. No more would they sell pig bones as those of a stoned-to-death martyr. So, there was pressure to rid the world of relics. Rid, rid and rid.

The Christian viewpoint changed. Later, people became Separatists knowing the reformed church has become just as corrupt as the old one. But some places—churches and holy communities—kept their relics, and hid them. They kept that superstition because they couldn't quite let it go. They needed it for hope, for fertility, for success, or for the right place in the after-life. They were too scared to get rid of them, too scared to keep them in the church, so they put them into hiding. Certainly, any relic would be too valuable to destroy. So mostly, they were stored, buried or locked away in priest holes. By now, of course, most have decayed, and gone into the earth, but picture these pieces being kept. Yes—just picture people worrying about superstition. But whatever happened, the cures ended, the miracles stopped, whether real, psychosomatic, or autosuggestive. The cult of relics ends, and the cures go with it. It is now time for rational humanity.

Ah—but something of these proportions, of this magnitude, cannot disappear as simply as that.

See, relics may be hidden, brushed under, or they may be ignored, but they are still there. Relics go on as friends. They wheedle their way into our lives. And although most of us are no longer religious, and Christianity takes a back seat, there are other ways; other attractions. But the relics are still around us; in different forms, yes, but they serve the same purpose: veneration. And I genuinely believe we are changing again. We look away from the machine, the city, the weapon. One day—not too far away—we will need relics to tell us we are human again; just as we do with stories. They both tell us that we are different, that superstition still hangs around our necks. For belief, we need both.

Jude

I knew it would happen—eventually. I had faith. I knew my body would give. Something deep down always told me—said to me one day that I would. I went this morning to the hospital, to check I was correct. I shall only tell the world when the moment is right. I want to savour it. It has been a long time coming—a whole lifetime.

We have wandered again. We have travelled through the dark. I have almost forgotten about Grimspound, now that another life-force arrives. I tell myself I have no need of that box. I have a future. We have travelled into Plymouth. We needed things—provisions and clothes. We need to make some money. Skinner's Bottom must wait for now. So, we have come here, out of the wilderness of Dartmoor and into civilization. In the shops, we are stared at. We are oddities. I don't care. Not now.

Des was right. There's a regatta on around the Barbican, celebrating the *Mayflower* crossing. Some hero sailor is trying to make the same trip in record time, following the exact route they took. I've set up a jewellery stall on the front. I'm trying to trade. Next to me, some old boys on pulleys are lowering themselves down the side of a boat, to paint it up a little. The profession looks ancient, like as if they have been doing it since time immemorial. Pete and Sarah are inside a circle of pink-skinned onlookers. They are doing storytelling and street theatre. At the moment, Sarah is juggling, while Peter captures imaginations with a tale matching her movements. I hear children in the crowd laughing.

I am interrupted from watching this by a customer. She wants to buy some earrings. I explain that they hand-made, and what they signify. Many of the designs are based on British Celtic symbols, which seem to please her. She holds up a few pairs, and I glibly hold up a mirror for her. Right now, though, I can't help but look at Pete. I am tracing his face. I am searching for clues. He is wearing a mask, but I know him too well. He does not want to be here, in Plymouth. He is, for some reason, scared; afraid of seeing someone. I can tell this, by his banter not having the usual confidence. I know by the way he pulls at his dreadlocks.

"How much for these then?" the woman asks, pointing at a pair of crescent-shaped earrings.

"Make me an offer," I say.

She is surprised. This is unexpected—a new way of buying for her. "A fiver?"

"Fine," I say. She smiles at me and hands over a note.

I place them in a brown bag and give them to her. This is my third sale this morning.

I offer different designs from the usual I think; that is why they appeal. See, we don't scrounge off the dole. This is how we survive.

Most of the boats are in today. Only the hardened fishermen are out in the Channel. Other local mariners squat around the front, smoking and chattering. They watch the performance too, and clap alongside the tourists. Across the quayside, sit tiny, tucked-in, garlic-smelling bistros and wine-bars. Tourists mill in and out of them, dodging stall-holders and eager seagulls. To the right, Robert Lenkiewicz's large wall mural stands proud, with its images of Pilgrim Fathers and Plymouthian life. A few visitors walk past me to view it, but don't look at what's on offer. A couple of goth kids come cover to the stall too, but they don't spy anything they want.

Pete is winding up the morning show, with a finale based on the story of the giant Gogmagog who was heaved off Plymouth Hoe in a wrestling match with the Trojan refugee Corineus. When the tale is finished, he sends Sarah's kids around with bowler hats to collect money. He knows the onlookers will dip into their pockets. It's been a good show, if not up to Pete's usual standards. Meanwhile, by the Mayflower Steps, some dignitaries have arrived to open the regatta. The crowd moves across to see this. Pete knows when to catch them for a performance, and this is not one of those times. He comes over to me, sweaty and breathless. Sarah has taken the children off to look at the boats. She promises them some sweets and a look around the shops as well. She will not be refused entry today. She is a tinker, but tinkers are all right at these sort of events. While it's all topsy-turvy we are accepted. It is just in reality we are not. As Pete comes across, the people chat to him. They see him as the wandering minstrel, the storyteller, not some lawbreaker or oddball.

"How's business?" he enquires, with the air of an experienced banker.

"Fairly good," I answer.

"Coming down here... being capitalists... not really our way is it?" he jokes.

I tell him I don't mind. Not this time. Not the way I am feeling. He is puzzled, and asks if I want some lunch. Sarah comes back to look after the stall, and we enter a well-to-do restaurant. We are no longer travellers it seems. He is a minstrel, and I am a trader. We have stepped out of a book of medieval brigands.

We sit. We talk. We eat. I want to know what's up with him. He wants to know what's up with me.

He finishes a mouthful, sits back in his chair and stares hard at me.

"I thought we were agreed. The past doesn't matter. Doesn't count."

"It does when you're like this."

"Like what?"

A pause.

"Family?" I enquire.

Pete is edgy. He hates to be pinned down. He mumbles something about his father and mother.

"You know..." he says.

But I don't.

He pushes his plate aside, the act indicating that is the end of this particular line of questioning. He asks me if I want a pudding. I don't answer. Instead, I contemplate his possible pasts. Now, they seem more important. Genetics. Heritage. Identity. Not just us any-more. Fed up with waiting for me, Peter orders two apple pies, which we eat with clotted cream in a silence we have never known. A man on the next table looks over at us. He has recognized our dif-ference, I can tell. He has seen what we represent. We leave shortly afterwards, me exiting first, and Pete squaring the bill with a bagful of ten-pences and coppers.

Sarah, meanwhile, has been chatting to another trader. He is older than her, in his late thirties, but there seems to be a chemistry between them. She told me she fancied him, when I returned from lunch. They talk now. I know what he is asking her. He is asking what she does, but I already know her answer. I know that if he is to make any progress with her, he will need to want the same. The children go with them round the harbour, and he carries Cari and Ally one after another on his shoulders. From here, they could be a respectable family from the suburbs of Plympton or Plymstock.

In the evening, the pubs of the Barbican are jam-packed. A vivid September sunshine washes over the Sound. Pete gave two more shows today. I sold nine more pieces. We feel good about that. I feel especially good, knowing what I know. We decide to walk up to the Hoe, where the giant Gogmagog got defeated by Corineus. We walk arm-in-arm, like an Edwardian couple, taking the air, out on a stroll. Pete is more relaxed now—back to his old self. Perhaps all that energy has gone into his shows. We edge around the Citadel, and consider the grey hulks sat in the Sound. Noise still sounds from the Barbican—bands are now playing their evening sets on the back of articulated lorry trailers. The place is still packed. Cars have parked on double-yellow lines, and the ice-cream kiosks do brisk business. Sticky, lolly-faced children run past us, pursued by worried mothers.

We reach Smeaton's Tower and peer up at the lighthouse top.

"Sit," I say to him.

He jokingly obeys, as if he is a dog.

I don't look out on the Sound anymore. Not now. Now, comes the telling. I boil. I have to pour.

"Listen…"

"What?"

"I've something to tell you…"

He shuts his eyes, like it will hurt. I have him, the storyteller, listening. Then, I release it.

"I'm pregnant."

He lifts his head. He stares forward. I smile at him. He still stares.

"Say something…"

"Wow…" he says, shaking his head in disbelief.

"I'm sorry I didn't tell you before, but I wanted to check. Yesterday… When you and Sarah were setting up, I went to the hospital… I bought a kit… but they confirmed it."

In a moment, he will get up and dance. I know him.

"What happened? I mean, how… Before, they said you could never conceive…"

"I'm just as confused as you are…"

But I'm not really confused. I believe it is the box. I know that something "higher" entered me and made it happen. Miraculous medicine. Fertility cult, maybe. A tonic.

I don't tell Pete any of this.

He gets up and dances, like he always does when some news is joyous and wonderful. We spin around the Hoe in a hopeless tango. The light starts to fade, and when we stop dancing, his face changes. The smile is taken.

"Okay. I've gotta tell you about my past now Jude… about my childhood. It's more important now, now that you're pregnant. See, I don't want any repetition. I don't want to make the same mistakes…"

The confession will be difficult, but I smile to encourage him. I have longed to know this. That evening, we walk and talk, talk and walk, and he tells me his past, the way I have told you mine.

Eddie

Union Street failed me utterly and completely. I only found disharmony. I sat in a couple of bars. I watched rookie sailors and squaddies freshly crew-cutted, move in for the kill with hen nights. I get offered acid and ecstasy. I spend the evening smoking and drinking hard. I have a hope that I will meet some leggy, red-dressed prostitute and we can just talk about the good times. I'm told Milbay Docks is the place now though and that's too big a step from here, right now.

It just doesn't happen. An old guy named Micky asks for some change for a beer, which I tell him I haven't got. I chat to the barman for a while, then a Scotsman who is driving a lorry on the ferry over to Brittany. He finds me intriguing, and likes my accent. I leave that bar when he staggers to the toilet. I pass girls in gaudy, ass-poking skirts, laced with perfume. Young guys pass laden with rich aftershave. Having said that, all of human life is found here. Old men, old women peer from barred, bolted windows of the flats opposite. Guys shout. Girls scream. Ambulances go by. Each place I enter, I am of interest, the moment I speak. But by one o'clock, I've had enough of being the specimen under the microscope, and of watching initiation ceremonies of Plymouth eighteen year olds celebrating their birthdays. I've had enough of sick, tits, piss, kebabs, curry, rave music, DJs, fried chicken and spicy spuds. I leave in a black taxi. I return to the *Drake's Lodge* hotel, where I spend five minutes gulping down several glasses of water to prevent a hangover. I can't get to sleep though. I am thinking too much. I hate that—when there is no noise or sound, and all you can hear is yourself and your own darkest thoughts. That's when you really come to the edge, and when you are too damn scared to look down.

I stayed in bed late. I finally rose at eleven, and grabbed a brunch in the hotel bar. I notice preparations are in process for some kind of festival in the Barbican. I spend the rest of the late morning wandering the cobbled streets. I touch rounded windows, ducking under the shadows of toppling storeys. I sniff the cracked timbers. There is a hellish stink of fish coming from the market on the quayside. I see blood dribbling from the iced-filled crates. Fish eyes stare; their gills done with. These were once the poor sods who tried to waddle from the sea to the land…

I check out all the in-between shops and up-spiral staircase places. I ease into dusty bookshops. I buy a surfing T-shirt. I take photographs of old age pensioners and drinkers standing outside the *Dolphin*. I visit the Merchant's House.

I take pictures of the displays inside. I gaze upon Robert Lenkiewicz's mural of Plymouth. I look at the faces. There is much in there: philosophy, metaphysics, mysticism, alchemy, cults, chivalry, pilgrims. I photograph it. I gaze between every cobblestone for traces. I think of piss running down New Street. I see dogs in the street scratching their ears. I see cats seeking fish. I see coils of rope stacked, lobster pots, and nets slung out for repair. Vessels are being painted by jobbers in the harbour. Men in small dinghies row around the larger ships, checking their seaworthiness.

I follow the road down to the Mayflower Steps. In the distance, out there in the Sound, the massive breakwater which protects the harbour from the Channel's force. Further… France, Holland, America. Home. There, the New World. Always the New World. Watching it from here, home of the Water Clan, and me thinking of mom's Thanksgiving meal: turkey, corn, sweet potato and pumpkin pie. I don't quite get to the steps yet. I'll save that for now. Instead, I turn and look at upstairs windows. They are now prettily-painted places, with window boxes. I look close. I crane my neck higher, and around a bit. There are windows up there, as small as your head. Some places, with just window bars. That's where, those sort of places, I think. One of the higher floors—yes, definitely.

The ope leads down into Southside Street, then I take a sharp right. A pub there is called *The Mayflower*. It is light, bright and airy, a yellow and green Formica job these days. I laugh to myself. So this, is what it has come to, this side of the Atlantic? A designer pub, but just step outside, and you can still see the tin cup snack bar of *Cap'n Jasper's* and your nostrils are still hit by the smell of rotting mackerel. It smells beautiful really. Oh yes, you can slap the interior design in there, but this is still the same place.

At Island House, I look for his name on the wooden board. I follow each name down from John Alden, Cooper, to Richard Ely, Sailor, "Pilgrims" it says at the top, "who sailed from here, The Barbican, Plymouth in 1620 in the *Mayflower* 180 tons." I look again, but my past is not here. Still, they say that not all the passengers who left are on this board, and "sly" Zip had said. See, this is the real reason I have come to Plymouth. This is what this whole thing has been about. Like we all do, I am tracing my heritage. I realize I haven't told you yet. See, I've been kinda waiting for the right moment. Yes—I'm not the only modern Hopkins who was over here. My grandpa, Zip, Doc—whatever—he visited the Barbican, when he was a G.I., over here in the Second World War, waiting for the Normandy Landings. There was some kind of memorial event. It must have been a little like the one going on this weekend. Yeah, I'm standing where he stood, and I kinda like to think where my other forefather stood too.

Back at the newly-smelling designer hotel, I anticipate my saga ending for now. But no, I am fooled.

I order a coffee, and glance through the *Western Morning News*. Some professor has written an article. It catches my eye. I focus. I read it. Then I read the headline again. I am back with the woman. I am in the hut circle once more. It couldn't be any clearer: "Holy Relic found on Dartmoor: Seventeenth-Century Mystery found at Grimspound".

XVI
The Key to Mythologies

Robert

Someone once told me that storytelling is always a way of searching for our origins. I believe there to be some truth in this. In my story (can I call it that now?) you have heard one such search. In the search for my origins, I have passed many signals along the way, things carved in the sand, and markers in time. One such marker now sits in our hotel room next to—because it seems a safe place— my wife's dressing table. In fact, it does not look out of place, except that this morning, a slight history exudes from it.

She is out. I am alone. It is a bright September morning. I went to bed late, so rose late. This has become a regular habit lately. When I returned from the Moor, I looked at the box all evening. I say looked, for that, for the most part, is all I did, though I confess, I did take one of her make-up brushes off the dressing table, to dust of the dirt. She asked me if I had seen it this morning. No, I had not. It lurks in the inside pocket of my jacket, laced with traces of peat.

I don't dare open the box lid. It would have been a struggle anyway. I would certainly have damaged it. Besides, even in its unopened state, the box speaks to me eventually. It tells me loudly not to open it. Its language is foreign and strange somehow, but we'll translate some of the meaning. All evening, I think of rubbing and polishing it. I think of holy spirits or genies swirling out of the double key-hole. I think of Pandora and her power. All this is strange, because I'd like to show you the symbols on the box. Yes, there are crosses, one large one on top, and others on each of its four sides, and pictures of life-embracing couples, legs twisted and apparently copulating. Clearly, whatever it contains, it is life-giving; full of fertile energy. Maybe touch of it alone, is enough.

I rang Bill. He had expected me. Told me he thought I would be planning some summer dig, on the pretext of a re-excavation of Grimspound.

He didn't expect me to find anything on my first visit of course. He'd been researching. Found some article by the *Dartmoor Archaeological Society* who excavated the place in 1891. They found a few objects apparently, but none had been possible to date properly; nothing, of course, about a reliquary. I told him I had waited. I waited to make sure it was safe, before I rang him. He'd be down, he said. I aim to meet him at the train station. I am to put something in the local paper to generate interest from the public and elsewhere. It might flush out a few leads; even the woman whom I had snatched it from.

"Of course," Bill observed, "it's entirely possible that the 1891 team completely missed it. Do you think it was away from the main excavation area?"

"I believe it was."

"Objects work their way up as well as down you know. Depends on the leaching, soil type, vegetation, wash outs, all manner of things…"

Bill paused.

"What am I doing? You know all this Bob…"

"I know I'm retired, Bill, but you don't forget all this you know…" I joked.

I describe the box to him. I sense him listening, ear pressed to the sweaty receiver in the laboratory back in Bristol.

I tell him about the engravings.

"Yes," he says, "Definitely. I have seen others resembling your description of that… Sounds Middle Eastern…"

"What?"

"Middle Eastern. Yes—those kind of images. You don't get them elsewhere. Too suggestive you know. Definitely a reliquary though… I mean some Christian sects loved those kind of images… Now all we've got to do is date it. "

I warned Bill about my inability to open the lid, but then, you know by now, that Bill has his ways. I want to tell him more. I want to tell him how I found it, about the woman and her anger, but he doesn't seem too bothered. For him archaeology is 99% luck and he thinks I got lucky. He is in full technical flow, talking about his dating processes. Eventually, he comes up for air, and senses that I want to speak.

"There are two lock systems Bill…"

"Interesting. Anyway, I'll be down… Look forward to it…"

The phone clicked down. He was coming.

I go back upstairs from the phone in the lobby. Then, I have to listen to my wife. She wants to know what the hell had happened to the car. Kids, I tell her. She wants to know.

She wants answers from everybody, including the hotel management. Kids, I tell her again. She is sensing I am lying, but then you know how she lies to me. It is our unwritten rule, remember. I promise I'll get it fixed and then she won't have to worry. I swear about the kids, to make it all look a bit more realistic. I am a pathetic actor. Actually, I couldn't lie my way out of a paper bag, but then we both play cardboard characters, so it comes naturally.

The thin thread of all this leads me here then. I need to fix the rear windscreen. I fling a plastic bin big over it, and sellotape it up, with a roll that the hotel manager has given me. There is still glass in the rear seat. I cannot move very quickly though. I keep thinking of her: that woman. I cannot believe my own evil. I stole it from her. I know that the box gave her something. She knew the power coming from it. If only I had reasoned with her more, we might have talked about the metamorphosis, instead of me just imagining it. I could still feel her anger when the stone went through; still feel the crunch of the glass. I thought of her clothes; I mean, I've seen undergrads dressed like that, but she was doing it for real. Like her life depended on it.

I keep thinking of the man who came up to comfort her. I can still see her sobbing, in his arms, but I couldn't really picture his face. In a way, I long to go back, to explain, but I suspect they will have moved on again. I still ring in a story to the paper; a journalist phones me back and I get him up to speed.

When that is done, I take the car in to *Autoglass* to have the rear windscreen repaired. They ask me to leave it. There are a few checks on the computer to be made, to see if they have the right screen in stock. Yes, they do, but no-one can possibly get around to it, until after lunch. I say that I will wait. The mechanic does a double-take on me. No-one waits like me. But you must understand—when you reach my age, things like time matter less. Besides I want to think. I twiddle my thumbs, to indicate my boredom. Maybe they will get on with it quicker. I listen to the tedium in the customer service centre. Actually though, it is good to be here and be distant from everything. You already know what is on my mind. I watch the water of the Sound. I watch the gulls on car dealership rooftops. Flex dips into the water the way it has always done. Shouts come from the boats and ships the way they always have.

When I get the job done, she will be attentive to me, like she was once. She and the Major have had words. She wants me to buy her flowers, like in the old days. She even wants me to swap stories. But no, that time has gone hasn't it? I have others now, whom I want to trade tales with.

Jude

I stop running. Pete holds me. He cannot understand what is wrong. Ally is crying, but I am trying to calm her. I am shaking uncontrollably. In the frantic run away from him, I have lost one of the earrings my mother gave me. I curse. We stand in an opeway next to a restaurant. Steam trails out of a grimy extractor fan in a frosted window. I have to lean against the cobbled wall to collect my senses. Pete is scared now; he has hasn't seen anything put so much fear into me for a long time. I explain, or attempt to tell him where this stems from. I tell him more about the photographer, the American, and what he seems to know about Grimspound, and how weird it felt for him to follow us—stalk us even—to Whiteworks. I fear him because somehow, I feel he will destroy something in me. Deep down, I know that the box had something to do with me getting pregnant. This man, he puts fear into me about my unborn child. I then think of the old man, the academic, who took the box away from me. There is some connection, I tell Pete. I know there is. Knowing it scares me. Even though I don't know where I seem to stand anymore with the world, I have been added into this story as an ingredient. I don't necessarily want to be in this tale, this unfolding, but I am somehow in the chronicle, along with the rest of them, blindly following.

Pete holds my rounded belly, my tor belly, then puts his arms around me.

"He's only a journo. That's all. He only wants a story... You know what he said. For the magazine yeah, that's all he wants us for..."

"But why is he here? There's a reason..."

"Jude baby, it's just a coincidence... He's a photographer right? He goes to things like this. He told us he was going to the Barbican, yeah?"

I nod with Pete, trying to calm my breaths. I want to believe him, but I am forced not to; not the way he chased me. He knew that I had more to tell. He knows there are more photographs to take: better photographs. Somehow, he has entered this as well. A chance meeting, and here he is, ruling my life. Then, that can be the way sometimes. We all know that. I look back into Pete's eyes, and reflect how our lives have changed since our first meeting, and now will change again from a chance meeting between my egg and his sperm. Waters uniting inside of me.

I weigh up the reasons for his pursuit of me, and why he shouted after me. Why does he want contact again? He obviously wants to talk to me. I know he said something about us being like Native Americans, about us having similar problems—trying to live an ancient lifestyle in a modern world.

Perhaps he was just interested. Maybe he really did want to promote our cause. He might even have wanted to join us. Am I being too cynical, too concerned, too worried?

We begin to walk back. My breathing becomes more controlled. I feel slightly foolish now. I have denied him opportunity. I have limited by own life by doing so. I feel regret about my actions now.

"We'll look out for him then," says Pete, "but only when I'm there... with you... eh?"

I smile.

"Yes. We could look for him."

"He'll still be there. The Barbican's not that big an area. I think we stand out enough—don't you?"

So, I have changed. I now want to meet him. I have to meet him to find out exactly what he wants. I want to give him the chance that I wish others would give us. On the way back to the waterfront, I still keep my eyes down-turned though, looking for my mother's earring. Pete looks into the crowd's faces. He listens for his accent.

I leave Pete gazing over the crowd to see if he can spot him. Another speech is being made at the Mayflower Steps; then a reminder of the firework display this evening. I walk back through the streets I ran along to search for the lost earring. I scour every inch of the ground, but it is not there. It won't become a relic that one.

When I come back to Pete, after fifteen minutes of searching, his expression is now the one which has changed. His formerly animated features, so used to the gift of the gab, have become sad and lonely. Wondering what's wrong, I nudge into him, to make him laugh.

"Can't see it anywhere…" I say.

He doesn't hear me. He is staring forward, arms by his sides, like a soldier on parade.

"Pete?"

I catch his eyes following a figure somewhere.

"Pete. Is it him? Is it Eddie?"

This time he hears me.

"Over there…" he says, but he does not point. A kind of bitterness runs over the words.

"Eddie?"

"No."

"Who then?

The words come slow.

"My father."

I turn to look.

"And my mother."

"Where?"

He doesn't point. I want to shake him. Here's the missing piece.

"It doesn't matter."

"You could speak to them," I say.

Pete stares down to me. Childhood pours from his eyes as tears. He sobs.

"No… Come on," he says. "We're going."

I look once more to see them, but they are now lost to the crowd, and he won't point them out to me. I argue with him; try and reason that he should at least tell them they are going to have a grandson or—daughter.

"And then there's Eddie," I say. "What about Eddie?"

Pete doesn't answer me. His entire body is too full of pain. He understands how it feels to be pursued now. He pulls me harshly, like I am a spoilt child, in the opposite direction.

Eddie

Think Christ for the written... sometimes: "On the 6th September, 1620, in the Mayorality of Thomas Townes, after being 'kindly entertained and courteously used by divers Friends there dwelling' the Pilgrim Fathers sailed from Plymouth in the Mayflower in the Providence of God to settle in New Plymouth, and to lay the foundation of the New England States. The ancient Causey whence they embarked was destroyed not many year afterwards, but the site of their embarkation is marked by the Stone bearing the name of the *Mayflower* in the pavement of the adjacent pier. This Tablet was erected in the Mayorality of J. T. Bond in 1891 to commemorate the Departure and the visit of Plymouth in July of that Year of a number of their Descendants and Representatives."

I just manage to read the last sentence, before I am politely ushered back by an official. Thick, red rope is being put around the Mayflower steps. It is here that the sailing will begin later on today. Other tourists are with me. I wonder about their history. Do they have a connection here? Their faces are smiling and don't mirror mine. I think not then. For me this is a serious matter. It is my departure point, my life-changing moment. How would the Hopkins family have fared if we'd stayed?

The arch over the steps is impressively Victorian. Two flagpoles—one bearing the Union Jack; the other the Stars and Stripes—sit on either side of it. The early morning sun casts a shadow onto the sidewalk. The official gets a man to clean the steps themselves from dropped orange peel and dust. Yes, it is now that I really think of Samuel. I think of who he waved goodbye to. I think of him rowing out to board, three hundred and seventy-plus years ago, on a day to change the world. It was a time that made me who I am. And now, the nation formed that day, still changing the world.

They lay red carpet. A temporary podium is being constructed. They fence off areas for the expected crowds. Someone informs me that the current Mayor will be coming down, and Royalty possibly.

A good opportunity to shoot some pictures then. Right now, at this very moment, I want Zip to be here; here because of what he had always said, and here because I want to see him pull in with his Medicine Show, and sell them happiness. He would help forgive the crowd's sins, and give them a tonic; the pep-up they need.

I have a phone call to make later. I tried earlier, but a very obliging women told me to phone again later, when the reporter would be back in for his shift. It concerns the newspaper article. I have to make contact. In the meantime then, I wander around the pier.

There are a few holiday-makers squatting on the end. Boys with orange lines fish crabs out of the water. Babies catch the sun in prams. Old folk suck morning ice-creams. Scaffolding for a bandstand has already been erected. Stalls are being set up. There seems to be some kind of storytelling street theatre over along the front. Even the bagmen and tramps have wandered down here to see what is going on. All humanity then—for a gathering and a celebration. It is a place of worship. A common aim then.

Cruise boats filter in and out of the harbour, like the one I took earlier this week. Two have set up against the quayside hoping to do business as floating bars. The Challenge catamaran, the *Mayfly*, they have named her, bobs gently in the middle of Sutton Pool. She is sleek and low, double-hulled, and strong enough to survive the Atlantic's dread heave. A lot of Americans have come over for this— rich ones, with more money than sense, to be honest. Investment and sponsorship deals can be seen aplenty. This kind of event attracts bankers from New York, and their London counterparts. This is no "founding of a nation" for them. Oh no. This is about celebrating the beginning of power; knowing their place in the world economy. I wonder whether they might celebrate the same third world refugees floating in, illegal shoeless aliens, dodging tumbleweed on the Mexican border. Didn't our forefathers once do the same? Jump barriers? Tread on someone else's land. Take someone else's identity. Alter their history. But then, no-one cares about that now. The sun is shining, and the great Waterclan are meeting.

By lunch-time, the place is full of milling people eating and drinking. There is music, fast-food trailers, stall-holders and entertainers. The ripe smell of the fish market is replaced by candyfloss and excited holiday chatter. I note the bagmen and tramps have moved back to the city centre. It is too happy for them. A parade begins at one o'clock. This interested me. It is a recreation: an Elizabethan costume parade. I push to the front and get out my camera. Puritan black and white passes by. Wide-brimmed hats. Gaiters. White ruffs. One man has a pointed beard. Straight out of 1620. There are children, as well, from local elementary schools. A loudspeaker bawls out a commentary: "They were shopkeepers, sailors, boat jobbers, and men and women on a mission to America. These were *the* Pilgrim Fathers."

I want to share my elation at all of this, but there is no-one here with any connection to me. I roll another cigarette in consolation. I smoke it deep. I snap the tugs bringing the *Mayfly* across. The crowd waits for the Mayor. The Royalty turns out to be the Duchess of York. When he steps out with her, he fits the bill exactly: silver hair, double chin, sweaty armpits, just like you imagine a British Mayor to be.

I photograph the two of them and they wave to the crowd. He gives a "honored-to-be-there" kind of speech and she says some pleasantries. I only move forward when it comes to her cutting the ribbon that leads down to the steps. Silk is wrapped around the two pillars. The snip comes. I wait for significance, but can barely see the ribbon shred. After this, a bottle of Champagne cracked on the *Mayfly*'s double hull. I am now caught in the bowels of the crowd.

What comes is unexpected. Nothing stirs in me. I am here, right here, where I need to be, and yet I feel no union, no emotion. I expected an ocean of warmth to wash over me. Water again. I watch a television crew move closer. It has taken a few goes, but the Champagne bottle has finally cracked. Patriotic songs are being sung. I am back in Iraq with the primitive, trekking for clean water. Then I am back in Massachusetts, doing shopping at some mall. Soon, I am back here. My camera drops from my hands. I wanted an image of this; the one to show. This was the one I wanted to justify everything. I guess I looked too hard for the "prick".

We watch the catamaran pull gracefully out of Sutton Pool. I don't wave like the rest of the crowd. Soon, I will be flying back home. You can do that now don't you know? I will pass over him at 39,000 feet. I can go to the other Plymouth in a day, and watch him come in. For now though, I stand decaying, destroyed, scattered, like all that I saw in the Gulf. I am gone. I am a relic of a former time.

Oh, but we can be hit by life at odd times. It gives us another good kicking when we are down. Maybe this is to make us fight twice as hard when we get back up again.

Over on the quay I see her. This time, her face is whiter, more haunted, but the same smile underneath. Here's the transformation I have sought. Here comes the photographic prick. I watch her for a second or two. I have to ask her about their reasons for moving on. I want to know. Unlike everybody else, she is not craning her neck to see the catamaran pull out into the Sound. She holds a child—one of Sarah's no doubt—Ally by the look it. I need to know why we meet here, why we travel in similar orbits, why we glide on the same plane. I must know why we are on parallel lines but never meet. I want to bend our lives again.

The crowd is thick here, but I barge through it. My camera catches momentarily in a woman's handbag, and this delays me. I rescue it, staring madly forward. People move out of my way.

As the catamaran leaves, there is a charity balloon race. She and the child are looking upwards now, at the red shapes filling the sky. She has her back to a slate wall. My eyes will meet hers when she looks down. We will make history here, the same way others make love. But when her eyes come down and meet mine, there is already a history. A barrier goes up instantly. Her expression turns to horror. I am the image she never wants to see. She does not look anymore. She runs.

"Jude… Wait! Please…" I shout.

I run after her. She cannot run fast because she is still carrying Ally. She passed into an ope of listening people. I see her dreadlocks bouncing. The crowd swells, but I am good at moving through throngs like this. Remember I have practice. Iraqi markets. They make you fast. For certain, both of us think of Grimspound, and what transpired there. She winds through more people hoping to lose me.

"Jude!" I bellow.

I am stared at; no longer a stranger, just strange, for anyone who encounters me. I run faster. Another ope. I turn the corner. The camera smacks on the stone edging, cracking the telephoto lens. I search again, but she is nowhere to be seen. She has buried herself in the very streets that nourished my family line.

XVII

The Articulation of Opposites

Robert

I'm frustrated. I'm twiddling each of my thumbs in opposite directions, just as my mother did, when my father was on a shout. My journey nears its end, but is not quite there yet. You (for your sins) have listened, listened to its successes and its failings. Somewhere, we will have gained new understanding. We have become wiser together: the teller and the told. And now you may tell it again. Take the tale forward to some new listener.

But then, although I am in reach of everything, of complete enlightenment—of finding out that little piece more about Stranger, it cannot be quite done yet. Bill arrives later tonight, so the box still sits unopened. It will be the ultimate pleasure to lift the lid. Like the Christmases we once had. The unwrapping is always the best bit. That moment of surprise surpasses the actual gift. I don't quite know what to expect anymore. Bill is certain: it really is a relic of some kind. The box is similar to others found in the same period—or from the century before at least. I can tell he's thinking Middle Eastern; not European. Certainly, not British. Not Celtic. No. It's from somewhere more distant. I've been digging, see; I'm expecting some power from it; some higher truth. See how I still believe in stories. I don't know the end, or the middle, or the beginning, but isn't that what a good story should do? Shouldn't it promote further questioning? That's what it should do with children. It did with my son I seem to recall.

So maybe this story will lead you to another, or for you to remember it and retell it in some new place. And surely this is the right way forward, by the telling of our experiences? Better that way than strafing the hell out of someone or some place, just because of differences of opinion. This is learning from others' mistakes, and yes, from your own too. That way we don't stand still. Instead, we grow and progress.

When you think of all of this, then I have one more request. Please don't accuse me of exaggeration, or of complete fallacy or falsification. I am not like that. Perhaps I loaded the tale a little, yes, but that is my prerogative as the teller. I have done merely what we all do, when it comes down to it. I told it, and made it more interesting. There may be those of you out there whose lives are so interesting that all they need is the telling, but do we really believe those kinds of people exist? Only in myth I think. The reality is we are forced to make our own myths; find our origins, save and recover them from the ravages of that old bastard of a warrior named Time. So take this one with you, wherever you travel. Have it, free of charge.

One other thing: I did try telling my wife, but she is the one who will not listen. She hears, but she does not listen. We stand now, both frustrated, both wishing we weren't there, on the quayside of the Barbican. We listen to speeches being made, as if they will offer full enlightenment, and make us more aware. We both know this stroll, this perambulation is poppycock, but still go through the motions. I drift, of course, and I have no doubt that she is doing the same. She has now made me aware that I still haven't read our son's letter. I promise her that I will read it tonight.

It is afternoon now. The air is warm, and we politely watched the Challenge catamaran leave. We stand in a crowd of waving arms. She bends down.

"Look…"

I examine her hand when she straightens again. She has found an earring; an old-fashioned one, in the shape of a rose.

"I wonder who that belongs to?" she asks.

It is one of her pointless questions.

"No idea. Could be anyone's. Best put it back—then they'll find it…"

She glances at me.

"Back where Bob?"

"There… Someone'll be missing it."

"No," she says. "I'll keep it. It'll be a reminder of today."

"You haven't got the other one though. You only wear pairs of earrings dear…"

"Doesn't matter. I'll just have it to keep… and remember…"

"Remember what?" I ask, full of incredulity.

"I'll tell you later," she says.

I don't bother to question here anymore. She often teases me like that. She has surprises and things she will only tell me about, when she is ready. Normally these days, it is changes in the curtain fabric, or a new choice of wallpaper—things which have no relevance or interest to me.

The pity is that it was one of the things I used to like about her: her girlish games with me. Now, it is just plain tiresome.

I suggest we walk along the edge of the quayside. We walk with a slow pace today. Our arms are entwined, but we aren't close or intimate at all. She toys with the earring in her right hand. We wind around to where some people from the Press stand. We overhear snippets of the conversation, about what Plymouth hope to achieve by the challenge. The Mayor's answer is some ramble about how people need to remember the close links between the two countries. I note an American photographer there. He's different from the others; you know the way you can tell sometimes. With, Americans, I find it's often the shoes. But with him, he's younger. Now it's more the trousers. I notice him changing his lens over; the first one was smashed and broken, as if he has dropped it hard on the ground. We watch for a while, then go back to the hotel. It begins to drizzle.

We don't speak in the lift. We have done very well today, to spend so long together without arguing. In fact, it is almost a miracle. Once inside our room, she places the earring on the bedside cabinet. She looks down at the reliquary and touches it.

"When are you going to move this disgusting old thing?"

I don't answer.

"Bob—it's dirty, you know…"

I undo my tie and turn on the television.

"Don't," she says.

"What?"

"Turn it off again please. I've something to tell you."

Hers is strangely matter-of-fact kind of telling. She sits on the floor, almost-Lotus-like, still touching the box, or rather banging it slightly with her fist.

"Robert… Bob…"

She moves her hand off the box, and reaches out to take my right hand. Her palm is warm.

"Yesterday," she says. "I saw 'him' again. We talked for a long time. We went for a walk on the Hoe. We agreed we had no future. We've finished it…"

Her bluntness, her openness, her willingness to confess momentarily shocks me. For a minute, maybe more, I am silent.

Then: "What do you want me to say?"

"Nothing. I just wanted you to know, and for us to try again from now on… Finding that rose earring… it was like a symbol… yes… a symbol."

She wants me to kiss her. She wants that kiss to recoil her pain. I hate this kind of talk: make-it-up talk; try-again chatter.

"Good," I say, which sounds pathetic and wrong, but for me, it is too late. Our story has stop-started, spluttered and failed. I still manage a smile though, for the old times.

Her guilt eases. She thinks she's done it. She goes for her shower. I walk down other corridors in my mind, but she seems to be making a new effort.

"You know Bill's coming down tomorrow don't you?"

"Yes. Fine. What time?"

"Evening, I think."

I hear the shower being switched on. Water hisses. She is saying something, but her voice echoes and booms in the cabinet, and I cannot hear her. I begin to think about what she has said. Perhaps we should end our days without all this pain, and just get the hell on with it.

"Oh," she says, standing in her dressing gown. "Reception said there was phone call. Someone wanting to speak to you about the thing you put in the paper. An American, I think. He'll phone back."

I am barely listening. I am thinking about her, my son, and her, and my son again.

"Eh? Say again…"

She repeats what she said.

I listen intently this time, certain that my heart misses a beat.

So, there is another story to go. Another wind, only I am not the one whistling for it. Somebody else is.

Jude

We sleep in the coach after spending a day wandering around the city centre's shops. Gratuitous spending is what Pete calls it, but the children need things. I need things. Besides, I tell him, we have traded, and so we are justified. We have come to market. He laughs, when I explain this logic. We weave in and out of the shops, becoming anarchy as far as the store detectives go. They must track our every move, each feel of the goods. I would give anything to see their faces when we pay at the tills. The shop assistants still check out money, to see if it is counterfeit, but it doesn't bother us. We are free. Well, not quite.

Glitzy shops dazzle goods at us, but we shine back just as bright. We don't need fashion the way others needs it. We are not chameleons or Cinderellas. We don't change our spots. But I do feel like looking around the shops for baby things. I will need certain items. I leave Pete and Sarah and her children playing on some wooden animals in the middle of the street. They giggle like crazy when I return with a maternity dress. Sarah laughs and jokes that it is like something Maddy Prior would have worn in the 1970s.

I've noticed. Somehow, we are on the pivot now. It could go either way. Green culture sprouts in the shops, on the counters, in our pockets but I question whether it is really in our hearts. See, it might just be another trend. Another fashion. I, no, make that we, have a hope that it will not go that way. We look for a New Age, an Age of Conscience. When does the third millennium start? How about now?

I listen. Adam sniffles. He has a summer cold. There are a few people returning home from the pubs. The police haven't said anything yet. They are doing their blind-eye bit. We are Entertainers now. Joe Public squats on our side now.

Despite everything, despite a frightened run and an awkward confession from my man, I am glad we travelled here. It is funny how different places can bring different facets out of people. As though we never knew Dartmoor hid something. I have not forgotten. That is impossible. I forget very little, in fact. So one day, when we are old and grey, when my child has children, when more travel, when more look under their fingertips, we shall be able to sit still and remember this. And that is fitting, for this place seems a place fit for stories—all of them—Gogmagog and Corineus—to those nights on the piss down Union Street. Fitting.

I try to sleep. I hold my womb. Adam still sniffles in his bunk. I lie awake.

The darkness presses down on me. My belly gurgles. When I eventually sleep, I dream. Pete tells me so in the morning.

"You kept grabbing me," he said. "And you kept saying something…"

And he whispers in my ear, because it is one of those things we normally don't like to tell—"… about a family."

Eddie

Some people collect stamps: gummed remnants and perforated squares. I have a friend in Boston, who has a collection of post-marked stamps for every year back to 1869. I like looking through his collection. I like to feel the inks; imagine all the places these letters were sent from and to. Nebraska to New Orleans. Oregon to Pennsylvania. The places and people change according to my mood. I have a collection too. I have never really thought of it before, but my collection is an odd one, and a precious one. Odd, because everything in it, is the opposite of reality; precious, because it is absolutely unique. See, photographers like me rarely keep the prints; only the negatives. I keep them in files, and there, everything is topsy-turvy and make-believe. Light become dark and dark becomes light. Reality can become unreality. Sometimes, then, there is the shock of the print itself. Reality steps back into the room. I can articulate opposites then, but I cannot change how the picture pricks me.

Scattered around my room then, are some of the negatives I have taken. I normally develop them myself (not trusting others), but this time, I have taken a chance at an agency, and the results are pleasing. I am being the slide-projector here, holding the negatives to my eyes with the window before me; sometimes taking a eye glass and running over the sets. There is enough light for me to reverse the image and see what is actually there. I catalogue them precisely. They have to be well-preserved if I am to use them for the magazine. I have files of these things from Iraq. I often feel like throwing them in the bins outside, but something tells me that one day, they may be useful, so I keep them for a rainy day, that black-sky pouring down day that never actually comes.

I don't need to catalogue them for you. You know what I have taken. I have told you. I have said I snapped or took wherever I did. I don't need to show you London or Glastonbury, or Grimspound and Dartmoor, or their camp at night, or the ones around the Barbican. I have a favorite already though, of the procession that passed through in costume. A child smiles in just the right place. That'll be used. That will remain.

But there is another reason why I complete this quick search. I look for Jude's face. Her, the traveller, the journey-woman. I look for her form in the crowds. I want to see her eyes in black and white. I find the sequence I took when I saw her. I was definitely facing that way. I push the negative to the window. I take my eye glass. I look. Her husband Pete is there, but I can't see her. What was that about the camera never lying?

I gotta leave this place soon. No part of me will be left, unless I carve my initials on the newly-painted window sill. *E. H. forever.* Then, someone in the future can work out my history and label me as a degenerate vandal. Like all hotel guests, I will steal the soap, and the shower gel and the shampoo, just to prove that it wasn't a dream, and that I have been there. I'll keep them for the future; to remind me. I gather up the negatives: my pauses on time; my pathetic fragments of history. I am resolved that tomorrow will be my last look around.

I roll a cigarette, dropping tobacco onto the carpet. I later pick up the leaf, strand by tiny strand. I kneel against the window. This is a pleasant place really, this *Drake's Lodge* Hotel. It should do well. I look at my watch. It is lunchtime. Downstairs is Emma, the manageress, whom I am attempting to chat up. She noticed that my camera lens was broken. I told I had a brief accident in the Barbican and she nods. There is something about her. She is blonde and wears her hair in a French plait, which looks good on her. I want to kiss the back of her neck. I try it on, and ask if she would like to join me for lunch. She declines, but says she'll meet me for a drink later, after her shift.

I worked fast, faster even than with that gasoline girl. She came back to my room.

"I thought it would be good though… Like everyone told me. Like the Union Street you hear about…"

We are naked in bed, and her blonde hair is tumbling over her beautiful, veiny breasts. She is half-asleep, but she still answers me.

"It's changed a lot. Just a load of night-clubs. That's it. Nothing more now. Just like the Barbican. A place to get pissed in…"

Her voice is beautiful, thick as clotted cream.

I hold her close. I don't want to let her go.

She wakes, now suddenly conscious of her body, and that she has only known me for two hours. For a minute, we lie in silence, both of us thinking about our decision to come up here.

She speaks first.

"I've not done anything like this before you know."

"Neither have I," I lie.

She kisses me once more, in the hope that I will not leave her.

But this time, I want her to have my number. I want to stay. Here is one story, at last, that I do not want to stop. I want it to run and run and run.

XVIII
The Mask of Antiquity

Robert

We are alone. It is the evening. Fireworks crack off in the Sound.

"Are you sure it's okay to do it here?" I ask.

"Why not?" says Bill. "It's as safe as anywhere…"

All her junk has been cleared off the dressing table. We've put some newspaper down, and the box sits on it. We see all four sides of it; the back reflected in the mirror. Bill is visibly drooling. In the mirror, I can see his dark brown pupils dilated. This is a real moment in archaeology—they don't come very often.

"I always had a feeling you'd find it," he says. "Intuition, eh, Bob?"

I have explained how lucky it was. I have told him about the girl. I have told him my story. My invention. He believes it accurate enough. The story doesn't matter now though. He isn't interested the way I am about people. All he wants is the object. We now have the final clue. The reason. It sits before us.

What I have not told him is my theory, this now wearying story. I cannot. See, I fear Bill. He is a realist, a scientist really. He is all chromatography and isotopic replacements. I can hear him already. He will be talking about settlement patterns, pollen analysis and flotation techniques. He hasn't my ear, or eye. Though we share some things similarly, on other perceptions our views are completely different. See, all stories have meanings; have truths behind them, like the way fairy stories tell you not to go off with strangers. Though I have confessed this to you, all the while, I have been searching for meaning—a moral or message—while Bill has just been looking for facts: archaeo-magnetic readings and oxygen isotope analysis.

Now, I believe I have come closer to the truth. There are a number of us joined here—connected, I believe—through Stranger (or should I really now say "Samuel"?).

But this group, as yet, is incomplete. I know not its true size or breadth, just that it is bigger. I know no real numbers either. All I know is that it exists. And no, it is not imaginary, and yes, it cannot be pinned down. And all these members of this story are all, might we say, pilgrims, chasers, journeymen and women, travellers, seers, and believers. They are all pursuers. There are two common pursuits within this. We look for the miraculous. We also look—and take this any way you want—for our salvation within the mask of antiquity. The way we look, and because it is a human condition, is through our relics—the things left behind, just as I leave behind this story. You are hearing my inheritance to you.

And, so you know those who look; those who belong. You may belong also, since you have listened. You may know many things that I do not. You may have greater perceptive skills than I. There is Stranger and Moses. There is Carver and his daughter. There is now, on the periphery, Bill and my wife. (I would not have thought she belonged until yesterday.) There is my son. He is out there somewhere looking for the miraculous: the better existence. I have read his letter. I have come closer to him, although I have my doubts as to whether I shall ever see him again. I have doubts whether he is really involved at all—and that it is just my old man's imagination playing tricks on me. Maybe I would just like him to be involved.

There are more though. There's the woman on the Moor. She knows. She knows I know.

Oh, and another as well. Of that, I am certain.

Ah, but deduction is easy. Facts are what are difficult, and unfortunately, what count. Bill is at work.

"This is what I call a find," he keeps repeating. "This is old. Must have been passed down to your bloke Carver. You can tell by the inscriptions: Middle Eastern. Would've come here in the fifteenth century. Stolen from some shrine or something… It's Christian definitely—but not conventional…"

"What about the illustrations?"

"Oh, fertility-orientated, obviously. They kept the strangest things you know… from bodies… you know," he laughs and points to his groin. "Would've gone to this for growth of crops, or perhaps in preparation for someone to become pregnant, a newly-married couple maybe, or someone who wanted to restore life into something… or just wanted a baby…"

Bill has un-wrapped a greasy tool roll, in which is a specialized collection of pliers, tweezers and lock-picking devices. It makes me think he might have a striped black and white sweater on, a black eye mask, and a bag marked "Swag". He is examining the lock mechanism.

"Dual system," he notes. "Might have to take it back for an X-Ray. It would save us a lot of bother."

I don't want this to happen. I need to know now. I have waited long enough.

Bill explains his theory.

"They would've carried this thing around. Some bugger selling pieces from whatever's inside, or else selling the chance to touch it. Oh yes, there'd be followers as well… the cult as it were. That was the way it was…"

He changes tack.

"Have you completed any translations from it?"

"No. I looked closely. There's stuff there—but it's in a language I don't read. Persian maybe?"

"So, according to you then, this is what our friend Stranger carried up onto the Moor, before he went to America… She won't budge Bob. Might have to use a bit of force if we're to do it today…"

Bill looked at me anxiously, awaiting my approval. I nod.

"Reformation brought an end to all this," continued Bill.

"Most of them," I observe. "Some people were sensible enough to hang on to them. Of course, that pilgrim Carver, he couldn't keep it. Oh no. It would've been against their ideals. That was all old religion and they were the founders of the new. But he still must've known its power. He'd never manage to ferry it across to America, without it being discovered. God knows what would have happened to him if it had been discovered. He wouldn't have received much mercy. Instant death—or thrown overboard, I suppose. Maybe he even planned to come back for it one day…"

I move closer to give Bill a hand. I kept looking down at it, away from the mirror.

"Bugger," swore Bill. "I think I got the first lock... but I'll have to saw the second one."

He takes a blade and pokes it between the lid and the rest of the box.

"Come on then... you old bastard... Show us what you've got..."

While he is sawing, he looks up at me.

"You realize that I shouldn't be doing this... We should've taken it back to the lab."

I nod, but Bill knows as well as I do, that now there is no turning back.

Apart from us two, no one else knows of it—in the department at least.

Besides, neither of us cares about his career anymore. We have waited a long time for this. We aren't about to leave it closed.

"She's coming..." Bill observes.

I could hear the blade cut into the metal, and then more softly into the wooden casing inside. I am barely able to look. My mind is a rush of unrelated images. I am telling the story over and over to myself. I am trying to decide whether this was the ending of that, or the beginning of another.

"I've done it, I think," says Bill.

He sits back. We look in the mirror at one another.

"This should finish the story then..."

"You and your bleddy stories Bob... Open Sesame!"

He takes the lid between both hands and eases it slowly upwards. The hinges, unopened for hundreds of years, grate back. It is inevitable that one snaps.

"Shit!"

The lid is now vertical. It rests against the mirror. Old, musty air greets us. We peer in. The metal covers an inner ivory box, tight against the edge of the outer box. Bill looks at its mechanism. He sees what damage he has done. The inside smells earthy and decaying: an old animal bones smell. Organic material, obviously.

There is a knock at the door.

Bill raises his eyebrows and covers the reliquary with a sheet.

I go to answer it. A tall, dark man is outside in the corridor. I am momentarily angry at being disturbed in our moment of glory.

"Yes? Can I help you?"

"Hopkins," he says. "Eddie Hopkins. I rang about the relic. I'm the photographer you spoke to on the phone…"

I look at him. Somewhere I have seen him before. Down on the barbican before… Then I know more. His face, his darkness. It is Stranger—alive and well. Before me, this man personifies my mind's eye.

"Eddie—ah—of course… Come in, and see…"

I find my sense. I apologize for being rude.

"Yes… Bill… this is the gentleman who has the connection…"

"My forefathers told me about all of this…"

Bill interrupts our conversation.

"Come over here. Look… I've opened the ivory box…"

We peer inside. I anticipate fulfilment; the world explained in a box. It is the "prick" which later, Eddie informs me about. An ending. A finish. A relic. An actual relic should be there, but no, in the mirror, I see only three disappointed faces. This pursuit, this journey we have all been on, has taken us to here, to peer into a very empty ivory box. We wanted bones, or preserved genitals, or a skull, a piece of cloth, a hand, or another part of the body, as representation, but there is nothing there; nothing, except the dust of two thousand years. Despair falls on our heads like crowns of thorns. The tips of the thorns pierce and jab. This is where the story seems to stop, and where the past looks at us, wearing a grinning mask. Stranger has given us a double whammy. Not only an empty coffin, but now this.

After a few minutes though, I realize that all is not quite lost though. I know that in the corners of that smile, we have formed ourselves and somehow become assembled like plastic fuselage sections of my son's *Airfix* kits. A cult, you might say, is born. Curiously, it is born from nothing.

Only small questions may be asked now. The relics we have kept are of no use to us. They were there before science, before we discovered our world was round, when men mixed base metals in the vain, misguided hope of producing gold, when men were bled to cure sickness. This was the time when relics could actually cure things, or release you of your sins, be it blasphemy, or being caught in the hay stack. This was when superstition ruled the globe, and when stories were real and you dared not question them. The relic cult was the last; the very last piece of the darkness, and when it disappeared then it was the start of those last, agonizing efforts to get out of that bed. Now they are poked, dated, pulled apart, destroyed replicated, doubted. They are no longer revered, not in the way that Carver first did when he first swore his oath.

And so to the small questions: What made him give up the "evil" relic cult to join the Separatists? Already use of relics would have been very dated. Perhaps he used them still in his own time, like a wise man. Maybe he was just uncommitted; saw the Separatists as a way out... a way of travel. More than likely then, he still had superstition. Perhaps he still lay in that bed. Maybe we should all climb back into it, instead of peering underneath it and testing the springs. Carver knew, and that is all. He knew about miracles, knew about how stories could actually work. He must have seen them happen with the relic. Once you have seen that, you cannot give it up. It becomes addictive, like the best tobacco.

Later on in the week, the phone rings. It is Bill. He has two things to say.

"I'm joining you, now," he says cryptically.

"What? Joining me?!"

"They want me to retire Bob. When I got back from you, they told me. It was in a letter from the Vice-Chancellor. You know, good time to go. Enhancements and so on..."

"Sorry Bill, I..."

Bill is silent, but when he speaks, the voice is not the acerbic tone I expect.

"It's all right," he says. "I know when it's time for a change. I was becoming a bit of an old codger there. Time for some new blood... Now I can get around to some real writing."

"Good," I answer.

"Anyway, that's not the real reason I'm phoning... I've had some people working on the box. You'll be interested in this..."

I hear him clear his throat.

"We were right. Got some experts to have a look at the symbols...They're Christian—but the inscriptions. You were right—written in Middle Persian. It is a fertility cult. Possibly Chaldean. Married couples came to it, if they found they couldn't produce any children. Even the air inside might have been enough, whether the bleddy relic was in there or not..."

"Medieval equivalent of the test-tube baby then, eh?"

"You could say that I suppose. We're still having difficulty over some of the lettering. Persian's all they'll tell me, whatever that means. You'll have to take another look at it with me."

Bill seems satisfied. This may be his last wondrous journey, his last knock on the door of the earthy past.

"We've had it valued..." he continues.

I don't listen to what he says anymore. I don't need to. I can tell. It is priceless. It is one for the British Museum, destined to be set in an artificially lit, temperature controlled secure cabinet. It will be peered at by American tourists, and will never perform any more miracles. A plaque will be mounted before it, giving possible explanations, possible translations, proposing its history, and a sign beneath it, will ask visitors not to touch; the very purpose of its existence denied.

Jude

We both feel in a kind of limbo. You may think that is no different from our normal pattern of existence. As a result of our recent experiences, things have changed. We cannot keep up this pretence. We shall travel again, probably westwards—the romantic direction to travel, I suppose. Like the pioneers. Like cowboys. Like pilgrims. But for now, we travel without direction. Sarah finds this difficult to accept. She feels my pregnancy has irrevocably changed me. But no, it is not just that. We have learned. I have learnt that I may not ignore the world. There are those who may not wish to join us, but who do feel some concern for us, who feel that what we do is right somehow, but in a way, are stronger by not joining us, for not rejecting, but fighting the system from within. And Pete, after telling me about making his *Airfix* model aeroplanes, has another story to tell the children: one of a father and son. Besides, Sarah has her own man now, and he will give her direction.

The Barbican festival has ended. The crowds have gone. All our kit has been loaded back onto the coach. There is a point in all our lives when it is time to go. To push forward. To forget the past. Progress, as it were. We aim to do this. No words have been said. It is understood. You may sense we have been broken. Oh no, we are stronger. We are more tolerant. Yet we shall fight harder. Our limbo is a result of us climbing a level of experience. A higher consciousness, as we might say. We start the New Age the way the Pilgrim Fathers started a New Age in America. Only our Age will the one of harmony, learning and peace, the Age they strove for. We shall try to be the group to do that now. Of course, our question is still "How?" So many have failed. Even the Pilgrim Fathers failed. I want us to find the way through. We shall articulate opposites. We shall unmask antiquity. We shall convert heretics.

I feel satisfied. A baby shall be born from me next year. Already, I can feel him or her kicking. I can turn my love inwards now, as well as outwards. We do not need explanation. I know that somehow, by touching that box, my body changed. A miracle occurred there and then. It was something beyond words; these words that I speak to you now. But I don't wish to touch it again. Nor do I need to know how it works. I can live without precise knowledge, but I cannot live without belief. Let it fall into another's hand. Let love exude from it.

So, I have a hold. The limbo will pass. It is here perhaps, that I reconcile past and future. They are not different places or separate entities. They are as easy to travel to and from as places on a map. And my faith in travel has not dissolved.

No, it has become more powerful. Only now, I have changed my views about certain aspects of it. I left my mother to escape; never to hurt her. I left to learn, and see new experiences. I had to take that road, and I thought I would never go back. That is wrong. See, travelling means absolutely nothing, if you don't go back to your origins, to compare your roots with your branches. Examine the present in the light of relics. So travelling is about going away. It is about journeying from John O'Groats to the Land's End; it is about going around the world in eighty days; it is stepping to see the Holy Land, but it is also about learning and putting into practice a better way of existence—our higher consciousness. Ah, but more than anything else, travelling is about two things: the returning and the telling of those experiences. That is the truth of travelling, of pilgrimage. Nothing else is. So I am resolved to go back, with plump belly to see my mother. To show and tell. Inevitably then, there might seem a mellowing, a cop-out, but that is false. There can never be a mellowing, only a hardening. So, maybe before we travel onwards, we shall go backwards.

I think about all of this as I wrap up the pieces of jewellery from the stall.

And something else…

Pete told me last night that he wants to find his mother and father. He wants to re-trace steps. He wants to show his father his grand-child before he dies. He fears the unmeaning when he passes on. Pete fears sorrowful stories of regret, when the child asks about the grandfather. He cried last night. Deep sobs in the back of the bus. He told me he had forgiven them. So, his parents made mistakes, but then don't we all? None of us is a perfect being. We are all flawed; joined together by our collective fuck-ups. We will do the same. So I say, go back and tell. Find the balance. Harmony. Acceptance. Check the proverbs: familiarity breeds contempt, distance makes the heart grow fonder. He wants them to join us, and us to join them, so we may travel in the same orbit; the same ship.

Amen, to all that.

Eddie

I mentioned him briefly earlier on. There is an artist I have an affin-ity with. He is called Paul Klee. One of his works is called the *Angelus Novus* or "The Angel of History". I feel a strange parallel with this angel. I have noticed it before, but I haven't told you yet. Now is the time. In the painting, the angel's eyes are staring, the way mine look now. The Angel's mouth is open, the way mine is now, and his wings are spread, the way mine are now. My overcoat catches the wind, and flaps against my thighs. The Angel's face is turned to the past, and I feel as though I am looking back over Plymouth. We see the past as a chronological chain of events, an ordered progress. I still did before I came here, but the Angel doesn't see the past in this way. No. He sees a single catastrophe which throws wreckage upon wreckage in front of him. I begin to see it as well. The Angel wants to stay. I want to stay. He wants to wake the dead. I want to call them. He wants to make whole what has been destroyed. When I think of it—that is the very thing I wanted to do in Iraq.

He cannot though. I find I cannot. It is impossible. A storm blows from the direction of Paradise, and has caught his wings with such force that he cannot close them. The Atlantic wind cracks at me. I smell America in the air. The storm forces him into the future to which his back is turned. I don't want to leave, but know that I must. The storm is called Progress, and I, with tears, have to join to it.

I no longer see the past as a chains of events preceding the now, and the present. No more as a history textbook. That is not the way it works. No, here I re-live it. It enters me. I spit at the storm of progress. I throw fire and brimstone into its eye. See, my problem now is that since I've come over here, it has given me a new direction. I have looked closer, photographed closer. I have listened properly and heard new stories. Old ones have been re-told to make me smile. But at the same time, I am lost (maybe I have always been lost), and the map of life confuses me even more now. I no longer know which point of the compass to follow. A magnet pulls the needle in all directions. I belong to some higher force, or some larger truth. I am a part of a collective. Some damned array of function and from somewhere that I just don't get. I thought I had come closer here to finding out the collective I belonged to: the very type I am, yet I know in reality, that I may be no closer even now.

But enough of this tongue-tied thought. It is just that many riddles have been opened up here; many more than I arrived with; more, in some ways, than Iraq. Perhaps it is because I feel at home. There is a spirit here. I have come from Paradise—a Promised Land—and travelled back.

Push forward to another century, and while the rest of humanity lives on Mars, I would be the one itching to drift back to Earth. And it isn't the homesickness. No, it is for the meaning, the meaning which, as a tide, has never before touched my shore. It has never left any driftwood, or pebbles, or seaweed even.

The Barbican is empty today. All energy has been exuded from it. All money has now been spent. The *Mayfly* has left. On the news they said she was making good progress some fifty miles south-west of the Isles of Scilly. Now the Barbican is just the stuttering old fool of a place she has always been, slipping and tripping in between Plymouth's tower blocks. One day, it will all go—remember the last second of the last hour?

Towards the Channel, heaving gray frigates bulk their way in across the Sound. I can just make out black dots of sailors. They are returning from the Gulf, and will be making up for lost time. A few babies made tonight. Watery exchanges of life enhancement. A few stories made and told…

I will ring London later. I'll speak to gay, nail-bitten Martin and tell him how it has all gone. I will say nothing of what has really happened. Well, you don't do you? No, I will tell how wonderful it all was. He likes people to emulate his positivity. I will congratulate him on his excellent choices of locations. He will ask for some copies, and I will send them to him. They will soon sit as decaying remnants in his high-tech domain, next to his dolphin prints. They will be relics of me.

Worse than this, I have broken all that I thought, that I admitted to you, and told Emma that I am going back. There is no bitterness. She knew it was coming; knew the chance she took with me. We have agreed to write, knowing that paper can never make up for the person. Still, she left her hair grip in my room. It will travel back with me, to remind me of when I pulled it from her hair.

Now though, I have another phone call to make—to some Professor. See, in my wallet are a couple of newspaper cuttings I kept. Something pricked me in them. I enter a phone booth and put in a one pound coin. I dial the number. Connections are made. I don't yet know it, but I become even further involved by this simple action. I dissolve into a story. There is idle chat at first; a getting-to-know-you dialogue. Then, I release it to the straining ear at the other end of the line.

"I may be wrong, but this grave you found earlier in the summer… Well, my name's Hopkins. I'm from Massachusetts. I think he was an ancestor of mine."

I explain things badly.

"The grave you found… I can't think why you found it. My grandfather used to tell me stories about him. It seems the same man's been buried twice."

I expect the voice to be incredulous, but it is not. I feel he knows me already. The voice is precise, and methodical. Its tones do not change, but beneath all of it, I sense a breathlessness, a vast energy, that has instantly found a new home.

"Tell me," it says, "anywhere in you family history—do you know the name Carver?"

"Carver. Alice Carver. I think she was called. Married Samuel… That's how the story goes at least…"

I am scared what more the voice might ask. I tell the voice it was who my forefather married. I describe his grave the way my grandfather told me.

"You're in," says the voice, as if I have gone through an initiation ceremony and joined some secret society.

Genuine surprise now drips from the phone. The voice now trusts me like a brother or a son, even. He gives me the place: a hotel upon the Hoe. He tells me he will fill me in, and that I can help with his theory of what happened. I can fill in the other half, where the truth, for him, became vague. I shut the phone box door, and lean against the glass, which props up the back of my head. For a second or two, I fly, even though the air is still, and I have never had the wings of an Angel.

Before I put the receiver down, breathlessly I tell him one thing more.

"Something else," I say. "My grandpa Zip. He has this weird object—in a glass bottle—a bit of skin or something I think, all black and leathery, preserved in formaldehyde. He used to make potions from it—a tonic… See, he ran a medicine show…"

Glass bottles.

Potions.

Fairy tales.

See how I am mythologizing? I am the Bothers Grimm. I am Hans Christian Andersen. And suddenly, people want to listen.

XIX
The Approach of Death

Robert

And so, you have heard my tale; my philosophies of life. There is no more. My sooth, as it were, is said. I return to the hotel. I have been to the Mayflower Steps once more; perhaps for the last time in my life. I have walked the Barbican's streets again. I have side-stepped lager cans on the pavement, and watched floating pint glasses in the green water of Sutton Pool. I walked with my eyes down. In between the cobbles are those gaps which once ran with the blood of fish. I might wish for a few strands of tobacco, or a scrap of ballad sheet music. I look hard, but know I will find neither. I sniff, wanting the putrid odours of bygone days, but I only smell the pot pourri and soap from the interior design shop on the corner. Even the old fish market is to be demolished I hear—to be turned into a café and glassware centre—part of a large project, reconstructing the Barbican for the new century. Work has also started on a new visitor centre opposite the Mayflower Steps. I read of "interactive experiences" and "tourism estimates".

We are leaving soon. Before that, I have an appointment at the hospital this afternoon about my blood pressure. The doctor will tell me to take it easier, much easier—and she will warn me. Still some love there then. Maybe it is getting better. Maybe her touching the box softened things, brought us closer, took away the heresy of the twentieth century. What can I say—we aren't so separate any more? The old union is still here, despite everything. I am satisfied enough for now though. I may have lost one family, but gained and joined another. Some things are missing, but that is the way of time. It picks and chooses what shall be left, what will survive and what shall become the new relics of our age left for the future.

That night, Eddie, Bill and I stayed up chatting—in fact, until the dawn eased over the Sound and our throats were dry from the intensity of the conversation.

We have agreed to meet again tonight before I return to Oxford, and Eddie flies back to the States. All of us are reeling from the shock of events. Bill and I will fly to Massachusetts to have a look at Zip's relic. We talk about the Chaldean Church in Iraq. Full circle then—maybe even restore the relic to the reliquary—after nearly four centuries of separation.

I open the door of our room. She is sitting on the bed. She has been crying; crying over the spilt milk of our marriage. I hold her. That old, crumbling, beautiful warmth comes over use again.

"Elizabeth… I have to tell you a story some time…" I say.

"Yes," she says. "This time, you must. Tell it to me now."

"Are you sitting comfortably? Then I'll begin…"

I tell her, and Stranger make us less estranged to each other.

That night I hold Elizabeth in my arms as though our lives are beginning again. For the first time in a long time, we make love and hold each other as we pass into the night. We shall leave in the morning, resolved to provide memories for each other, and keep more. For you know, that time moves on, and it is so very short.

And remember, unlike Chaldean relics, time doesn't have much of sense of humour.

Now, go. Do the same.

Make children.

Tell them stories.

Jude

We have split from Sarah now, or rather, she has split from us. She has gone her own way, as we all do eventually when we travel. She is to follow a different path, and has lined up new horizons. It wasn't the fact that I had changed. No, she has other concerns now. She is with her new man Simon. He deals in clothes from the Far East, and travels abroad regularly to find new goods. Her children will miss our tales. They have told us so, and the youngest Ally, cried her heart out. But in the bigger scheme of things, stories don't matter. They are inconsequential, unimportant things. They are now a family, and what is more important—a story—or a family? I know which I would choose. And so, for now, Sarah has gone. They are travelling eastward to where the sun rises. She will write, she says, but she cannot really: us being of "no fixed abode". She knows that one day we might lock in again, cruise in the same orbit, same trajectory, and touch once again.

We travel westwards in a rich motion over a landscape of wonder. Endless possibilities beckon. Inevitably, there will be endless learning along the way. We are off to West Cornwall—to St Ives, where Pete's origins are. There will be more mileposts to touch. More encounters. We are a-roving again, Pete, me and the bump. I do feel I belong now. The world accepts me and I accept it. I blossom. Soon, I shall flower. I will hold a child. I will bathe it in the ocean off Porthmeor Beach. I will sing him or her songs. I will still tell it stories. It will belong.

Pete has found his past again. We smile at one another. It is a look that tells me we should be as one. He is not smoking anymore. I have convinced him of his future. He is sucking Polo sweets instead. He shows me one on his tongue.

I am tidying up the interior of the bus. I brush Dartmoor peat and moss off the floor. I hang up bunches of dried flowers from the ceiling. I gather materials to be recycled: old bottles and old newspapers. I feel my mother's single earring. I take it out of my lobe. I never did find its pair. I will wrap it in newspaper and save it for a rainy day. A keepsake, then. Suddenly, the earring becomes less important. It is the petal-like pages of the newspaper that my eyes focus upon. I note the dirty smell of the black print; the dots of the photograph. There are words, printed words; words which are real and not just of the air. In the *Western Morning News*, I am reading an article about a holy relic found on Dartmoor, at a place called Grimspound. There is a telephone number to ring. Some professor.

"Pete Bolitho," I say first, faltering, but then my voice grows stronger, "please... can you turn the bus around...?"

"What is it?" he says.

"I've just found your father."

Eddie

The end is about turning and altering. You know me, or you did know me. You knew one part of my life. I am at Heathrow. Airplanes fly overhead, to Holland, to America, to Iraq. They become high, dental floss trails, adorning a purple sky. Distant. High. Far apart. Journeys of significance, of wonder: pilgrims finding their relics, their objects of veneration, each for their own deity. I have a coffee in my hand. People are watching me, as I spill some of it slightly, as the cup is overfilled. Have you ever noticed why we view strangers with suspicion? It is because they have no history. You draw meaning from me, because I provided a history (free of charge, incidentally), of my life. But normally, we have nothing to draw meaning from. Nothing to worship. We see them as having their own friends, their own dreams, their own cult, and ours and theirs must not meet.

Oh no.

It is East and West.

Christian and Muslim.

Them, and us.

But it does not have to be.

And yes, I believed I was once like that, but then, time moves on. Death beckons. And you travel. And you collide. You leave some things behind, and you gain others. I want to leave behind this lifestyle. I want to gain Emma. Plymouthian sexy. I fantasize about her. She has a body like whipped cream.

But for now, I am leaving. I know now. I have met Robert. He's a one, that guy. He's like Zip. We have agreed to keep in touch. I told him all that I knew. He says he and Bill want to come over some time soon, to visit Zip's grave, see where he sold the tonic water, talk to the Native Americans. He wants to unite relic with reliquary. He wants to see New Plymouth, and see where Carver and Samuel came to. I have to take him up to the hill, on the farm, where according to Zip, our family thinks he and Alice were buried. He will fly across the Atlantic and be there in seven hours. He is a rusty nail, but he can still "prick" me like no other I have known. I am still filled with wonder about his discovery. What was incredible was our individual knowing while the other never knew. This was the prick that drew the blood and burst the sack of my soul. So you thought you knew me, inside out, back to front, upside-down. Well, I've news for you. You don't.

See, I've let the trolley go, and people are staring at me. My luggage rolls lonely down the corridor. My ticket will be unused. There will be an empty seat on the 747, and the desk will repeatedly call my name for boarding. People around me, watch me intensely. It is because, to them, I have no history. But then, they know nothing. Not a bean. I am resolved to return then. I will go back to Emma. I will alter the story, and make her smile again. We will have strawberries and champagne for lunch again. I will plant myself back in Old Plymouth.

Yes—a plantation back here.

I am moving, but it feels like I am not using my legs. I pass people like clockwork toy, arms jerking, eyes opening and closing, heart whirring. I am not about to make a mistake. I told Emma, I had to go back to Cape Cod. Instead I shall stay. I reach the end of the walkway. I am bursting outwards, pushing, explosive, erect, fertile, the way I was with her. The skin is ripping. I will shatter. I will scatter, but I will root, and send a piece of me deep into the earth here.

In doing this, I am turning in the face of history. I am blasphemous to my history. I, who though he knew himself, am becoming a stranger to myself. I will remain. I have Continental Drift—only in reverse gear. The last call for my flight comes. But the wind is too strong in the other direction. It feels like dust catches in my eyes. No, this Angel shan't fly. American progress, conquest, conflict will go on and on, but I, shall shield those I love from the wreckage.

In this, I declare my membership of a new cult.

XX
The Relics

This is what remains:

Robert

A dusty *Heinkel He 111* found in the attic, a found son, and a grandchild.

Jude

A pair of earrings, a puzzle solved, and a baby bold.

Eddie

Some photographic negatives, Zip's bottle, and a tale told.

You

?

Appendix I

List of passengers who sailed upon the *Mayflower* during its trans-Atlantic voyage of 6 September to 9 November 1620:

John Alden	Samuel Easton	Degory Priest
Isaac Allerton	Richard Ely	Somon Prower
John Allerton	Thomas English	John Rigsdale
Mary Allerton	Moses Fletcher	Alice Rigsdale
Bartholomew Allerton	Edward Fuller	Thomas Rogers
Remember Allerton	Mrs Edward Fuller	Joseph Rogers
Mary Allerton	Samuel Fuller	Henry Sampson
John Billington	Samuel Fuller	George Soule
Eleanor Billington	Richard Gardiner	Myles Standish
John Billington	John Goodman	Rose Standish
Francis Billington	William Holbeck	Edward Thompson
William Bradford	John Hooke	Edward Tilley
Dorothy May Bradford	Stephen Hopkins	Ann Cooper Tilley
William Brewster	Elizabeth Hopkins	John Tilley
Mary Brewster	Giles Hopkins	Joan Tilley
Love Brewster	Constance Hopkins	Elizabeth Tilley
Wrestling Brewster	Damaris Hopkins	Thomas Tinker
Richard Britteridge	Samuel Hopkins	Boy Tinker
Peter Browne	Oceanus Hopkins *	John Turner
William Butten	John Howland	Boy Turner
Robert Carter	George Kerr	William Trevore
Dorothy Carter	John Lancemore	Richard Warren
John Carver	William Latham	Gilbert Winslow
Alice Carver	Edward Leister	William White
Richard Clarke	Edmund Margesson	Susanna White
James Chilton	Christopher Martin	Resolved White
Susanna Chilton	Mary Martin	Peregrine White
Mary Chilton	Desire Minter	Roger Wilder
Francis Cook	Ellen Moore	Thomas Williams
John Cook	Jasper Moore	Edward Winslow
Humility Cooper	Richard Moore	Elizabeth Winslow
John Crackstone	Mary Moore	
John Crackstone Jr.	William Mullins	One Mastiff dog
Edward Doty	Alice Mullins	One Springer Spaniel dog
Francis Easton	Priscilla Mullins	
Sarah Easton	Joseph Mullins	* born at Cape Cod.

Appendix II

Robert Bolitho studied archaeology at the University of Liverpool and completed his Ph.D. on the burial mounds of Western Britain. He then held post-doctoral fellowships at Liverpool and London, eventually becoming Lecturer, Reader and then Professor of Archaeology at the University of Bristol. He was also awarded a J. Paul Getty fellowship in the History of Memorial Art. Among his many publications are: *Grave Concerns: Barrows and Burial Culture in British Pre-History* (1979), *Techniques of Archaeological Excavation* (with William Evans, 1980), *Death in the Celtic World* (1982), *Life and Death in Renaissance Europe* (1984), *Understanding British Graveyards* (1985), *Cemeteries in Britain and Ireland* (1987), *Post— Processional Archaeology: An Introduction* (1989), *Archaeology: Theory and Practice* (fourth edition, 1991) and *Grave Tales: Memorial Inscription in Western Europe* (1992). Now Emeritus Professor, his most recent work is *The Cult of Relics: Trans-national Reliquaries in Europe and America* (1995). He is currently researching esoteric aspects of the Chaldean Church in the Middle East.

Lightning Source UK Ltd.
Milton Keynes UK
UKHW020631241022
410994UK00001B/139

9 781782 013044